T0323890

DATURA

LM DEWALT

central
avenue
publishing
2012

Dedicated to my Mamá Hilda, Papá Augusto, Nana, Pop, and Grandpa.
I miss you all so much.

DATURA

✆ ONE ✆

The sweet scent of roses filled my lungs. Sunlight blinded me and the moisture from the grass seeped between my toes as I walked. I wasn't alone in the colorful garden surrounding me, I felt it, yet I saw no one. I turned my head, admiring the vivid colors splayed around me. White concrete benches surrounded a pond filled with lily pads. The benches were encircled by ivy-lined arches that blocked the tranquil scene until I walked into it. A rustling of clothing reached my ears and I turned to look.

"Ian." He leaned against one of the archways, looking at me with a smile on his perfect face. "What are you doing here?"

"Waiting for you." His hand reached for mine. "What took you so long?"

I looked around for any other sign of life. Besides the birds darting in and out of nearby trees, I saw none. His eyes called to me. His heart beat faster as he awaited my next move. I felt my heart speed up in response. I pressed my hand on my chest and felt the steady beating beneath the warmth of my skin.

"Am I dead too?"

His eyebrows raised in confusion. "Why would you say that?"

"My heart...your heart... they shouldn't be beating...I killed you..." My mind flooded with questions my lips could not form.

"What are you talking about?" He closed the distance between us and the warmth of his hand wrapped mine.

I stared at our entwined fingers and my fingers tightened around his, a sense of peace and safety filled the empty spot in my heart. It wasn't until then that I realized there had been an empty spot.

"Our hearts...they shouldn't be...beating." My eyes reached his and I was more confused to see green eyes instead of the usual violet. "What happened to your eyes?"

"What are you talking about? Nothing's wrong with my eyes. Nothing's wrong with our hearts. In fact, everything is perfect." He smiled at me. I tried to form a smile but my face felt frozen. My heart beat furiously. A splash in the pond made my head jerk as I tried to catch a glimpse of the cause. A ripple in the water was all that was left. Whatever it was had been too quick for me to catch and I worried that my instincts were slipping. My vampiric senses seemed slower, less intense, somehow.

"Where are we?" I asked, focusing on him once again.

"In the garden, my love." His eyes swept our surroundings.

"Whose garden?" Nothing looked familiar. Not even Ian. I knew it was him. I knew his face, his voice, the feel of his skin, except, it was...the wrong temperature, too warm. His eyes were the wrong color. His heart was wrong...all wrong. I killed him.

"Our garden. Remember your roses? You insisted on them so I filled it with as many colors as I could. It was a surprise...for your thirtieth birthday." He pointed to the white roses. He wrapped his fingers around a white bud and plucked it from the stem. He placed it in my hand. "These are your favorite."

I'm thirty? I shook my head. I should be only nineteen. This made no sense. My hand jerked away from his and I stumbled backward. I looked at the barely-open white bud in my hand. My heart sped as the feeling of emptiness took control of me again. I felt it in my soul and searched my mind for the cause. Something was wrong...very wrong. But what? Ian didn't move toward me. He stood and stared, as if waiting for me to come to my senses.

Dead. He should be dead. I tried to replay events in my mind. I knew I killed him; I was sure of it. This didn't make any sense.

"Vampire!" I stumbled back again and this time landed on the bench. It was warm from the sun. I jumped to my feet, wanting to run but not being able to move. "You're a vampire...I'm...a vampire."

He tilted his head and laughed. "Are you feeling alright? Did you hit your head when you fell, my love?"

"This is wrong. You should be dead, really dead!" I focused on the images my clouded mind was sending. "You're a vampire. I'm a vampire.

You made me. I destroyed you."

His eyes softened as his face filled with concern.

"Why are you here…with me?" I asked.

"We live here. Ever since we got married. I should get you to a doctor."

"We never married! You just used that notion to separate me from my parents. You had no intention of ever marrying me!"

He took a step in my direction and I turned and started running. I ran as hard as my legs allowed, feeling like my heart was going to jump out of my chest, pain shooting through my side. The scenery remained the same. The bench remained at my side. The emptiness in my soul turned black as my vision blurred and the colors faded. I pushed my legs harder, trying to get away from the laughter filling my ears. Blue eyes flashed in my mind… sad, yet comforting eyes. Were they the cause of the emptiness?

The more I ran the closer Ian came to reaching out and touching me. Dead. I have to be dead. What other explanation could there be? Could we be in heaven? Human again? But death meant no heartbeat. A fact I knew all too well.

"Stop, Lily!" His voice was clear and demanding. "I can't reach you if you don't stop moving!"

My legs slowed but my mind told me to keep moving. Never let him catch you! My mind screamed at me.

"No! I can't be here! I have to go! I have to go back! I don't belong here with you!" I screamed as I tried to run faster. My side ached and threatened to double me over.

"I love you, Lily! Don't leave me! Don't go to him!" His voice was pained.

Him? Who? I desperately searched my memories. Blue eyes, warm lips, blood…sweet, powerful, blood…

"Him who?" I demanded.

"You don't love him. He was only a distraction. He could never make you happy…truly happy. It's me you want. It's always been me. Stop fighting it. We have everything now. Our happiness. Our humanity. We got it all back. Don't you see?" His fingertips brushed my back as he stretched his arms to grab me and sent a pulse of electricity through my body. My vision cleared. I turned toward him. My legs stopped. My breathing struggled to slow. My hand clutched the burning pain in my side.

"I do see." I straightened so I could look into his green eyes; eyes that had once been violet and cold, filled with hatred and greed. Something suddenly clicked in my brain. "I see what this is. This is a dream. My dream. Not yours. I call the shots here."

His smile turned sinister, like I remembered, like it had always been.

I leaned forward toward his face and felt his hot breath on me. His eyes closed in anticipation, waiting for me to speak. "I loved you once. I will never make that mistake again," I whispered before my lips brushed his and then pulled away. All I could see was black again. Complete silence surrounded me. No birds, no Ian, no splashing, but best of all, no heartbeat.

"COME BACK, LILY. Don't leave me. You can't leave me. Please, not now." A familiar voice sounded like a melody in my ears. Christian. Christian was begging me to come back. From where? Where did I go? I struggled to open my eyes so I could see his angelic face and look into the deep blue eyes that held my future. Nothing but blackness surrounded me.

"Christian? Why is it so dark?" I felt the damp softness of the ground beneath my body.

"I can't stand this pain," he pleaded, his voice growing weaker. "Please help me through this. Stay with me. I need you."

"I'm trying but...I can't see you. I don't know where you are."

"Shh...it's okay. Everything is okay. You're safe." Another voice. A well-known, safe voice. "Relax."

I tried again to open my eyes, turn my head toward the sound, but couldn't. It was as if a weight sat on my chest, keeping me pinned.

"Is she hurt? Did you check her head?" A worried female voice asked.

"No...I don't think so. She's just in shock. She'll be fine." Aaron? The name brought a small comfort to my screaming mind. The man who had taken me into his life, into his fatherly embrace, was near, comforting me, holding my head off the ground. I sifted through memories for some image of him but I could see nothing but a blur, a combination of faces, arms, hands reaching for me.

"I'll stay with you. Take my hand...hurry." In my mind's eye, his blue eyes pleaded with me. His hand reached for me in a tangle of other hands, pushing his out of the way. I felt only his fingertips, couldn't stretch my arm enough to grasp. His back arched. His body writhed with pain but still he tried to keep a smile on his lips. His breathing was pained, in quick gasps through clenched teeth. I couldn't reach the security of his warm hand. But why would I be able to reach, to feel the warmth of his skin?

4

Christian was gone. Ian had ended his life and I had been unable to stop it. The reality of it hit me like a ton of bricks. The pain passed through my body making me the one squirming. I had failed him.

With all my might, I hoped I was dead. I hoped I was in hell, where I belonged, for all the lives I had taken, for all the suffering I had caused. Coldness settled over me and I felt movement. Someone carried me now. Whoever it was took his time. My head dangled. The heaviness on my chest continued but it burned now. It felt like my heart was on fire but I knew I should not be able to feel it. I wanted to cry. I wanted to scream. I wanted to run though I still couldn't move my limbs.

Christian was dead and I had caused it. I had to be dead if I was hearing and seeing him. I felt relief, if only for a brief moment, as the realization of what that meant hit me. If I was, indeed, dead, then what I was hearing and seeing really was Christian and that meant he was here with me. That also meant I couldn't possibly be in hell because he would not be there. Christian did not belong in hell with Ian and I. Nothing made sense. The blackness was driving me crazy. I needed to see. I needed to stop feeling the cold and the empty.

"This is good. Put her down here…careful." A female voice directed whoever was carrying me. Kalia? Her sweet, motherly voice was unmistakable yet it made no sense. All of us dead?

"Lily, honey? Can you hear me? Aaron, hand me your shirt…make a pillow." I felt my head being lifted and then placed gently back down onto something soft. "Her eyes are opening."

The orange light blinded me and I blinked against it. My head felt heavy and my eyes burned, my vision blurred. I struggled to focus my eyes on the faces around me.

"Christian, where are you?" I turned my head to the side as if it had a fifty-pound weight resting on it. "I can't feel you. I can't see you."

"Shh…shh…it's okay, Lily. You're safe. Lie still." Aaron's voice sounded so close, yet, I couldn't will my eyes to focus on his sweet face. Christian's face was the one I longed to see. My Christian. My human. My soul mate.

"Where are you? Come closer, please. I can't find you." My eyes moved as if of their own free will, my aching head staying still. I couldn't find him. I could make out two faces but I somehow sensed that neither was the one I wanted…needed…to see.

"Lily, please stay still. Don't over-exert yourself…not until we're sure nothing's broken." Aaron was beside me on the ground, his cold hand holding mine.

"Where is Christian?" I demanded. I wasn't waiting anymore. "I can't see him. I don't hear him anymore. Please go get him."

I heard Kalia's slow gasp. A moment of silence and then…

"Christian's gone…don't you remember?" Aaron's voice was soft as a whisper. "He died, Lily."

A throbbing pain hit my head as I tried to force my body to sit up. It was no use.

"No! That's impossible. He can't be…he was…talking to me. I heard him, just now. I saw his face. Please go get him," I pleaded. How could they not have seen him? They were all here. I heard all their voices. Three of them. The only ones that mattered.

"I'm so sorry, honey. I wish we could tell you differently, but…he is gone…to a better place." Kalia held my other hand. Her fingers squeezed mine in her comforting way.

"That's not true! I heard him! I felt his hand. I saw his eyes. He's hurt but he's alive. Go get him!" I tried again to get up but failed.

"He's dead, Lily. Ian killed him and you tried to save him but it was too late. Please understand that. He was not talking to you." Aaron's voice sounded firm. "There was a battle. We lost Christian. You killed Ian. I wish I could tell you otherwise but unfortunately…"

"NO! I don't believe you. I can't…" I managed to yank my hands away from them and roll to my side. Curling myself into a ball I felt the blood tears roll down my face. My eyes focused on a patch of dead grass at the base of the tree I had been placed beside. Blood made a puddle that seeped slowly into the ground. My head ached and my chest burned as if a match had been lit. I let the blackness reclaim my senses. I wanted to go back to that place I had been before, where Ian had been human, where I could take that humanity from him, the way he had taken mine, the way he had taken Christian's.

I felt something moist in my hand. It was clenched into a fist. I concentrated on moving my fingers, uncurling them. One by one they opened. I focused my eyes on that spot, on the crushed rose bud lying on the palm of my hand.

☙ TWO ❧

"Lily, can you hear me? Look at me, please." I turned my head toward the soothing voice and blinked a few times trying to clear my vision.

Kalia knelt next to me, her cold hand comforting on my shoulder. I could see Aaron's legs as he hovered next to her, waiting. "Can you sit up...with my help maybe?" she asked. I thought about it a moment and nodded. She moved her hands behind my back and pushed me gently as I tried to lift my body from the ground. My head spun as soon as I reached a sitting position. Her hands never left my back.

"Where am I?" My voice came out in a whisper. I looked around but all I saw were trees.

This time it was Aaron kneeling and looking at me with a sad expression. "You're behind the cabin. We carried you here a little while ago. Can you see me?"

His face was a little blurry but I could see him well enough so I nodded. I blinked a few more times bringing his features into focus. I couldn't help but smile when I saw his gentle eyes, despite all the recent horror I remembered. He forced a smile back at me.

"We have to get to Christian." I tried to stand but Kalia kept her hands on my shoulders, pushing me down.

"Don't try to get up yet, Lily. You've been unconscious for a while. You need some time to recover." She loosened her grip but did not remove her hands.

"You don't understand! Christian needs me. He's in pain. He..."

"Stop it, Lily!" Aaron's voice was demanding. "There is nothing we can do now. It's over. Please understand that."

I shook my head. I knew it wasn't true. It wasn't over. It couldn't be over and I refused to believe anything Aaron said. He didn't know. But I did. I knew Christian was looking for me.

"It's not over. He was just talking to me. I heard him!" It was Aaron's turn to be shocked at the harshness of my voice. Kalia's hand stroked my back, trying to calm me.

"Take me to the cabin. I'll show you..." I tried again to stand but failed. My head was still spinning.

"I'm sorry, Lily. We did everything we could. We tried and..." He hung his head in shame. I shook my head but he wasn't looking. "Christian is dead."

"It's true," Kalia's voice was shaky. "I wish we could tell you something different but..."

What was the use in arguing with them? They weren't going to believe me. Yet, as hard as I tried to convince them, I wasn't sure I was convincing myself. How was I seeing him and hearing him when they couldn't? I felt emptiness in the pit of my stomach. I knew there had been losses in this battle. Exactly how many, I wasn't sure, but I knew I didn't want to ask yet.

"Okay. You win. Now take me to the cabin," I said trying to stand again and noticing Kalia wasn't trying to stop me this time. "If what you say is true, then we have work to do."

This time Aaron helped me up. His hands hovered around me in case I lost my balance. I didn't. I started walking as soon as I felt steady.

The closer we got to the cabin, the more anxious I felt and the harder it was to breathe. I tried to forget what had occurred inside what had last been our home, all the violence that had taken place, not to mention the love of my life ripped from this world. I tried to forget, at least for the moment, that we had not one, but two bodies waiting. One body, I knew, had to be completely dismembered before we could dispose of it. That part, I realized, I kind of looked forward to yet it made me shiver. But good things had also happened there. Fiore and I had truly become friends. It was also the place where Christian and I had made love for the first time.

When we reached the steps, I stopped. I listened for the heartbeat I so longed to hear but encountered only silence. I took a deep breath and forced my legs to carry me up the steps to the door. Aaron stopped me as my hand reached the knob.

"Why don't you stay out here with Kalia for a moment? Let me look first, that may be best." He nodded at his wife. She returned the motion.

"No." I clenched my fist around the metal knob. "This was all because of me. I have to be the one to deal with it."

They both nodded and waited for me to make the first move. I turned the knob and peered inside. The cabin was covered in darkness. I could smell the remains of the fire in the fireplace and the stench of burnt hair. Kalia reached around me to flick on the light. Nothing could have prepared me for the sight we encountered. Ian's lifeless, headless body lying on the floor was the first thing my eyes rested on and I covered my eyes. No matter what Ian had done to deserve this end, he had still been my first love, and my maker. Aaron's arm gripped me around the shoulders. I took to a deep breath in hopes of regaining my composure.

"Um…where is he?" Kalia whispered behind me.

I lowered my hands. "Where's who?"

"Christian. I don't see him…"

I looked toward the kitchen doorway where I remembered Christian had fallen. There was nothing there. "I don't understand…"

"Wait here…both of you." Aaron walked toward the kitchen, scanning the area. He looked toward the bedroom but the door was closed. His head turned to the right. "In here…Oh my God!"

As soon as Kalia released my arm, I ran to the kitchen. I don't know how I hadn't heard the sounds coming from Christian's mouth. He was laying on the floor, curled on his side, his breathing coming in fast, labored gasps. His eyes were wide open and his hands, in tight fists, clenched a kitchen towel. I dropped to my knees beside him, my hand going to his forehead. His skin felt sweaty and clammy, cold. His eyes widened with the feel of my touch.

"I told you!" I spat. "I knew he was alive. I knew it!"

"But how?" Aaron's voice was full of confusion.

"Aaron, not now…" I leaned close to Christian's ear. "Can you hear me?"

"He can hear you, Lily, I'm sure of it. Talk to him." Kalia's gentle tone coached.

"Let's get him to the bed," I said turning to Aaron.

Without hesitating, he dropped to his knees and lifted Christian's body from the floor. Kalia ran ahead of us to pull down the covers on the bed. I never let go of Christian's hand as Aaron lowered him to the bed.

"How much longer?" I asked, wanting desperately for his pain to end.

"I'm not sure." Aaron looked at Kalia.

"It takes about twenty four hours. I'm guessing the rest of the night and most of tomorrow." Kalia settled in the empty chair next to the bed. "Aaron, can you please take care of the rest? We'll be out to help in a minute."

I didn't take my eyes off Christian's pained face as Aaron left the room, closing the door behind him without saying a word.

"I can't leave him. I know I should be out there but I can't…"

"Lily, honey, it's supposed to be you but…I'm sure we can make an exception, considering the circumstances. I have one question though." She leaned forward in the chair, waiting for a response. I turned to her and nodded. "How did you know?" Her voice was gentle, not accusing.

"I didn't really know. I only hoped." I lied. How could I explain what I saw when I couldn't even make any sense of it? I didn't want to think about that right now. All I wanted was to focus all my energy on Christian. I wanted to take his pain away. He didn't deserve any of it. "What's happening to him?" I ran my hands through my tangled hair. "Is this what I think it is?"

"His heart is no longer beating so it certainly looks that way," She stood and walked to the other side of the bed. She sat next to him, taking his other hand. His eyes widened again at the unexpected touch. "I don't know if you remember what it feels like to die but…"

"Vaguely. It seems like so long ago. I remember feeling paralyzed. I wanted to cry out for help but couldn't make anything come out of my mouth. I also remember Ian watching me from across the room but I could do nothing to make him come to me. The more I tried to scream the more it felt like my lungs would explode. I couldn't move my limbs then suddenly, it all went away. I can't stand knowing he's going through this."

"There's nothing you can do but comfort him right now. His organs are shutting down. His senses are changing. You can't ease the pain but be assured that it will pass."

"Before you go…do you think I did this?" I looked at her face.

"I honestly don't know, but that doesn't matter right now. Take care of him. Leave Aaron to me." She knew why I asked without my having to say it. She knew me so well. She gave Christian's hand a gentle squeeze before she rose to join Aaron.

The front door opened and closed with a bang as they took Ian's remains outside. Guilt filled my body and threatened to overflow. Why did all this have to happen? Why couldn't Ian just leave me alone? Christian's fingers twitched in my hand and brought me back to the present.

"I thought you were dead. I thought you were taken from me forever." I lay next to him and put my arm across his damp chest. I don't know why I was surprised not to feel his familiar heartbeat or warmth. I put my lips close to his ear and whispered. "Please don't hate me for this. I don't know how this happened but I'm glad. I couldn't bear the thought of losing you. I couldn't stand the thought of going on without you."

"Lily?" Fiore called from the other side of the door. "May I come in?"

"Please."

I sat up as she entered the room, leaning back against the pillows, still holding Christian's hand. Her clothes were torn and dirty, and mud was spattered on her beautiful face. It was hard to think that she had fought on our side, especially considering her true feelings for Ian and the fact that she had aided him in keeping both Christian and me prisoners in Ireland. She rushed to the other side of the bed, her eyes looking over Christian.

"Aaron told me. He asked me to check on you while they're outside."

"I'm fine. I hate to admit this but I couldn't be happier about what's happening to Christian. He was not taken from me after all. How are you? And the others?" I wasn't really sure I wanted to hear the answer but I asked anyway.

"I'm okay. I can't believe how many young vampires Ian made, totally inexperienced, more of an inconvenience than anything. That finally explains what he was doing when he left us. I took care of Fergus. He was more of a challenge than the newborns. Beth is on Ryanne's trail. Pierce and Riley are still looking for Maia. I came back here as soon as I could." She explained everything with such calmness, like relating the events of a typical day. "I'm going to see if Kalia and Aaron need some help. Call me if you need me." She took one last look at Christian's scrunched face before she left the room with an understanding smile.

His body was soaked in a cold sweat. Beads formed on his forehead and upper lip. I pulled the covers down to the bottom of the bed before getting up to go to the bathroom for a washcloth. I wet it and returned to the room to wipe the sweat off his face and try to make him as comfortable as possible.

When I reached the bed and sat down next to him, he had the blanket tucked under his chin. Strange. He couldn't possibly be coming out of it yet. He shouldn't be able to move, yet he had sat up and pulled the covers back up?

Putting that thought out of my head, I set to wiping his face and neck

11

with the cool water. His breathing finally slowed to a more normal pace, not perfect, but better. All I could do now was wait for him to die...again.

∽ THREE ∽

The room brightened and warmed as the sun rose, announcing the start of a new day. Hushed voices came from the living room and, though I was more than curious to know who was out there, I couldn't bring myself to leave Christian's side. His body was still drenched in sweat and his limbs twitched from time to time, but he finally closed his eyes when the light started shining through the window.

"It won't be much longer, I promise. I wish I could make it stop. I wish I were the one feeling all the pain. I'm so sorry I can't stop it."

There was a light knock on the door. I didn't bother getting up this time. Sensing Kalia, I telepathically gave her permission to enter. "I wanted to see how he's doing."

"Better, I think. He's not breathing as fast. I don't know if that means anything." She sat on the bed on his other side and looked at him with a mother's tenderness.

"That is a good sign. He's not feeling as much pain anymore. He seems more peaceful. How are you holding up?"

"I've been better. I have been trying to figure out how this happened but I really have no idea. Ian killed him. He drained him enough to stop his heart. I saw him do it. He never had a chance to do anything to turn him."

"Don't worry about that now," she interrupted. "There's no point. When the time comes, we can ask Christian. Maybe he'll remember something."

"What about the others? Did they find Maia?" I sat up, stretching out my tense muscles.

"They followed her through the forest. One of the newborns caught up and distracted them. When they finally got rid of the newborn, they followed Maia's scent but lost it at the river." She stopped and searched my face. I wasn't sure how I felt about that news. Part of me was happy she wasn't here but part of me was worried, for Kalia and Aaron's sake.

"What about Ryanne?" I asked. I could picture Ryanne's face the first time I met her, when Ian took me to Ireland as blackmail to keep Christian alive. Ryanne was never comfortable with me and her disapproval always showed. I knew now it was probably because she was helping Ian keep Christian locked up in her basement. She ended up playing babysitter for Ian's captive and she didn't like it one bit. She and Fergus no longer had the freedom to come and go as they pleased.

"She took to the air when Beth had to fight off three newborns. By the time she was able to get away from them, Ryanne was out of sight," she explained.

I shook my head in disbelief. Maia and Ryanne were still out there. Fergus was dead and Ryanne was his mate. She was not going to forget that any time soon. I wrapped my arms around my knees and rocked back and forth. Kalia stood and came to my side. She sat behind me and wrapped her arms around me.

"Don't worry yourself about any of that. You need to be strong for him now more than ever. He's going to need you." She turned her face toward Christian and he opened his eyes. "Oh, he's waking. I'll leave you now. If you need me, you know where I am."

"Kalia?" I whispered. "Is Aaron angry with me?"

She laughed softly. "Of course not. He loves you."

As soon as she left the room, I looked at Christian. His eyes were open but he didn't seem alert, so I walked to the window and pulled the curtain aside. The sun's brightness made me squint and my eyes watered until they adjusted. I wasn't looking for anything in particular when my eyes settled on the mound of fresh dirt piled in front of a tree. My stomach sank when I realized it had to be Ian's grave. I gasped and turned away from the window.

What's happening to me? Am I dead?

I was not expecting Christian's voice so clear in my head. I looked down at him but saw he had not moved.

Can you hear me?

Yes.

My breath caught in my throat. *Are you in pain?*

Not much...anymore. I can't move. I want to get up but I can't move anything. What's happening to me?

I sat back on the edge of the bed. His eyes were open so I turned his face toward me so he could see me. He closed his eyes against the light. *Your body is shutting down, dying. You're going to be able to move again soon, I promise.*

I hadn't shut the curtain in my haste to get away from the sight of what had to be Ian's grave. I stood to go back to the window and closed it, and darkness covered the room once again. I snapped my head toward the window and saw the curtain still moving as if a breeze were somehow coming through the closed window.

"Ian?" I whispered in fear but to my relief received no answer.

Am I going to be a vampire too? Like you? Christian's voice snapped me back.

Yes. You will be exactly like me.

Good.

It was like him to be so calm…always so calm. *Good, I'll be a vampire, like you.* As if that was the most normal thing in the world, like when he found out the truth about what I am. Even then he just accepted it. He wasn't disgusted. He didn't run away screaming like I'd expected him to do. Any other man would have run without a backward glance, but not Christian.

As the hours passed, I heard talking in the living room, where I knew everyone was gathered, waiting for Christian and me to reenter. They knew it would be any minute now. I never felt as anxious in all my years as I did now, waiting for him. How changed was he going to be as a vampire? Would his love for me change? Would he resent me? Would he leave me because of it?

"Never." His voice was hoarse but it was his voice. I jumped off the bed again. "I will never leave you."

"Oh my God! How do you feel? Can you move? Are you okay? Do you need help? Should I get…?" I rattled off questions in my nervousness.

He cleared his throat. "One question at a time, please. I feel…different…strange. I think I can move but I might need help. Should you get what?"

I couldn't help but laugh. Relief washed over me as I sat back on the bed. I grasped both his hands and pulled him to a sitting position. He pushed his body forward to assist me as I pulled and fell off the end of the bed with a loud thump. Within seconds, the door flew open and Kalia and Fiore were in the room, wide eyed.

"What happened?" Fiore asked, looking from Christian to me with her mouth open.

"I guess I didn't know my own strength," Christian answered with a laugh.

This time, Kalia and Fiore helped him to his feet while I stood frozen, unsure of what to do next.

"Kalia, let's leave them alone for a while. They'll come out when they're ready." Fiore took Kalia by the hand and pulled her out of the room before she could respond.

Christian stood at the foot of the bed. The sight of him took my breath away, as it always had, but this time was different. His blue eyes looked somehow bluer, deeper, more intense. It felt as if he were staring straight through me and into at my soul. His dirty blonde hair looked darker against the paleness of his flawless face. He seemed taller, though I'm sure that was all in my head. When he spoke, his voice sounded deeper, sexier, as if that were even possible. I stood still, unsure of what to do, and stared with my mouth hanging open. I couldn't force myself to close it, let alone will my legs to walk.

"Okay then. I'll come to you." And he did. He wrapped his arms around me and I felt myself collapse against his chest. His hand went into my hair and it no longer felt hot against my skin. He kissed the top of my head. I relaxed in his embrace.

"I can't believe this. I thought…"

"Shh…I know. It's okay. I'm here. I'll always be here," Christian reassured me.

He backed away enough to look at my face. Again the sight of his perfection took my breath away. His lips met mine with a fire I didn't expect from his cold body. Everything that happened in the last day melted away with the heat of his mouth. My whole body went limp but he wasn't going to let me fall. I knew that. He would never let me fall.

We parted slowly, not wanting our kiss to end but knowing everyone was waiting for us and there were still things we needed to discuss. As much as I wanted it at that moment, we were not the only ones there. His hands held mine as he led me to the side of the bed and we sat on the edge.

"How are you feeling now?" I asked.

"Dizzy from that kiss." He smiled. "I'm thirsty, though. It feels like my throat is on fire."

I swallowed hard before I spoke. I knew I was going to have to deal with this but I didn't feel ready. "You need to feed."

"I don't feel hungry. It's…different. I hear this strange pulsing or humming in my ears."

"It's not food you want. Your body is no longer alive. Your stomach won't growl anymore. The smell of food won't start your mouth watering. It's blood you need." I knew I wasn't ready to teach him how to hunt, especially not humans, and hunting animals with Ryanne and Maia on the loose was not an option at the moment. "Will you settle for a *little* blood, for now?"

"What do you mean?" He looked around the room as if searching for an answer.

"I mean my blood."

His eyes widened. "I can do that?"

I nodded and went to the desk in the corner of the room. I reached in the drawer and pulled out the letter opener. I sat next to him again. Sliding the edge of the opener across my wrist, gasping at the instant sting, I raised it to his mouth. "Drink." I ignored the pain as his hands enclosed around mine and his lips clamped around the wound. His eyes locked on mine. I could feel the moistness of his tongue as he lapped the blood his body so desperately needed.

My free hand reached his head and my fingers tousled his damp hair. If there was ever a more intimate moment between two people, I couldn't imagine what it was. There could be nothing to bring us closer than my blood coursing through his veins. My head spun and a sudden chill shook my entire body but yet I felt like my body was on fire. He'd had my blood once before, when I used it to close a knife wound on his hand, but that had been out of necessity. The feeling had been desperation to heal him. This was pure desire.

"That's enough…for now. You'll want to drink little bits at a time," I explained, though I didn't want it to end.

He withdrew his mouth from my wrist and licked his lips, never taking his eyes off mine.

"I'm still thirsty." His eyes looked hazy but his lips formed a smile.

"I know but we have to take it slow at first. This is new to your body," I explained.

"I feel so…drugged? I don't know quite how to explain it, like I'm floating." He stood again and ran his hand through his hair, fixing the mess I'd created. "Is all blood like that or is it only yours?"

"It's not just mine, I'm sorry to break it to you, but all human blood. Animal blood doesn't have such a strong effect. It quenches our thirst and sustains us but it doesn't have that hypnotic quality." Maybe hypnotic was the best way to describe the feeling. It didn't matter who the donor was, the end result was always the same: hypnotizing, mind-numbing.

"I saw something in you…scattered images. You were lying under a tree, Kalia and Aaron were with you, I think." He stood and reached for my hand.

"You will. You'll get something from anyone whose blood you drink. That must have been what I was picturing, what was happening after the battle was…over." I stood now, wanting to pull him out of the room with me so I didn't have to think about any of the events leading up to this moment. It was all too confusing. Ian's headless body was in the living room before Aaron buried him, yet, I had seen him only a short while before that. He had a beating heart then but I knew better. I didn't want to think about any of that. I was too happy having Christian at my side again.

Christian watched my face and nodded. "Okay. Maybe I can have more later…I guess we should make our entrance. They expect it." His arm wrapped around my back, strong and steady. "Ready?"

I took a deep breath. "As ready as I'm gonna be." I couldn't help but worry about Aaron and what he thought of me. Could I have done this? Could I have been the one to make Christian a vampire? It was very possible that I suppressed that memory because of all the stress.

"Later. We'll worry about that later."

FOUR

As we entered the living room, conversation ceased. Everyone focused on us, except Aaron. He stared out the window with a stiff back. I followed Christian to sit on the floor in front of the fireplace, which was the only space available. I tried to listen to their thoughts, but everyone closed their minds.

"Beautiful day, huh? So, what is everyone doing?" I asked, trying to break the uncomfortable silence. Christian looked around the room as if he'd never laid eyes on it before, which he hadn't – not with vampire eyes, anyway. Kalia smiled at his child-like wonder and everyone else relaxed a bit, except Aaron.

"I'm going for a walk," he said and left, letting the door slam behind him. My stomach sank.

Kalia looked at me with tender eyes. "He'll be fine. He just needs a little time and he'll come around."

"But, time for what? I did not do this. Why doesn't he believe me?" I knew I pleaded with the wrong person but I didn't care. I did not want to lose my new family. If anyone could make Aaron understand, it would be her. Aaron was the only one who had no access to my thoughts, but it would help so much if he did. "I don't even know how this happened."

"I know dear. Christian, how are you feeling?" She leaned forward in her seat.

"I'm okay. Actually, I never felt better." He smiled and hugged me closer. "It's what I wanted, to be with Lily forever."

"Do *you* know what happened? Do you remember anything at all?" Pierce asked.

Christian shook his head. "I only remember what happened in the beginning, after Ian started talking to Lily. I hid in the bedroom, against my will, I might add. I heard a struggle and came out to see if Lily was okay. After that, I only remember very hazy bits and pieces."

"What do you remember, Lily?" Kalia asked.

"Well, I heard someone outside. I made Christian hide, like he said, and then Ian busted through the door. We argued, fought, and I lost the sword. The next thing I knew Christian was in the room and Ian grabbed him." I took a deep breath, trying to gather strength to continue. No one moved. "Ian bit him and I knocked Christian out of his grasp, out of the way. Ian came toward me but something was wrong. He was slow and awkward, stumbling like a drunk. He acted like that was my fault. He accused me of letting him drink poisoned blood." I looked from Kalia to Pierce, hoping they had some explanation.

"That was my doing. I put a spell on the charm around Christian's neck. I'll explain later. Go on," Pierce said.

"He said some things, we said some things, I swung the sword and… that was it." I explained as Christian gripped my hand, encouraging me. "I tried to do CPR on Christian but it wasn't working. I kept trying until I heard Maia. She looked shocked or scared when she saw Ian and she just ran. She didn't try to do anything to me. She ran and I ran after her. That's all I remember." I lied, leaving out the part about seeing Ian alive and well later. I didn't know how to explain that part.

"That doesn't explain much," Fiore said, smiling at Christian. "Well, Christian, welcome to our world."

Everyone nodded and I couldn't help but smile at how easily they accepted him. Pierce stood. "We'll figure it out later, I suppose."

"I'll go find Aaron and talk to him. In the meantime, we need to figure out what our next move is. I think we're pretty much done here," Kalia said.

I hoped with all my might that Kalia would be able to get through to Aaron. I couldn't wait to get back to Astoria and the semi-peaceful life we had created there. The only difference was that Christian would be a vital part of that life now, no longer someone I had to hide, or hide from.

As if hearing my thoughts, Christian asked, "Where do we live?"

"I hadn't thought about it. I guess we'll have to wait and see what Aaron says." I knew where I wanted to be and that was anywhere Christian was, whether that was at his apartment or at the Benjamin house. "Where do you want to live?"

"Anywhere you are." He smiled and squeezed my hand. I somehow already knew that.

Kalia walked in with Aaron behind her about a half hour later. He didn't say anything to the others, who were chatting while they waited, but walked directly toward where Christian and I stood by the kitchen sink.

"Can I talk to both of you outside?" He looked a bit nervous.

"Um…sure," Christian answered.

We followed him out, where the setting sun painted the sky the bright orange of flames. We walked a few feet from the front of the cabin, where he paused and faced us.

"I wanted, first of all, to say that I am sorry about my reaction. I don't want you to think that I don't trust you, Lily. It's, well, what was I supposed to think?" He raised his voice and I backed up a few paces. He took a deep breath, calming himself before continuing. "You say Ian didn't do this and there was no one else. I still have no idea how this happened but I suppose, in time, we will get our answers. I know everyone is exhausted right now and would probably like to go home." He smiled trying to ease the tension.

"Believe me, Aaron; I would like to know too. I don't understand it either. All I know is…I'm glad it turned out this way." There. I said it. And I was glad Christian wasn't gone forever. I couldn't take that back.

"I can imagine. I can't even fathom having to go on without Kalia. This is why I want to forget about this for now. Christian…" He turned to him. "Welcome to our family. If I would have had to choose someone for Lily, I couldn't have done better than you."

"Thank you, Aaron. I appreciate that more than you know." Aaron nodded and started walking toward the cabin. It was the end of the discussion.

As we entered, all talk ceased again.

"I say we head out. There doesn't seem to be anything left to do here," Aaron announced. Everyone agreed.

I cleared my throat. All eyes focused on me, including Christian's. I bit my lip and smiled at him. "On behalf of Christian, and myself, I want to thank you all for helping us. You have no idea how much we appreciate it. This had nothing to do with any of you and yet you all came. I wish there were something we could do to repay you."

"No payment is necessary. We are family and that's what family does." Beth smiled and looked around the room. Agreement was unanimous.

"I think I speak for all of us when I say I know you would do the same if any of us needed help," Riley said. "Now let's go home. I'm famished."

In the moments that followed, goodbyes were said and plans to meet again soon were made. As I stood by Christian's side, as my new family welcomed him with open arms, I couldn't help but glow. What I had avoided all along was now something I couldn't live without. It made me wonder why I hadn't realized it sooner. Christian squeezed me to his side, again knowing what was on my mind.

AFTER EVERYONE LEFT, we packed what few belongings we had gathered there and extinguished the fires. The question of where we were going still unanswered, I stopped cleaning out the refrigerator. "Where are we going? I mean…Christian still has an apartment."

"Nonsense," Kalia said looking at Aaron. When he didn't disagree, she smiled and continued. "You're coming home with us. That is, if that's what he wants."

Christian stopped in the middle of pulling the bag out of the trashcan. His eyes questioned me. I nodded. "I would be honored. I will go wherever Lily is happy."

"Great. That solves that. Fiore, what about you?" Aaron turned to her. "Are you coming with us or do you have other plans?"

"I hadn't really thought about it. I figured I would go back to Italy for a while, but…" She turned to me. I smiled. "If you have enough room, maybe for a while…"

"You're coming with us!" I blurted.

Christian stiffened but said nothing.

"Then that's settled," Kalia said and went to turn off the bedroom lights.

"Shall we?" Aaron said as he piled things into his arms. We followed with our own loads.

Not a word was said about Maia. No one seemed to want to even think about her.

ᴄ⟶ FIVE ᴄ⟶

Kalia and I gave Fiore and Christian a tour of the house and after Fiore went to the guest room, Christian and I went to my room… our room. He took everything in with his new vampire eyes, opening doors and walking around the room.

"So this is it?"

"This is it."

"When I tried to picture what you were doing during the day, I tried to imagine your room, thinking you might be in it."

I smiled, realizing I used to do the same thing about him. "So, do you like it?"

"I love it. You have a lot of books," he said as he looked at the shelves in my sitting room.

"Most of those were here when I moved in. I usually borrowed books from libraries," I explained. With all the moving around I'd done in my past, it was just easier to borrow books than to accumulate them, much easier to pack.

"I need to email my landlord."

"Maybe we should wait on that. We haven't exactly figured out what to tell people." I sat on the bed, kicking off my shoes.

"What do you mean?" He stood in front of me, waiting for me to invite him.

"Your bed too," I patted the mattress. "I mean, we have to tell them something. You've been missing. They don't even know if you're alive. We can't just go back to normal."

"Oh, right. I forgot. As far as work, I have to stay away. I'm sure the police questioned the university and my landlord."

"That's true," I explained. "The reason I knew you were even in Ireland when I escaped was that Ian told me the police had questioned him. They called because you were missing and students had seen us together in the parking lot. That's how I knew to go back to the cottage for you."

"Right. I wonder if my apartment is considered a crime scene."

Picturing the CSI team walking around getting prints and photos of everything, I laughed. Christian laughed too. "What are you laughing at?"

"CSI? You watch too much TV."

"You saw that?" This was going to take some getting used to. Ian had only been able to see what I wanted him to see. But Christian? I didn't intentionally put that image in his head, yet he saw it anyway.

"I guess I did. Wow! Are we *that* connected?"

"We must be. I can't remember ever being *this* connected to someone. It was different…you know." He nodded, knowing it was a subject I didn't want to discuss.

"How do you think this happened, me being like you? Do you have any theories?" He leaned back against the pillows, throwing his arms behind his head. It was strange to see him on my bed. Many times I had wished we'd been here and now he finally was. That made me smile.

"I wish I knew. It would make things with Aaron so much easier. Maybe someone came in after I ran outside but…no, I had just left you and I ran into Aaron right outside the door. If someone had passed he would've seen." I sat up searching for the TV remote. I spotted it on the night stand next to Christian. He looked at it and, with his arms still behind his head, the remote took to the air and landed on my chest. I jumped up. "Ouch!"

"What was that?" Christian sat up and turned his head, looking around the room.

"I have no idea. That's not the first time something like that happened." I picked up the remote and examined it, not knowing what I was looking for. "Ian? Is that you?" I asked, bracing myself. No answer.

"Do you think so?" Christian asked but shook his head. "I don't think that's possible. He's quite dead."

"I know. Neither do I but I thought I'd try." I stared at the remote in my hand. "Can I try something?"

"Sure."

I crawled to the bottom of the bed and set the remote down at his feet. When I lay back down, I asked him for it. "No. Don't move," I said when he tried to sit up. "Just think about it."

"You think?"

I shrugged. He concentrated and scrunched his nose. The remote lay where I put it but after a few moments, it twitched. He turned to me with a wide-eyed look. I nodded, excited. "Try again. Give me the remote."

As he stared at it, it rose about two feet off the bed and flew at me so fast I didn't have time to react. It hit me square in the forehead, again. "Ouch!"

"Oh no!" he cried as his hands pushed my hair aside to look at my forehead. "It's red. I am so sorry!"

Suddenly, I was doubled over with laughter. I laughed so hard my body shook. Christian stared at me, not moving. "What is so funny?"

I couldn't stop laughing long enough to answer him. I saw the frustration on his face but it didn't matter. "What is so hysterical?" he asked again. I calmed myself enough to talk by taking a few deep breaths. "Please, Lily. I'm going nuts here."

"Beth said you were powerful. She said that when she first met you and at the cabin she said you were special. I had no idea what she was talking about, until now. Do you realize what this means?"

He shook his head. "You got hit in the face with a remote?"

"Besides that. You did it, like you pulled the covers over yourself in the cabin, when I had pulled them off because you were sweating. You closed the curtain when the sunlight bothered your eyes. I was in the room for that one. I thought it was Ian, somehow."

"So, you think I can do that with my mind?" He looked confused.

"That's the only explanation I can think of. I wanted the remote. You knew it and you made it move before you actually reached for it." It made sense. That had to be what Beth was talking about. Christian was powerful enough to use the part of his brain that had been dormant while he was human.

"I guess I did." He still didn't look convinced.

"It was definitely you." Most of us had special gifts that weren't awakened until after we became immortal but I had never seen this one. "Truthfully, it doesn't shock me one bit that you would be so talented."

"Even though I hit you twice?" He laughed.

"We'll have to work on your aim." I hit the power button on the remote and settled down with my head on his chest. "We have all the time in the world to perfect it."

He wrapped his arms around me and held me, kissing my head and whispered, "I love you, Lily."

"I love you, Christian." I turned my head up to look at his face. "How are you feeling? I mean, how's your thirst?"

"It's there but it's manageable. I guess I have to hunt, soon, huh?"

I knew I couldn't put it off too much longer but I had no desire to leave the peace of our room yet. "Yeah, soon. I don't want to move right now."

"Neither do I." He flipped me to my back and lay on top of me, our faces inches apart. As usual, butterflies invaded my stomach. "I can't believe this is really happening." He gently kissed my lips. "All my dreams came true."

"You really feel that way? I was afraid you'd resent me. I thought…"

"Are you kidding me?" he interrupted. "Don't ever think that. This is what I wanted all along: to be with you, forever."

Relief, and disbelief, washed over me as his lips found mine again and his kiss wasn't so gentle this time. The room started spinning as his lips and his tongue danced with mine in perfect harmony. Moans escaped both our mouths and his hands pressed against my back, holding me tighter still, our bodies like one. His lips left mine as they traveled down the side of my face, finding my neck as I arched my head back granting him easier access. My head clouded and my breath sped as he nibbled on my skin, once in a while letting his tongue touch the sensitive flesh, sending chills up my spine. I felt him pull back a bit as a gasp escaped his lips.

"What's wrong?" I asked trying to pull my face aside enough to look at him but he dropped his face to the pillow. "Christian, what is it?"

"My mouth," he mumbled. "It hurts."

Relief washed over me as I realized I hadn't done anything wrong. "Is it your fangs?"

I felt him nod against my shoulder. "Let me see." He leaned over me but kept his mouth closed awkwardly. "It's perfectly normal. It's okay."

"Yeah but I want you. It's overwhelming. I can taste it," he explained, showing his protruding fangs as he spoke.

"That's normal too. Why do you think I wouldn't let myself go with you when you were human?" I kissed his lips but he pulled away.

"No. I'll hurt you." His eyes filled with pain.

"It's okay. I want you to," I whispered as I pulled his face toward mine again and lost myself in his kiss. My hands held the sides of his face and after a few moments of passion, I pushed his face back toward my neck. He kissed me, with closed lips at first, and then a gasp escaped my open mouth as his teeth brushed against my soft flesh. I moaned when I felt the burn, followed by the hypnotizing ecstasy of his drink. The room continued to spin out of control as every horrible thing that had happened lately left me with each swallow of his throat. The burning started in my own throat, barely noticeable at first and then strong enough to make my mind snap back to reality.

Gently pushing his face away from my neck, I found his lips again, moisture still on my neck as blood escaped before the wound began to close. I kissed the side of his face, all the while pulling his body closer. His breathing echoed in my ears as my mouth found his neck and my teeth sank into his flesh, sweetness flooding my mouth in a frenzy of colors and fire and love and relief, complete and utter rapture. His body relaxed as he melted against me. I drank him in and lost myself in him until my mind warned me to stop. Reluctantly, I released my hold on his neck and kissed his chin before I let my head fall back, exhausted. We lay still for a while, neither of us speaking. His arms finally wrapped around me and a sigh escaped his lips.

"Wow!" he said and kissed the top of my head. "I had no idea it could feel this way."

"I know. Incredible, huh?" I looked at his face. He had a drop of blood on the side of his mouth and I wiped it away with my finger.

"And yet we're fully dressed!"

"Now do you see why I couldn't let myself go with you before?" I asked looking at his smiling but thoughtful face.

"I do. I was insecure though and thought you didn't want me as much as I wanted you. Silly?"

"Ridiculous!" I answered and got up. "As soon as the stores open, we have to get you some clothes."

"Guess so. Fiore will need stuff too," he answered and turned off the TV we weren't watching anyway. "I don't feel thirsty anymore."

"You did feed twice," I explained. "Not much but still."

I heard my phone vibrate and went to retrieve it from my bag. Rain pounded against the windows and I knew Christian's skin and eyes would need minimal protection on his first immortal outing.

"What is it?" he asked as I opened it and looked at the screen.

"Looks like a text," I clicked to open it. "It's a picture." I waited for it to load as Christian came to stand at my side. I covered my mouth to restrain a scream.

"What is it?"

I couldn't speak so I turned the phone for him to see. He grabbed it from my hands and scrolled to look at the number. "I don't understand."

It was a picture of Christian, lying on his side, gagged and blindfolded. It looked like he was on a carpeted floor.

"I need to see Aaron. Now!" I grabbed his hand and ran for the stairs.

⌘ SIX ⌘

"**A**aron! Kalia!" I called as I ran down the stairs pulling Christian along. I heard Fiore's door open then her footsteps right behind us. Kalia, with paintbrush in hand, and Aaron rushed in from the kitchen.

"What's going on?" Aaron asked walking into the living room behind us.

"This." I held out the phone. Kalia stepped around Aaron to take a look. Fiore put a comforting hand on my shoulder.

"What is it?" she asked. I looked at her and shrugged.

"It's a picture of Christian. It must have been taken when he was captive, but where did it come from?" Aaron asked.

"There's a number if you scroll down," Christian said. Aaron did and shook his head.

"Do you know the number, Lily?" I took the phone back and looked at the number for the first time. I went through numbers in my head, trying to match it to one I knew. "No. I have no idea. It's not…" I looked around but they all looked as confused as I felt. "Is it Maia's?"

"No," Kalia said looking at Aaron. He shook his head.

"Why would she send something like this anyway?" Aaron asked. "Why would she even have this picture? She wasn't in Ireland."

"I don't know, but who else would've done it? Ian's dead," Christian answered and grasped my hand tighter. "What are you thinking?"

"I honestly don't know," I admitted. "I don't feel safe here. I don't think *you're* safe here."

"What are you saying, Lily?" Aaron grabbed my other hand that still grasped the phone. "It's over."

As much as I wanted to believe it, deep down I knew it was too good to be true. It had been too easy. It had been too fast and I had gotten what

I ultimately wanted: Christian. "I hope you're right, Aaron. Maybe who ever sent this will try again."

"No one will let anything happen to you." Kalia made everything sound so easy I had no choice but to believe her, for now.

"What are your plans for today?" Aaron asked, also looking a bit more relaxed.

"Fiore and Christian need clothes," I said turning toward Fiore.

"I guess we do. Sounds like fun. I can't wait to see this town and now I have two tour guides." She smiled at Christian's annoyed look. I didn't think he liked the idea of sharing me with Fiore. Kalia covered her mouth so we wouldn't see her laughing.

"Yeah, guess so," Christian answered and tried to smile but with much effort.

"Do you want me to go along? I could help," Kalia asked, hopeful. I knew how much she loved shopping.

"Sure. If we're not taking you away from anything," I added.

"Not at all. Aaron has some work to do so I was going to putter around the house anyway. I'll get ready." She kissed Aaron before going back to the kitchen to wash her brush.

"I FEEL FUNNY with all this stuff on my face," Christian complained as we entered the mall. He kept touching his face and fidgeting with the sunglasses. I explained to him that even though it was overcast, I didn't want to take any chances when it came to his well-being.

"Here," I held out my hand, "I'll put the glasses in my jacket. Trust me; no one knows you're wearing make-up."

"Then why does everybody keep looking at us?"

Fiore laughed, tossing her gorgeous dark hair over her shoulder. "They can't help it. We're irresistible to the mortals."

As we walked down the corridor of the lower level, I did notice that all eyes turned to us as we passed. Christian's facial expressions changed with each person who passed, but he didn't say anything. "What's wrong?" I finally asked.

He leaned in and whispered, "I can hear everybody's thoughts. It's terrible. They don't shut up even for a second!"

"You can hear it too, huh?" I asked. Christian nodded. "You'll learn to control it. You'll be able to shut it off when you want."

"I hope so. It's enough to drive a person mad!"

That could be fun!

"Fiore!" I gave her a sharp look.

"Oops. I'm kidding. Did you really just stomp your foot?" she said and laughed.

"Yeah, guess I did. I don't know where that came from," I said.

"It was actually kind of cute," Fiore teased. Kalia and Christian shook their heads.

"It was. It was very child-like and adorable," Christian agreed. Fiore made gagging sounds.

"Children, please," Kalia said as she led us around the bend. "Let's go to Macy's. We can split up inside. I'll go with Fiore."

Once in the store, Fiore and Kalia headed for the women's department and Christian and I went to the men's. We started with shirts and after loading our arms with as many as we could hold, went to find some pants to go with them. We picked some dress pants, though he only wanted jeans, and found the fitting rooms.

"Why do I have to try any of this on? I only grabbed my size," Christian asked, overwhelmed by the heaping piles in our arms.

"I'd like you to at least try the pants on. I don't know if it's my imagination but you look taller." I handed him five pairs to start with and nudged him toward the fitting room. "I'll wait right here."

He took the load from me and obediently went in. I looked around to find the underwear department. After a couple minutes, Christian stood in the doorway with a smirk on his face.

"High-waters?" he asked, spinning around.

"Um…yeah. I thought so. I'll go get more." I took all the pants with me and waited until I was out of sight to laugh.

I grabbed each pair two sizes longer and picked out three more I thought would look good on him. When I returned to the fitting room, I called for him but got no answer. I tried mentally but still nothing. I poked my head in the doorway. "Christian? Are you in here?"

After throwing the clothes on top of the return rack, I walked around the men's department. Maybe something caught his eye and he went to look while he waited. I passed a few women in the tie department and listened to their thoughts in case one of them had seen him. They hadn't. I started running through the rest of the store. In the lingerie department, I caught a glimpse of him in a saleswoman's mind. He was headed out of the store. As I passed the jewelry counter, on my way back into the mall,

Kalia and Fiore caught up to me.

"What's going on?" I asked in a panic though I had a feeling I knew.

"He's following a man. He just passed through here," Fiore answered and grabbed my arm. "Hurry. He's hunting!"

"He's hunting in the mall?"

"He sure is. He's headed toward the escalator," Kalia said and led the way.

"What if we don't get to him in time?" I scanned thoughts as we passed people, hoping I wouldn't see anything out of the ordinary.

"Wait…" Fiore stopped and almost pulled my arm out of its socket. "He stopped. He didn't get on the escalator."

"There he is!" Kalia pointed. He stood by the escalator, eyes on the back of the man he was following.

"Christian!" I called and pulled out of Fiore's grip. "What are you doing?"

"I don't know," he answered with a terrified look in his eyes. "I…"

Kalia and Fiore caught up. Kalia put a comforting hand on his back. "It's okay. We're here now."

He turned wide eyes to us. I held his hand tightly in mine. "I'm so sorry, Christian. I should've known better. It was too soon to bring you here."

"What are you talking about?"

"Were you following him because you're thirsty?" I whispered.

"I don't know…maybe. I didn't feel thirsty until I smelled him. He was in the fitting room next to mine." He looked down at himself and gasped. He still wore the much-too-short, now stolen, pants.

"We're leaving. We'll get you clothes later," I said and Kalia nodded. She and Fiore could shop for him later.

"What about these?" He pointed at his legs.

"Consider yourself a fugitive because we're stealing those. I'm not taking any chances by taking you back there." He looked shocked.

"Trust me, you'll be stealing much more than pants in the future!" Fiore winked at him.

I elbowed her in the ribs as we led Christian back out to the car.

"I'm so sorry, Lily." He looked at the floor as we walked.

"It's not your fault. You didn't know any better, but, I do. It's way too soon to have you out in public. You haven't learned to control your urges yet."

Everyone made small talk on the way back home, avoiding the incident with Christian. I was thankful for that. What kind of teacher would I make for him when I hadn't had one myself when I was new to this life? Ian didn't bother to teach me about my new talents. He didn't explain all the changes my body had gone through. But I knew I had to do just that for Christian. I had to teach him everything I knew so that he wouldn't ever have to wonder. Kalia's warm smile told me I would not be alone in my efforts to help him acclimate to his new life. She would be there to guide me and fill in the blanks when I could not.

We found Aaron in the living room watching TV when we entered. I knew by the way he looked at Christian's pants, and the fact that we had no packages that he knew the shopping trip had not gone well. He smiled at us and kissed Kalia before returning to the sofa.

"This movie just started if you want to join me," he said and patted the sofa.

"Maybe we will," Kalia said looking at Fiore. She glanced at me.

"You guys go ahead. We're going upstairs. If he's getting clothes, I have to make room for them." I led Christian to the stairs.

"What the hell happened to me?" he asked as he closed our bedroom door.

"You didn't do anything wrong. You were just following your instincts," I explained.

"It felt like I had absolutely no control. One minute, I'm trying to take off these ridiculous pants, and then, I'm zipping them back up, my throat is on fire, and I'm walking like a puppy dog behind some man."

"Yeah, but you stopped. You didn't go through with it. You had enough self-control to restrain yourself," I led him to the bed to sit.

He shook his head. "Self-control has nothing to do with it. I knew exactly what I wanted. I wanted his blood."

"That is what we do. We are predators. We hunt and humans are our prey. You just have to make sure it's the right time and the right human," I explained.

"That was an awful feeling. I hate the thought that I might have killed that man." He finally raised his eyes to mine and I could see the pain.

"But the point is, you didn't. What made you stop just then?"

"You did. I heard you coming and it snapped me back. And then, once I heard your voice, I couldn't remember what I was doing by the escalator."

"You still stopped. That's all that matters."

"This time. What if you hadn't found me? I could've killed him in front of everyone!" He looked at his lap again.

"But you didn't." I turned his face to look into his eyes. "I have to teach you to hunt now. It's time."

He sighed. "Is it my only option for survival?"

"It is, unless you want to live off my blood, or animals, for the rest of eternity." I laughed to lighten his anxiety, and mine.

"Yours would be fine with me, but..." He scrunched his nose, "Animals? I didn't think we could do it as our only source."

"We could, I suppose, if we really had to. Their blood does not taste as good and it doesn't sustain us as long. Unfortunately, you'd have to feed much more often if you were to survive that way."

"So, you don't recommend it then?"

"Not really. I will teach you all you need to do to kill only criminals. It feels more moral that way," I explained, hoping it wouldn't trouble him as much if he knew he was bringing justice to the victims.

"Then I guess I will be a proper vampire and do things your way."

Proper vampire...whatever that means.

∽ SEVEN ∽

We walked down the dark street as rain poured down on our heads. The streetlights reflected off the wet pavement and gave off a glowing effect that made the deserted street look almost magical. The wind was still for once and I didn't have to fight my hair.

"It's amazing how comfortable I feel, not one bit cold," he said as we passed darkened, closed stores.

"And you always thought I was cold. Remember?"

He nodded and smiled, remembering what seemed like so long ago when in reality it was not. We had been through so many trials together that it felt like we had been together for years rather than mere months.

"Okay. We're hunting my way," I explained as we crossed the street. "My way means no innocents ever."

"So how do we know?"

"We listen. Any human who has committed a crime will think about it without realizing. The crime committed will always be in his or her subconscious. Especially when guilt is at play, they never get over it." It was my theory anyway. "I want you to stay with me at all times and do exactly as I tell you."

"You are the expert," he said and put his arm around me, which caused me to walk crooked.

The bar we found was to my liking: dark, loud, and full of smoke. He seemed nervous as he looked around the room and focused on each face. I led him to a table near the back of the room, closest to the pool table. As soon as we were seated, the man behind the bar walked over to get our drink orders. Christian looked at me with raised eyebrows.

"Two gin and tonics, please." The man nodded and hurried back to the bar. I turned back to Christian. "We can dump those under the table and it won't be too noticeable."

"Oh. No color, I get it," he looked around again. "How do you ever focus on only one mind?"

"It takes practice, believe me. Try focusing on just one person for a while," I coached. He looked at the bartender, concentrating.

"I can hear everyone else, him too but everyone else. It's frustrating."

"It's okay. Don't expect to get it on the first try. No one does."

We listened to the room as we pretended to enjoy our drinks. Christian's eyes gleamed and he licked his lips, obviously thirsty. I followed his gaze and noticed two college aged guys had walked in and were ordering drinks from the bar. I listened to their minds for a moment. "Perfect," I said and took Christian's hand.

"What?" He looked back at the guys.

"Those two," I nodded toward them. "See the smiles on their faces? Both of them think they got away with date rape. One planned it and the other one went along with him."

"You got that by looking at them?"

"Years of practice," I assured him.

"But they're just kids," Christian protested. "They look like most of my students. I don't know..."

"Does it make a difference how old they are? I mean, think about their victim. What do you think she's going through?"

"Still, they're so young." He frowned.

"They're both over eighteen and old enough to know better," I explained, hoping he would understand what the girl was dealing with because of them. "It was too easy for them. They'll do it again."

"You really think so?"

"Absolutely. Did you see them looking around when they walked in?" He nodded. "What do you think they were looking for? A woman sitting alone."

"Oh. Since you put it that way...I couldn't imagine something like that happening to someone I love. This is still terrifying," he whispered.

"Welcome to my world."

"That was by far the most terrifying yet exhilarating thing I've ever done. I almost hate to admit that." Christian looked at the bodies of the boys whose short lives had come to an end. We both felt full and were in no hurry to drag them into the ocean since no one else was crazy enough to be on this cold, wet beach at this late hour. Luring them here had been easy. We shot some pool with them and the more they drank, the easier it was to get into their heads. Even Christian had been able to pick up on the thought that what they really wanted was to get high. So with a promise of giving them what they wanted, we talked them into going to the beach with us.

Keep doing what you're doing. When we get there, I'll grab one, you grab the other. Go straight for the throat and don't hesitate. Even if they scream, who'll hear them over the rain and waves? I communicated instructions to him on the way down the hill so there would be no questions once we began. He nodded but kept silent, even in his head, keeping his doubts to himself.

"You did great, by the way," I assured him as I finally stood and began dragging my meal to the water's edge. "Be careful of the rocks."

"Don't worry. I can see everything!" He smiled, finally relaxing a bit.

"Do you feel satisfied?" I asked as I threw the body as far as I could into the water. He followed my lead, tossing his twice as far as mine. Show off.

"I think so. The burning in my throat is gone. What if they wash back up?" He rinsed his hands in the salt water and dried them on his jeans.

"I used my blood to close the wounds." I motioned to my neck. "Don't worry. No signs of foul play, right?"

"Is this how you always do it?" He stood behind me and wrapped his arms around my waist.

"I never imagined I'd be having this conversation with you." I turned to face him, his arms still around me.

"I bet you never imagined we'd be killing together either but here we are. Will you tell me about them?" He looked serious.

"Who?"

"The ones you've killed."

"Why would you want to hear about them?" I pulled out of his embrace.

"Because it's part of who you are and I want to know everything about you."

"On the way home," I said and grabbed his hand to lead him back up to the street.

As we walked hand in hand, I told him everything I remembered and he listened without asking questions until I finished. I even told him about the waitress, Lori, from Washington, whose abusive ex-boyfriend I had enjoyed killing. He looked calm as I described the details to him.

"So, you're like an avenging angel?" he asked with a smile.

"If you want to think of it that way, I guess. I didn't always kill this way. I've killed plenty of innocent people, before I knew any better," I explained, remembering what it had been like in the beginning.

"Is this how all vampires do it?"

"Unfortunately, no. Ian killed as he pleased. He wasn't a picky eater. He killed anything with a heartbeat. The others in Ireland hunted the same way," I shuddered remembering my first night there, when Fiore had lured two drunken men home for *dinner.*

"How do you justify the way you do it?"

"I make it easier on myself by thinking of the victims. They may never know what happened to the person who violated them, but will never have to worry about it happening again, not by the same person, anyway. Imagine running into the person who raped you?"

"What about Fiore?" He scrunched his nose, having caught the image of the dinner party from my mind.

"I hadn't thought about it since she's been with us. I'll have to talk to her." I stopped walking and wrapped my arms around his neck. "Do you think any less of me?"

His lips brushed my forehead. "Of course not. I understand your reasoning. Besides, you are a very sexy teacher." This time, his lips found mine and I lost myself in his kiss, forgetting about everything, including where we were standing, until a car blew its horn and made us jump.

"Just because we're immortal doesn't mean we should tempt fate. Let's get back on the sidewalk and go home."

"So, HOW DID it go?" Fiore called from the living room as we entered. Kalia and Aaron were with her, paging through what looked like photo albums.

"It was horrible! I made such a mess of things!" Aaron's jaw dropped so I elbowed Christian. "I'm kidding."

"It went very smoothly. He's a natural," I said and everyone's relaxed. "What are you all doing?"

"We're showing Fiore some photos, filling her in on the family history." Kalia moved over on the sofa so I went to sit by her. Christian made himself comfortable on the floor in front of me, his cheeks glowing with new color.

"Who's this?" I asked pointing to a picture of a thin man with long dark hair; a severe contrast to Aaron's blond, standing next to Aaron in a library. Both were dressed in clothing not of this period.

"Oh, it's Aaron's great-grandfather," Kalia answered. "Can't you see the resemblance?"

"Since you mention it, some of the facial features are similar but definitely not the hair," I examined the photo. "He looks about the same age as Aaron in this picture."

"He was only two years older than me when he was made," Aaron said, holding his hand out for the album. Kalia handed it to him. "I do miss him. I wonder what he's up to."

"I can't believe you have another vampire in your family! It must be strange being so close in age with your great-grandfather." Christian sounded shocked. It all must seem so surreal to him. Not long ago, vampires were only legend to him and now he was one of them.

"His name is Aloysius. He's a nomad so he's hard to track down. I haven't seen him in years," Aaron explained handing the book back to Kalia.

"I take it he doesn't have a cell phone," Christian said.

"Not him. He still hangs on to some of the customs of his time," Aaron explained. "I have letters upstairs from him and they come from all over the world."

"So you have no idea where he lives?" I asked as I paged through the album.

"The last letter I got from him was about a year ago. He was in Germany then." Aaron grabbed another album and began turning the pages.

"Does he have a wife?" I handed the album back to Kalia. "He's alone in all the pictures."

"No. His wife, my great-grandmother, died in childbirth. She was the love of his life. He's had women, I'm sure, in all his years, but nothing serious." He put the album on the coffee table.

"That's so romantic," Christian said. Fiore laughed.

"Is he the one who made you?" I asked.

Aaron looked at me and his expression changed from melancholy to plain sadness. "Yes. I had cancer and, back then, there wasn't much the doctors could do for me. Aloysius insisted."

"So what happened then? Did you have to leave your family?" I asked.

"Actually, I had to pretend to die. I lied still in a coffin for hours while my family mourned and cried over me. That was really difficult. Sometimes they would talk about something funny they remembered and I had to fight not to laugh or reach out and comfort them. I was relieved when I was finally put in the ground. After I was buried, Aloysius dug up the grave and got me out. That same night, I left the state and came here."

Kalia patted his hand and smiled. "And I'm so glad Aloysius did what he did." She said. Aaron smiled.

"So, any thought on the text message? Have you heard from Maia yet?" I wanted to know more about Aaron's fascinating history but there were more urgent issues that were nagging at my mind. I couldn't help but feel like we were still walking on eggshells.

Kalia looked at Aaron before she spoke. "No, nothing from Maia, but I say we don't let it concern us unless it happens again. There's nothing to do right now. We don't even know where that message came from. Aaron called the number under the photo and got a recording saying the number is not in service."

"That's it then," I said and stood to go upstairs. Christian followed and after a few moments, we heard a knock on our door.

"May I come in?" Fiore asked.

"Sure. It's unlocked," I called. Christian sat on the edge of the bed.

"We were talking while you were gone," she said. "They told me about their feeding habits, and yours, and I want you to know I'm okay with it."

"I don't think we need your approval," Christian said with a frown.

"I don't think that's what she means," I said and motioned for Fiore to continue.

"I'm easily adaptable. I'll do it your way as long as I'm here." She sat between us and Christian stiffened. I rolled my eyes.

"Thank you. It means a lot to me. What do you mean as long as you're here? Planning on going somewhere?" I felt a knot in my stomach suddenly.

"I mean while I'm here...well, I don't think you need a third wheel. There's an unanswered question still hanging in the air and I'll just be in the way. I'm sure you'll want to live alone." She looked at both of us.

"I hadn't thought about moving. Wait, what question? I don't...oh!" I looked at Christian and his eyes dropped to the floor. The question he asked me in the cabin, the one everyone in the living room had heard. The one I answered but Christian took back because he knew I was unsure.

"I forgot you all heard that," I groaned.

"Well, I'll leave you alone now. It's my turn to hunt and Kalia said she'd go with me." She kissed the top of my head before she left the room and I heard Christian's sigh.

I went to the closet to make room for the clothing Christian would need and he followed.

"What's wrong, Lily?" he asked sitting on the floor next to me as I was taking things out of the bottom drawer.

"Nothing, why?"

"You seem sad. I thought you'd be happy since Fiore won't be killing innocent people anymore." He took the papers from my hands and set them aside. "What's bothering you?"

"Besides the horrible text?" I said a little harshly. "I was wondering… are you planning on asking me again?" I turned to look at his reaction. His face was calm as ever but a glint appeared in his eyes.

"I didn't think it was what you wanted." He pulled more papers out of my hand and took both my hands in his.

I swallowed hard before I spoke. "What I didn't want was to have to bury my husband, like I knew I would have to do since you were, after all, human."

"Come with me." He pulled me out of the closet. "We're going for a ride."

"Where?"

"You'll see," he said and grabbed my car keys on the way out the door.

As we passed the living room, he called to Aaron. "We'll be back shortly." We were out the door and in the car before Aaron could answer.

He drove in silence though I tried to ask questions. He said nothing except that I'd see when we got where we were going. I tried to figure it out as we passed familiar buildings but he laughed every time I got it wrong. Finally, he pulled onto the street with the Japanese restaurant where we'd had our first date. I knew we weren't going there, considering it was closed and he no longer ate.

"What are we doing here?" I asked as he opened my door and pulled me out of the car.

"We're going to the beach." He walked with a serious look on his face and it made me keep my mouth closed. As soon as we reached the break to the path, he stopped and turned around. "Hop on."

"I can walk," I protested when he squatted.

"I want to. Please get on." His pleading eyes were nothing to argue with

41

so I bit my lip and got on his back.

I thought of the time we had been here, during our first date; he had lost his footing and slid part of the way down the hill. I was thankful he was much steadier tonight. As soon as we reached the bottom, he quickly stepped over logs and rocks. He didn't set me down until we were at about the same spot where we'd sat and had our first kiss.

"Have a seat," he said and dropped onto the wet sand. At least, with the rain, the sand was wet and heavy enough so the wind, which had started again, couldn't blow it in our faces. I sat next to him and leaned against his side. After a few seconds, he pulled away and turned to face me. "Do you remember that night?"

"How could I forget? But it didn't end well." I had gotten carried away kissing him. I panicked when I started losing control and pushed him away. I thought he wouldn't want to ever see me again. He shook his head, catching the memory from my mind.

"Don't worry about it. This place means the world to me. It's where we had our first kiss. It's where I realized I wanted to spend the rest of my life with you." His smile made his eye squint and I couldn't help but smile too.

"I guess since you put it that way..." I started, but his face turned so serious I stopped talking.

"I want to do this right so, please..." He was suddenly on one knee, my hand in his, his knee sinking in the wet sand. The world was spinning and there were butterflies in my stomach. He cleared his throat. "Lily Townsend, you know how much I love you. I loved you since the first time I saw you and I will love you for the rest of time." He took a deep breath. "Will you marry me?"

My body moved without my permission and I knocked him backward on the sand, landing on top of him. My lips smothered his and in between kisses I managed to utter, "Yes, Christian. A million times, YES!"

The world continued to spin as we kissed under the pouring rain and felt no need to warm up or to come up for air. Being dead sure had its advantages.

⤙ EIGHT ⤚

In the days following our happy announcement, Kalia and Fiore ran around making wedding plans like chickens without heads. Aaron seemed to take it all in stride and even offered to officiate our ceremony; another new thing I learned about him. He told me about some of the couples whose ceremonies he'd performed, which included Pierce and Beth.

Sitting in the kitchen one day, looking at lists of possible bands for the reception, which Kalia and Aaron had insisted be held at the house, I asked, "If Aaron is the official, who's going to give me away?"

They all stopped shuffling through papers and looked up at me. "Me, of course," Kalia said.

"Women can do that?" I asked.

Fiore was the only one to laugh. "Sure. Why not? After all, there's nothing traditional about this wedding."

How true! A traditional vampire wedding? Fiore was a little reluctant when I asked but agreed to be my maid of honor. Pierce was asked to be Christian's best man, since Christian had no family and his friends, who all lived in other states, couldn't see him the way he was now.

"I wish my parents could've met you," he said with a wistful look. "They would've loved you."

"What's not to love, except maybe the fangs," Fiore added.

"Besides that!" He slapped her arm, a little too hard since she rubbed it.

"They'll be with you in spirit, Christian," Kalia said trying to smooth things over. Ever since our engagement, Fiore and Christian had thrown even more jabs at each other.

"You need to pick a band before you leave on your trip. We can take care of the rest while you're gone. Don't forget you have an appointment at the bridal shop tomorrow morning, Lily." Aaron was taking a bigger role in the wedding plans than I had expected and I was relieved he accepted Christian as easily as he did.

"I know. I'm already nervous about it. What time is our flight?" I asked Christian.

"Late afternoon. You'll have plenty of time," he said and went back to discussing music with Aaron.

We were going to Pennsylvania to tie up some loose ends for Christian before our wedding. He had some belongings in a storage unit there and a bank account to close.

"It won't be the same without Maia here. I wish she'd come home already, or at least answer her cell." Kalia sighed. Aaron took her hand to comfort her.

"She'll be home when she's ready," he said but didn't look at any of us. I could tell he wasn't sure having her here was a good idea. With the exception of Kalia, who considered herself her mother, the rest of us felt the same as Aaron about Maia at the moment. Had she been the one to kidnap Christian? Had she sent the picture to my cell phone? Was she planning to avenge Ian?

"Lily!" Kalia's voice was a mere whisper but still harsh and I jumped.

"I'm sorry, but you can't tell me those thoughts haven't crossed your mind." Christian took my hand under the table as I ranted. "But if she did those things, it doesn't mean it was entirely her fault. Ian was very convincing when he wanted something. He was an expert manipulator. He obviously brainwashed her."

"Don't worry about it, Lily. Kalia's just being a mother, right?" Aaron looked at his wife, only guessing at what she may have heard in my mind.

"Yes. I'm sorry too." She stood and left the room. Aaron followed her and we heard their bedroom door close.

"Well, I feel awful about that," I admitted.

"It's only logical that you're a bit skeptical about Maia right now. I'm sure Kalia will calm down," Fiore assured me. I smiled in thanks.

"I say we finish this upstairs," Christian said. I nodded and got up, gathering my pile of folders.

"After the bridal shop, would you mind picking up some clothes for Christian, just the essentials? I'll make you a list of his sizes," I asked, hoping Fiore wouldn't take offense at having to shop for my soon-to-be husband.

"No problem. Anything for you," she said and winked at Christian.

We carried all the wedding folders upstairs and settled on the bed to look through them.

"So, Mrs. Rexer, what kind of music would you like for your first dance with your husband?"

The sound of it made me laugh nervously. Christian's expression changed.

"I'm sorry. Please don't take it the wrong way, but you called me Mrs. Rexer."

"It is going to be your name, unless of course, if you want to keep yours…"

"No. Lily Rexer is great. I love it. It just caught me by surprise, that's all," I explained taking his hand. "As far as music, I'm most partial to the '30s and '40s. Maybe even some '20s. But hey, don't you like Frank Sinatra?"

"I do. I also like Louis Armstrong and Dean Martin, though he's later, why?"

"See how easy we can compromise? I like them too. Pick a band willing to play a variety. Remember, our guests will be vampires and they are very old."

He looked over the lists while I lay on my stomach and pretended to look too. The truth was, my mind was on the wedding gown. I wanted a fancy and classy gown but not too full. I was too short to pull off a large, round dress and I did not want to look like a cake topper. I wanted one capable of making his knees go weak when he saw me at the end of the aisle.

"If you keep picturing stuff like that we're not going to get any work done."

"UGH!" I hit him in the face with a pillow. "Stay out of my head, especially now. How am I going to pick out a gown? You're not supposed to see it."

"I can solve that," he said with a wide grin.

"How?"

"Don't wear one."

"What do you expect me to wear, nothing?" His smile grew even wider and his eyes glowed.

"UGH! You are incorrigible!" Whack! The pillow again.

He was on top of me in seconds and as the clothes came off, the lists of bands and folders of caterers and florists ended up, one by one, on the floor. He kissed me so passionately I had forgotten what we had come up here to do in the first place. The fire of his mouth awakened every part of me. I couldn't get enough of his smell, his hair, his face, his tongue, his soul.

He pulled away. "I can't believe you're going to be my wife. Thank you, Lily. You've made me the happiest man…er, vampire alive." I pulled his face back to mine and as our bodies became one, I sank my teeth into his throat to fill myself with his existence.

"COME ON, LILY! We have to get going or we'll be late!" Fiore called from the bottom of the stairs.

"I have to go. I don't want to but I have to," I pleaded with him to unwrap his arms from around me so I could get dressed.

"No. Not yet," he whined.

"Haven't you had enough?" I teased, still trying to squirm my way out of his arms.

"With you, never. But okay. It is for a good reason. You're going with the girls to pick out a wedding dress. It's a big deal. Do me one favor?"

"What?"

"Pick one with the least amount of material. You know, a sexy one."

I hit him with the pillow again before I ran to the closet, ducking as the pillow flew over my head.

"Here I am," I announced as I reached the bottom of the stairs. Fiore and Kalia were already in the living room, purses and car keys in hand.

"Can't you two wait until after the wedding to make that kind of racket?" Fiore teased. If I could blush, now would been the perfect time. Kalia smiled and, with her arm around my shoulder, led me out to her car.

Three women helped us in the bridal shop. After several attempts at offering us coffee and us declining, they finally gave up and started showing us dresses. Everything they showed me seemed all wrong. I wasn't sure exactly what I wanted but I knew it was none of those. They were too fluffy, or covered way too much, or not the right shade of white. I guess I did know one thing: I wanted something form-fitting that would not make me look shorter than I already was. My height, or lack of, had always been kind of an issue with me.

"I can show you some others. If you'll please follow me," the woman said and the three of us obeyed.

"What is it you want?" Fiore whispered.

"That! That's it!" I said and pointed to a mannequin. "I want that one."

"This one?" the woman asked.

"Yes. Is something wrong with it?" I asked.

"Nothing's wrong with it. It's lovely, but it's way below your budget."

"Oh. I don't care about that. I love it! Kalia, what do you think?"

"It would be lovely on you, Lily. Can we see this one, please?"

The woman hurried out of the room with the mannequin under her arm. The gown was white, sleek, with a champagne-colored sash at the waist offset with rhinestones.

"If you please, in this dressing room? If you need help I'll be right outside the door," she said and led me to an open room. The gown was already hanging on a hook.

"Thank you." I entered the dressing room and stripped off my clothes. The silky gown felt like heaven sliding over my body. I looked at my image in the mirror and realized for the first time that not only was it very low-cut, with a mesh panel between the breasts, also accented with rhinestones, but that it was backless too. Christian was getting his wish granted after all.

"What do you think?" I asked when I stepped out. Kalia and Fiore turned from looking at veils and Kalia's hand flew to her mouth. Fiore's face froze. "No?"

"I'll leave you alone for a bit," the woman said and left us.

"Are you kidding? You're the most beautiful bride I've ever seen!" Kalia said. Fiore just kept nodding.

"Oh, here, try this veil," Fiore came over with the veil and placed it expertly on my head. "Wow! You have your gown and on the first try. It just needs to be hemmed a bit." I spun for their benefit.

"Kalia, what's wrong?" I jumped off the platform in front of the mirror and rushed over to her. "Why won't you look at me?" She stood facing away from me. I put a hand on her shoulder.

"I don't want you to see me crying," she said as her face streaked in red.

I looked around to make sure none of the sales ladies had returned. "Don't. You're going to make me cry." Too late. I felt the tears rolling down my face. Fiore rushed to get a tissue out of her purse so I wouldn't ruin the white dress.

"You're perfect." Kalia had gotten her tears under control but for me it was like turning on a waterfall. Fiore kept handing me tissue after tissue as

Kalia nervously eyed the door to the sales floor. "Um, Lily?"

"Yeah?" I blubbered.

"Were you crying like this the day Christian, you know, died?" Fiore looked at her with a wide-eyed expression.

"Worse, I think. Why?" I couldn't imagine why she would ask such a question now.

"Were you bent over his face by any chance?" Fiore seemed to come to a conclusion to Kalia's question.

"I tried CPR for a while but I finally gave up. I laid over him, kissed him, and cried. Why? What made you think of that now?" I looked at both of them hoping they would enlighten me.

Fiore nodded at Kalia.

"I think I know how Christian became one of us," Kalia said in a hushed voice.

"I don't understand what my crying has to do with anything."

"If you say you cried worse then, that's a lot of blood, blood pouring into his mouth as you grieved." She backed up to a chair and fell into it. I didn't know what to think, let alone what to say.

"Lily? Say something." Fiore had a hold of my hands but her voice sounded far away. I could picture Christian's lifeless body on the floor and the anguish and desperation I felt when I couldn't bring him back.

"I did do it," I pulled out of Fiore's grasp. "I made him what he is. I did this to him. I did exactly what Aaron forbàde."

"You didn't do it on purpose. Don't you see? It was an accident. You were trying to revive him. Not trying to make him into a vampire. No one can blame you for this. Aaron will understand." Kalia was on her feet again and trying to calm me.

"Everything okay in here?" the woman asked. "Have we decided?"

I snapped my mind back to the present situation so I could get it over with and get back to Christian.

"This is the one I want. Is there any way to change the color of the sash?" Kalia and Fiore looked relieved. I was back to dealing with the dress.

"Absolutely. We can change the rhinestones too to match whatever color you choose," the woman beamed at her sale. "Do you have a color in mind?"

"Burgundy," I said.

"It'll be lovely, Lily. Christian can wear that color too." Kalia smiled ear to ear again.

All the way home Kalia and Fiore tried, in vain, to assure me I did nothing wrong. I couldn't be held accountable if what happened had been an accident. I hadn't intentionally made Christian a vampire, they insisted. They also reminded me I couldn't think about my wedding gown at all since Christian was so in tune with my thoughts. It would be easy to do since it was out of my mind already considering the most recent development.

I ran past Aaron and up the stairs as soon as the car stopped in front of the house. I would let Kalia explain her theory to Aaron. I needed to face Christian and get the inevitable resentment over with.

"Did you have any luck?" I found him packing a suitcase. The look on my face made him drop what he was doing and come over to me.

"Yeah." I pulled out of his embrace. "We need to talk."

"You're not changing your mind, are you?" He looked scared.

"No…I don't know…" I shook my head. "This is hard."

"You know you can talk to me about anything, right?" He led me to the edge of the bed.

"Okay. This is Kalia's theory and I think she might have it exactly right." I swallowed hard. "When you died and I tried to revive you, I couldn't. I finally gave up and held you and cried."

"You did everything you could," he assured me. I put up a hand to stop him.

"It gets worse. Apparently, I cried so hard over you that all the blood tears pouring down my face ended up going in your mouth." I stopped, letting it sink in for a moment. His expression didn't change. "Don't you see?"

"Not really," he said.

"I made you what you are. Ian took your blood and I gave you mine." I stood and looked at him. He was quiet, still waiting. "I did this to you!"

"Do you think that's really how it happened?"

"What else could it be? No one else was there. When Maia came in, I ran after her. I left you alone. No one could have gotten past me, or Aaron and Kalia."

"It does make sense. How did you two come to that conclusion today?"

"Kalia started crying when Fiore put a veil on me and then of course, I started. Once I start, apparently, it's like a dam lets loose." He laughed.

"Do you have any idea how happy this makes me?" He stood and took my hands.

"What are you talking about?" I couldn't believe my ears. *Happy* was not what I expected.

"I'm here because of you. Your blood made me what I am and because of it, I get to be with you forever." He leaned to look in my eyes.

"You mean you're not mad at me?"

"Of course I'm not. This is what I wanted. I thought you knew."

"I did know but the reality is a little different. It's confirmed now that I did this. I made you an immortal, frozen as you are for eternity. You still want to marry me?"

"I will never change my mind. Don't you see? You're an even bigger part of me than we thought. I'd love to be frozen with you." His face lit up with excitement. A knock on the door interrupted my response.

"Come in," I yelled.

"Sorry to interrupt, Lily, Christian," Aaron said walking into the room and pulling me away from Christian. He wrapped his arms around me and kissed the top of my head.

"What's this for?" I asked but didn't pull away. I wrapped my arms around him and squeezed.

"I'm sorry I ever doubted you," he whispered into my hair. "Will you please forgive me?"

"There's nothing to forgive. How could you have known? I didn't even know. But does this mean you're okay with it?"

"You didn't do it on purpose, but that doesn't matter. I could never deny you this happiness anyway. I think sooner or later, had things turned out differently, I would have relented," he laughed.

"Thank you, Aaron. You have no idea how much this has bothered Lily. She thought she was disappointing you." Christian put his hand on Aaron's back as Kalia watched from the doorway.

"I can't hold it against you, can I? Especially when you didn't know." He went back to stand by Kalia. "Besides, had this one not already been a vampire, I don't know if I could have stopped myself." He squeezed her to his side as her face glowed.

KALIA AND AARON drove us to the airport. Fiore had come home before it was time to leave and we finished packing Christian's suitcase with some of the clothing she had gotten him. With Fiore's sense of style, Christian was going to look great. We said our goodbyes and boarded the plane to Pennsylvania, to the Lehigh Valley, where Christian was born and raised.

After an eight hour commute, we were more than ready to get off the plane. We rented a car, and since this was his town, he happily did the driving.

The weather happened to be cloudy in Pennsylvania and the temperature, though not uncomfortable to us, was noticeably lower. At least it was dry. We did, however, remember to bring jackets so we could blend in.

"Do you want me to show you around?" he asked as we drove down a crowded highway. Though the speed limit was fifty-five, everyone was going much slower, and as hard as I tried, I couldn't find the reason. I kept expecting to pass an accident scene or a disabled vehicle but we didn't. The highway was just too small for the population growth in the area, I guess.

"Why don't we get your stuff done first? Then we can take our time." I grabbed the door handle as he switched to the outside lane, way too close to the car in front of him.

"The bank first then. The storage place isn't far from there. Am I making you nervous?"

"I'm not used to this closeness on the road." I couldn't help but laugh with him. I trusted him and I knew his reflexes were much faster now than ever.

"I used to live right behind the highway. The mall's back there too." He pointed as we crossed an intersection. "My bank's straight ahead."

He parked the car in a small lot between the bank and a pharmacy. As we walked in the door, all the tellers were busy with customers so we took a seat in the waiting area. The man who had been talking on the telephone as we passed two desks finished his conversation and headed to the waiting area. As soon as he looked at us he froze and his jaw dropped. I looked at Christian.

"What's wrong, Nate?" Christian asked, suddenly fidgeting. I tried to remember if we'd remembered to cover our skin.

"Mr. Rexer?" he asked but still wouldn't approach.

"Of course. What's wrong Nate?"

"But how?" he asked. Everyone in the bank stared in our direction. The tellers were on their tiptoes trying to see over the counter.

"How? I don't understand...Is something wrong? Are you feeling alright?"

"Uhh...Right this way, please." All the color had drained from Nate's cheeks.

We followed him and sat down in front of his desk. He remained standing, still staring at us.

"I know it's been a while, but I don't understand. You look like you've seen a ghost," Christian said reaching for my hand.

Nate laughed nervously. "Excuse me for saying, but I thought you died."

Christian laughed. "Well, as you can see, here I am. Where did you get such an idea?"

"From your wife, sir."

I looked at Christian and automatically dropped his hand.

"I don't have a wife. Well, not yet," he said and looked at me, reaching for my hand again.

"Your wife was here. She closed your accounts, about a month ago." He finally sat down and started typing on his computer keyboard.

"You let someone close my accounts?" His voice showed his anger. The man, Nate, dropped his hands from the keyboard.

"She had all the proper documents. She showed me a marriage certificate, ID, death certificate." He stood again and started pacing by his desk.

"Did she happen to tell you her name?" Christian yelled.

"Of course. One moment, I'll look." Nate sat back down and started typing.

"Never mind!" Christian grabbed my hand and pulled me out of the bank and into the car before Nate even had a chance to protest.

∽ NINE ∽

The tires screeched as Christian tore out of the parking lot. Luckily, no other cars were coming since he did not even bother to look. I had questions but it didn't seem like the time so I kept my mouth closed. Even his mind was completely blank as his grip tightened on the steering wheel. After a while he finally pulled over on a dead-end street and turned off the motor.

"What are you thinking?" I finally asked.

"I don't know. What am I supposed to think?" His tone was harsh but I knew it wasn't directed at me.

"There has to be some logical explanation for this. Maybe we should go back to the bank, ask more questions. Maybe we should go to the police," I said trying to read his blank expression.

"First of all, we can't go to the police. In Oregon, I'm missing. Here, I'm dead, remember? Secondly, the bank knows me. I've been going there for years. They wouldn't have made a mistake about something like that. Someone is really out to get me." He finally turned to look at me. "I'm so sorry, Lily. I'm broke now. That was all the money I had."

"I don't care about that. I have plenty. We can always get more," I swallowed hard before asking my next question. "Was there a woman, before you left, that is maybe angry with you? Maybe someone trying to get revenge?"

His expression turned sour. "Why would you say that?"

"I'm trying to figure it out. Someone posed as your widow and closed your accounts. What am I supposed to think?"

"There was no one. Not for a long time. The last woman I dated is happily married with children now. We're on friendly terms when we run into each other. I can't think of anyone who would do something like this." He stared out the window again. "I know I should've waited for a name but I was so furious I was afraid I'd blow up in Nate's face."

"That's understandable. Do you think there's a possibility it could have been someone we know?" I couldn't bring myself to say the name. It made me sick to my stomach to think she could be that evil.

"I don't know what to think. I need to get into my apartment when we get back to Astoria. I have to see what was taken from there." I nodded. That would be difficult but not impossible.

"Let's go to the storage unit and then head home. I don't want to be here anymore. I'm sorry," he said as he started the engine.

"I understand." I reached for his hand. "Christian, I love you. Don't forget that. I don't care about money."

"I somehow already knew that." He leaned over and kissed me before turning the car around.

KALIA, AARON, AND Fiore were surprised to see us back so soon, especially since we had taken a cab home from the airport and not called for a ride like they'd expected. Fiore threw herself into my arms as soon as we were in the door and I couldn't help but notice Christian's look of disapproval.

"What's with you?" she asked backing away.

"We had a bad trip," he explained.

We told them what happened at the bank.

"Have you heard from Maia yet?" I couldn't avoid the question, as much as I knew it hurt Kalia.

"No. I don't know what to think anymore," Kalia said. Aaron walked over and put his arms around her.

"We have some good news though," Fiore said, trying to break the tension. "Aaron tracked down Aloysius and he's coming for the wedding!"

Christian and I exchanged looks. "Wow! That is great," Christian said.

"We need to go to Christian's apartment," I said. I couldn't drop the issue yet. "He wants to see what was taken from there."

"Do you think that's a good idea? What if someone sees you?" Kalia's face was drawn with worry.

"We'll go in the middle of the night. No one will see us." I knew how to keep to the shadows.

"It's very possible his apartment was cleaned out already. I wouldn't be surprised if someone else is living there." Aaron considered the possibilities.

"Someone stole my money so I'm thinking they stole more than that, considering they have my bank account number. They had all the proper documents to close my accounts, with the exception of a forged death certificate," Christian said.

"When do you want to do this?" Aaron asked.

"The sooner the better," I answered. Christian nodded.

"I'll go with you," Aaron said. "We can go tonight if you want."

We all looked at each other. Kalia agreed. "You'll need a look-out. Lily can do that. Your transmitted images could be very helpful if someone shows up. Aaron and Christian can do the rest."

"It's a plan then. Tonight," I said.

"Tonight," three voices replied.

"So, I'm DEAD," Christian said, closing our bedroom door.

"Well, technically, you are."

"Very funny. But the bank saw me. Now they know whoever closed my accounts lied. They'll contact the police."

"Most likely, but there's nothing we can do about that until they contact you. I'm not even sure they know how to contact you yet. In the mean time, we have to figure this out for ourselves," I suggested.

"You think Maia did this, don't you?" He opened the suitcase and started shuffling through things.

"I do," I answered without hesitating. "It's the only thing that makes sense."

"She's not going to stay away forever. She'll have to come back. Everything she owns is here," he said, stepping away from the suitcase with one arm behind his back.

"I know. That's why I think we should leave, as soon as we're married," I replied, knowing how much it would hurt Kalia to lose both of us. "I don't see how we have another choice."

"I know. Even if it was her, what can we do? Aaron and Kalia love her."

I nodded. They considered her a daughter and it would be devastating to them if they lost her. They were already suffering because of her staying away and not contacting them.

Christian motioned for me to sit on the bed with him.

He cleared his throat. "I may not have money now but…I can still give you this." He brought his hand out from behind his back.

"What is it?" We'd gotten some things he thought were important from his storage unit and left the rest. I couldn't imagine what he was hiding in his hand.

"Every bride-to-be must have an engagement ring. It was my mother's," he said, taking my left hand. He slowly slid the ring on my finger as he looked at my shocked face with a smile.

I held my hand in front of me. My breath caught in my throat.

"It's beautiful!" I wrapped my arms around his neck. "Are you sure you want me to wear this?"

He pushed away from me to look at my face. "Of course. That's why she gave it to me before she died."

I examined the ring, holding my hand out. It was white gold with a round garnet in the middle. On either side of the stone two little diamonds sparkled in the light. The fit was perfect, as if it had been made for me.

"You didn't think you were going to go without a ring, did you?" he asked with a smile.

"I didn't really think about it. The only thing that matters to me is that you're mine." I wrapped my arms around him again. He kissed my neck, sending chills up my back.

"I love it! Did you know garnets are my favorite?"

"Actually, no," he admitted. "I guess you have something in common with my mother."

SHORTLY AFTER MIDNIGHT, Aaron came to our room to see if we were ready. I laughed when I saw the three of us had dressed in all black, as if we were going to rob a bank.

"We're ready," Christian answered and we followed Aaron downstairs. Kalia and Fiore waited in the living room to see us off.

"Good luck. Not that you'll need it," Fiore said.

We left the car down the street and walked the rest of the way to Christian's building. Christian and Aaron walked in as soon as they reached the front door. I went to the side of the building, where I stayed in the shadows. It was my job was to stay out of sight, watch, and listen for any sign of movement from the other apartments. I did so intently, hoping I would be able to deter anyone who suspected something. I held my breath when I heard footsteps until I realized it was Christian and Aaron coming back.

*There's a padlock on the door…can't break it without being heard…*Aaron thought.

I pointed to the window I knew was to Christian's bathroom. It was the smallest window but the only one on this side of the building.

That's really high…what if it's locked? Aaron thought and looked at Christian.

Try opening it from here… Christian's eyes widened at my suggestion. I nodded encouraging him. *It's worth a try.*

Aaron watched the exchange between us with curiosity. We could hear his thoughts but he couldn't hear ours. I couldn't imagine how frustrating that must be. Christian stared at the window, his brow scrunched.

It's not working. It's probably locked. Christian suggested.

Then concentrate on the lock.

As I watched the street and Aaron stood by us, I heard a click. Within seconds, the window slid up a few inches. Aaron smiled and Christian's eyes lit up.

"We can't fit through that," Christian whispered for Aaron's benefit. "You'll have to go." I nodded.

Aaron and Christian put their hands together so I could stand on them and launch myself from there. The window was higher than I was used to jumping, but once I was hanging from the ledge, Christian managed to open it all the way so I fit through it. I was thankful there was no screen to knock out. Standing on the bathroom floor, I waved to them before going to the hall. It took a moment for my eyes to adjust to the darkness.

The living room smelled like Christian but there was another smell mixed in, one that turned my stomach. Ian had been here. I put it out of my mind for the time being and started looking around.

What exactly am I looking for?

Anything out of place. You've been here. You know what it should look like, Christian's thoughts replied.

On the coffee table, I spotted an envelope. It didn't have a return address so, rather than waste time, I shoved it in my back pocket. Nothing else in the living room looked out of place so I headed to the bedroom. His bed was as he'd left it, unmade, with his scent strongest there. A picture frame was laying face down on the normally empty nightstand. That was new. I picked it up.

What is it? Lily? Christian asked.

It's…

My neighbor's coming! She's in a different car! Get out now!

Stay in the shadows…I'll take care of it…

I closed my eyes and pictured the side of the building, the driveway, as it should be – empty except for cars. I had no idea if it would work, considering I'd never met his neighbor. I pictured her getting out of a car and seeing nothing unusual as she walked to the front door. I concentrated and walked with her, seeing every step of the way to her apartment. She put her key in the lock, looking behind her once and shaking her head. Then, I heard the car that dropped her off backing out of the driveway and speeding away into the darkness.

Are we clear? I finally took a breath.

We're clear. That was awesome, by the way! I saw everything you did.

My hands shook as I held the picture. Putting images in people's minds took extra energy, not to mention I was looking at something that didn't make sense. I grabbed my cell phone out of my pocket and snapped a photo. After replacing the frame on the nightstand, exactly as it had been, I took one last look around the apartment and decided everything else looked as it did the last time I was here. I knew I shouldn't take anything else so I headed back to the bathroom.

I'm coming out. I warned so they could move out of the way. I hung on the outside ledge and dropped silently to the ground. Christian got to work on closing the window.

Let's get out of here! Aaron started running toward the street with us right behind him.

When we reached the car, we finally spoke.

"So, what did you find? What was in the frame?" Christian asked.

I took my cell phone out of my pocket and scrolled to my photos. I looked at it again, my stomach turning. Christian turned in his seat so I handed it to him. His eyes widened.

"It's the woman that took me to Ireland!"

Aaron looked at it. "And you have your arm around her. You're smiling."

My breath caught in my throat again as I took the phone back and looked at it. "It's not Maia.

⤳ TEN ⤳

We showed Kalia and Fiore the picture I had taken of the photo in Christian's room. Neither of them recognized the woman posing with Christian. I felt relief that it wasn't Maia, but it was short lived because now the puzzle had gotten more complicated. Were all the events of the recent months connected? How many people were involved? With Ian dead, we should finally be free of all the trouble he had caused.

"Oh…that reminds me," I reached into my back pocket. "I did take one thing." I handed Christian the envelope and saw the immediate surprise in his eyes. He pulled the contents out, considering it was already open, and began reading to himself.

"What is it?" I asked, though he handed me the letter.

"Apparently, I had a wife," He turned to Aaron. "And she wasn't very happy with me."

"What?" Fiore looked angry.

We all looked at him. "According to this letter, I left her. I wanted a divorce and she was going to fight it. She begged to work things out."

All of us sat speechless.

"How is it signed?" Fiore was the first to speak. I handed the letter back to Christian.

"Love, Sam. That's all," he said. He crumpled the letter in one hand.

"Sam? As in Samantha Maureen Fitzgerald? Like on the passport you saw," I said. I turned the envelope over to look at the postmark. It was postmarked from Allentown, Pennsylvania.

"Whoever is responsible for this did some serious planning." Fiore took the wadded paper from Christian, smoothed/ it and handed it to Kalia.

"So let me get this straight," Kalia started, placing it on the coffee table. "You had a wife, left her, she wanted you back, and then, you died before you could make a decision?"

"That sounds about right." I stood, ready to go upstairs and forget about this for a little while. I reached out to take back the letter when Kalia grabbed my hand.

"What's this?" she asked, moving my hand toward Aaron so he could see.

"It belonged to Christian's mother. He gave it to me today." I couldn't help but beam as they admired my ring.

IN THE DAYS following our new discoveries, we solved nothing but paid no more attention to the puzzle. With the wedding date fast approaching, we threw ourselves wholeheartedly into the preparations. Aaron had all the proper documents made for Christian, since we needed to get our marriage license and he no longer had access to them. Kalia, Fiore, and I went to the bridal shop for one last fitting, the invitations were sent, the band picked, the flowers ordered, and the backyard was cleaned and landscaped to prepare for the ceremony and reception.

It was to be a small, intimate wedding. Aloysius was arriving the day before and Aaron was beside himself with happiness. We listened to stories about him every chance we had. Though Aaron didn't see him that often, he seemed to have a close relationship with him anyway and had nothing but good things to say.

As the big day got closer, I felt more anxious and though I tried to hide it, Christian picked up on it.

"What's wrong?" he asked when we were finally alone in our room, after cleaning the entire first floor.

"Nothing, why?"

"I don't know. You look...sad?" Christian had the remote hovering above his head, commanding it with a wave of his hand. His practice was really paying off.

"I'm just nervous." I dodged the remote and climbed up on the bed.

"Cold feet?" He waved the remote to the nightstand and moved to my side.

"Not at all. It's just been too quiet lately. I keep expecting something to happen and when it doesn't, it makes me more anxious." I snuggled into his awaiting arms.

"I'm not going to let anything happen to you. I *can* protect you now."

"I know. I guess I'm afraid something will happen at our wedding. Tell me I'm being silly." I looked up at his face.

"You're being silly," he said and kissed me. "Our wedding is going to be perfect. You'll see."

"I hope so." The knot in my stomach stayed.

We were all anxiously awaiting the arrival of Aaron's great-grandfather the next day. It was also the last night Christian and I would be in our own room before the wedding. Kalia was trying to make it as traditional as possible. Christian would spend the night in the living room with the men. Fiore and Kalia would spend time with me, once they finished decorating the backyard and the gigantic tent they had rented. I was glad I wouldn't be spending the evening alone.

As usual, the day dawned cloudy. The weather was much warmer than usual but it threatened to rain any minute. Aaron and Kalia left for the airport shortly after seven. The rest of us made sure everything was ready for Aloysius's arrival.

"It seems strange not having to worry about what our guests will be eating," Christian cleared the kitchen table of our newspapers. "Why is there a refrigerator?"

"It was in the house when they bought it. It's not plugged in," I explained and went to open the door. Christian smiled when he saw Kalia's art supplies neatly stacked on the shelves that in any other household would contain food.

"This is going to take some getting used to." He smiled. "What happens if we do decide to eat food?"

"Nothing really. We just have no need for it anymore. It doesn't even seem appetizing to me. I think the only smell I still enjoy is the smell of coffee, cookies baking and chocolate, of course. Even so, I still don't have the urge to eat or drink those things," I explained.

"It's just weird not to hear my stomach growl."

When we heard the front door open, Christian and I exchanged looks of anticipation.

"I guess it's time," Christian said as we met Fiore in the hallway.

"Lily, Fiore, Christian, this is Aloysius," Aaron said, setting down a suitcase.

An impressive man moved into view. He was a bit shorter than Aaron but with the same facial features and green eyes. The biggest difference was that his long hair, tied in the back, was a black as deep as ebony. He dressed casually but impeccably, from his blue button-down shirt to his black jeans, and polished dress shoes. He stood and surveyed us from head to toe and for some reason, none of us dared to move. It wasn't until he extended his hand to Fiore that the room seemed to relax.

She took his hand first, then Christian, and finally me. When his fingers closed on my hand, he held my wrist with the other hand. He stood like that for close to a minute, not saying a word, but his eyes widened. I looked to Aaron for an explanation but none was offered. What had they told him about me? He nodded and smiled then motioned us into the living room.

"We're so glad you could make it," I said and looked at Christian so he knew I was speaking for both of us.

"Me too. I'm glad Aaron contacted me. I wouldn't have wanted to miss something so important." His manner was serious but his smile was warm. I relaxed a little more, trying to put his reaction at touching me out of my mind.

Aaron and his great-grandfather started chatting and trying to catch up when we all noticed how anxious Kalia looked. Her fidgeting was unusual for a vampire.

"What's wrong, Kalia?" Aaron asked. We all turned to her.

"We have a lot to do tonight so Lily will have to go upstairs early. I was wondering if we could do what we planned now?" She looked at Aaron and winked.

I didn't know what I had expected when I saw her so anxious and I realized at that moment every muscle in my body had tensed. Seeing her wink, I let myself relax.

"I don't see why not," Aaron said and Kalia ran to the kitchen. Fiore's smile confirmed she was in on the secret.

Kalia returned with her hands behind her back and a look on her face as if she was ready to burst. Aaron stood to go to her side and motioned for Fiore to join them.

"We wanted to do this tomorrow but then we realized you would need to prepare," Kalia said through her smile. Aaron looked at her with encouragement. Fiore laughed at the look on my face as Christian and I sat on the edge of our seats. "Aaron, Fiore, and I have a wedding gift for you." She stepped toward me and handed me what was behind her back.

I held what she handed me but couldn't manage to open it. Impatient, Christian took it from me and opened it.

"Round trip tickets to Lima, Peru?" he asked, shocked.

Kalia clapped her hands together but stopped mid-motion when I threw my arms around her, all but knocking her over. I did the same with Aaron and Fiore.

"I know how much you love the place," Kalia explained.

"You didn't think we'd let you go without a honeymoon, did you?" Fiore asked. Christian had hugged her and Kalia when we heard Aloysius clear his throat. We turned our attention to him.

"I hope you don't mind if I travel with you. I have an apartment there and would love it if you used it. I have some things to take care of and I promise to give you all the privacy a honeymoon requires." He waited for protests but there were none. "You won't even know I'm there."

"We would be honored," Christian answered.

"Thank you so much. I can't believe you all did this. How long were you planning this?" I asked.

"Not long. You know how hard it is to keep secrets from each other," Kalia explained. We all laughed.

"I can't believe it. A month in Lima! I can't believe it." I couldn't wait to get upstairs and pack.

"Go ahead. Go pack. We will start setting up the chairs for tomorrow," Kalia responded to my thought. I looked at Aloysius.

"We'll have plenty of time to get acquainted after the wedding. I know how busy this time can be," he said.

"Once you go up, Lily, you have to stay there." Kalia led me to the stairs as the others waved us on with smiles on their faces.

"I can't believe we're going to South America," Christian said as he opened our suitcases on the bed. "This all feels like a dream."

"Tell me about it! So much has changed." I dropped a pile of clothing on the bed and walked over to wrap my arms around his neck. "By this time tomorrow, I'll be your wife."

He backed away enough to look at my face. "Any regrets?"

"Absolutely not," I answered without hesitation. "I can't think of anything I want more."

"Neither can I," he answered and kissed my lips. "Let's get this packing done before they kick me out of the room."

We packed our suitcases and made sure we had our tickets and passports ready to go for tomorrow night. We would be leaving for the airport from the reception and would have no time to do anything besides change our clothes and grab our luggage. Shortly after we were done, there was a tap on the door.

"Time for the groom to leave the bride alone with the girls," Aaron poked his head in the room. My stomach did a somersault. This was not going to be an easy night.

I kissed Christian goodnight but had to be pulled away from him by Aaron. He laughed as he dragged Christian, who kept his arms stretched out to me, toward the stairs. I stayed frozen where they left me. If I felt like this now, I couldn't imagine how I was going to get through tomorrow. It didn't make a difference though. All I cared about was that tomorrow I would be Lily Rexer. Everything else could wait.

⫷ ELEVEN ⫸

"**W**e're here. Let the festivities begin!" Kalia sang as she entered my room with Fiore, Beth, and Riley trailing behind. They all carried shopping bags in one hand and rolled sleeping bags in the other.

"What a nice surprise!" I went to greet everyone.

"Make room," Beth said as she unrolled her sleeping bag on the floor. "It's a slumber party, without the slumber, of course."

"Where are the men?" I asked, settling myself on the sleeping bag Kalia unrolled for me.

"They're out back. They have their instructions and are finishing up the preparations. Then they're going to play poker or some such manly thing," Fiore answered.

"This should be interesting. Men decorating for a wedding! I can't wait to see how that turns out." Riley rolled her eyes.

"They should have no problem with the detailed diagrams Kalia drew. She'll know if even one little thing is out of place," Fiore explained and laughed.

"We have gifts for you," Beth announced. "Since everyone was in too much of a hurry to throw you a proper bridal shower." She looked at Kalia who dropped her eyes.

"Mine first," Fiore exclaimed and pushed a package toward me.

It was wrapped in shimmery, silver paper with a red bow. I carefully slid my shaky fingers under the tape and pulled the paper off the box. Lifting the lid, I encountered red tissue paper. Fiore smiled with anticipation and everyone leaned in as I peeled the tissue paper aside to retrieve the contents. My jaw hit the floor.

"For the honeymoon," Fiore said and pulled the contents out. She held up a red silk and lace nightie for everyone to see. It was very short with a slit down the front from the breasts to the bottom. "Here's the rest."

She tossed what looked like red string at me until I realized when I held it up that it was the matching panties. If I could have managed it, my face would've matched the color of the lingerie. Putting my embarrassment aside for the moment, I reached for the next package. All chatter stopped when we heard a tap on the door. Kalia grabbed the nightie from me and hid it behind her back.

"Yes?" she yelled. The door opened a crack and a head appeared.

"Is there room for one more?" Maia asked with a wide smile.

Throwing the package aside and jumping to my feet, I was in a fight stance: my knees bent, my fists balled at my sides. Kalia raised her arm to stop me from diving across the room and tackling Maia. Fiore positioned herself between us, her arms out at her sides like a barricade.

"Oh my God! Maia!" Kalia yelled and ran to throw her arms around her. Maia hugged her back but never took her eyes off me. "We've been so worried!"

"I know. I'm really sorry about that," she replied, eyes still on my face. "What are you doing, Lily?"

I couldn't speak without screaming so I said nothing. Riley and Beth now stood firmly at my sides.

"Where have you been?" Kalia asked, standing away from her to look her up and down.

"It's a long story," Maia started, her eyes still wide on my face. "Why are you acting like that, Lily? Do you honestly think I'd hurt you?"

Fiore turned her face to look at me. I leaned to the side to look past her and felt Riley's hand close around my arm. I shook it loose.

"Where were you?" I asked as calmly as I could manage.

"I don't want to get into it right now. This is obviously a celebration." Her eyes glanced at the gifts. "All I'm going to say right now is that Ian lied to me and he hurt me. I had to get away for a while. I didn't know how to handle it when he dumped me. I felt like such a fool for believing him. I'm sorry I didn't call."

All eyes were on me now, awaiting my reaction. "Are you trying to say you're innocent?"

She looked at Kalia, who also waited for an answer.

"Of course, I am. I didn't know who he was. I honestly believed he loved me. He lied to me from day one," Maia answered, keeping her eyes locked on mine.

I searched her mind but she already had her shield up. I relaxed my stance, mostly so everyone else would back off. "Why should I believe you?"

"Lily, please," Kalia pleaded. "I've known Maia the longest. If Ian did what he did to you, why wouldn't he have used her too?"

"I can attest to that. He was very smooth when he wanted to get his way," Fiore said.

This was the eve of my wedding and I wanted so much for it to be a happy occasion. Fighting with Maia now and hurting Kalia in the process would be the worst thing that could happen. As much as I wanted to tear her heart out, I wanted our wedding to be perfect, for Christian.

"Okay," I said. Kalia smiled instantly. "But we *will* talk about it, later."

Maia stiffened but smiled anyway. "Thank you. I guess congratulations are in order."

Before I could say anything rash, Fiore tugged me back down to the floor. "What are we waiting for? Back to the party." I kept my eyes on Maia. Kalia led her to the floor beside her.

There was nothing more uncomfortable than having someone I didn't trust, or believe, join in the celebration but for everyone else's sake, I kept it to myself. I opened all the gifts they handed me and tried to act as happy as I should have felt. While we were cleaning up the wrapping paper, Kalia finally asked what I had forgotten to ask.

"Does Aaron know you're back?" She looked at Maia with so much happiness in her eyes that it made my stomach turn.

"He does. I talked to them for a while and they told me to come join you for the *girly* party. They were getting ready to play cards. Your fiancé looks like a nervous wreck, Lily."

"Totally normal," Fiore said, jumping in defensively before I could answer. Maia smiled but said nothing. "I should go get your gown out of my closet."

Fiore left the room and Kalia stood, stretching. "I'm going to get all the stuff to pamper you and make you more beautiful. Maia, some help?" She said and Maia followed her out of the room.

The rest of the night was spent with everyone taking turns telling stories about the loves of their lives while four pairs of hands worked on me. They shaped my eyebrows, slathered my face, and theirs, in a mud mask, and set my hair in rollers. We even took turns doing each other's toenails. The whole night felt like a real slumber party, like the ones I'd had with my best friend, Elizabeth, when I was a child.

"I'll do her fingernails," Maia announced, picking out a color from the array Kalia had carried in. I stiffened as she looked at me. All eyes were on me and no one breathed.

"I hadn't thought about my fingers." I bit my lip to keep from screaming what I really thought about her touching me.

"You're the bride. You have to have your nails done. People will want to see your ring." She shook the nail polish bottle.

"I guess so then," I replied through gritted teeth.

"Can I talk to you while I do them? Alone?" Maia said and looked at Kalia.

"Ladies, come with me, please. We can go to my room in the meantime." Kalia escorted them to the door. She winked at me before closing the door.

I braced myself.

⤟ TWELVE ⤞

"So what do you want?" I looked at my hand as Maia took it in hers. "I don't exactly feel comfortable sitting here with you."

"I know you don't believe me, and I think you're the only one. I just want to clear the air between us. Please, just hear me out."

"Why should I believe you? Or even listen to you? You've been nothing but hateful toward me since I got here. The truth is, I have no idea why you've treated me the way you have."

She paused what she was doing to look up at me. "Honestly, I'm not even sure why I've acted the way I have. Maybe it's just that I feel a little jealous."

"Jealous of what?" I tried to control myself and not give into the urge to slap her face or drag her out of my room by her hair.

She dipped the nail polish brush back into the bottle but didn't pull it back out. "I guess I was used to being Kalia and Aaron's one and only. I liked having their full attention all the time. I didn't have that when I was a mortal and I didn't want to lose it."

That made some sense. "But I never wanted to take that from you. I didn't want anyone's full attention. That's not how I am, but you never even gave me a chance."

"I know I didn't, and I'm sorry. Then when Ian saw you, I could feel what he was feeling and I hated you for it." She kept her eyes on my hand, avoiding my eyes.

"That was absolutely not my fault. He's the one that lied to you. I never did."

"Yes you did." She raised her eyes to mine again and I could see the anger in them. "When you came in, he acted like he never met you before. You didn't correct him. You just played along with him."

"You're right. I did do that, but I had no other choice. He was a very dangerous man and I knew that. I guess I also wanted to see what kind of game he was playing by acting like we had never met."

Maia finally tightened the lid on the polish bottle and set it aside. I guessed she was letting the first coat dry before continuing.

"I felt the feelings he was feeling then. I hated it. That's why I hurt you."

"And what exactly was he feeling?" This had to be good.

"It was kind of surprise and desire, all at once. Maybe more like lust, I don't know, but I knew he wanted you and I couldn't stand it. It hurt me," she said and stood. "I never wanted any man the way I wanted Ian."

I sighed, knowing exactly how that had felt. "I definitely understand that. I felt like that at one point, for a long time actually. Even when he had abandoned me, I still loved him. I saved myself for him for years, hoping he would find his way back to me. I regret that now."

"Did you still love him then, when I brought him home?" She looked down at me with a stone face.

"I don't think so."

"Did you hate him? I want to hate him. I want to despise him for the lies and everything he did, but I still can't." She sat back down and looked at her own hands, which she folded on the vanity table.

"I'm not sure that I hated him at that point exactly. I think I did feel some love for him still, but it wasn't the same. I was angry with him for leaving me. I was angry that he used you to get back to me and I was angry with you for bringing him here."

"I didn't do that on purpose." She lifted her face again and her expression shocked me. She actually looked hurt.

"How am I supposed to believe that? It's hard to believe that it was just a coincidence. I mean, you met him in Europe, for Christ's sake. It's not that small of a world."

"But I never knew he planned it 'til after. I met him at a party. For me, it was love at first sight. He said it was that way for him too. We spent every day together after that and he said he wanted to meet my family. How could I have known?" She swallowed as if fighting back tears. It was getting harder to fight my own instincts. I wanted to trust her. I wanted to believe her, even though it just didn't feel right.

"He never mentioned me?"

"No. It never dawned on me as something strange when he'd ask me questions about you. I just thought it was normal that he was curious about my family since he asked about Kalia and Aaron too."

"So you had absolutely no suspicions?"

"Not at first. But then he would ask more and more about you and it was starting to bother me, especially when he'd ask about who you were dating. Of course, I told him no one, since I didn't know about Christian." She smiled as if proud of herself.

"Well, you know exactly why I kept Christian a secret, but Ian knew about him anyway." He had been talking to me since the night I left Olympia. I just thought it was all in my head.

"I could tell then that he was more than just a little curious about you, but I tried to ignore it. I just wanted to be with him. I wanted him to love me. I didn't care about anything else."

"I know that feeling all too well. Still, you had nothing to worry about when it came to me. I was already in love with Christian," I admitted.

"I didn't know, remember?" She shook the nail polish bottle again.

"That's true. So now what? What exactly are you trying to gain from this conversation?" I asked, wishing she'd get to the point already so the preparations could continue.

"I guess I just want us to start over. I don't want to be jealous of you. I hate feeling like that." She bit her lip, just like me, and waited.

Trusting Maia was the last thing on my list of things to do, but for the sake of our wedding, and Kalia and Aaron, it was probably the first thing I *should* do. I sighed and, straightening my back, held out my hand before she could start polishing. Her eyes widened and a smile spread across her face. "To starting over," I said as she took my hand and then decided to throw her arms around me instead. Hesitating for a moment, I decided it was best to play along. I wrapped my arms around her.

"You have no idea how happy this makes me. Thank you," she said as she released me.

"No problem," I said as her focus went back to my nails. "Trust me, in time, you'll get over him." She nodded but did not meet my eyes. My stomach turned, refusing to trust her.

KALIA AND THE others were ecstatic to learn of our agreement to start over and forget about all the mistrust and anger between us. There was less tension in the room because of it and it seemed much more like a party.

You okay, Lily?

All eyes turned to me again. I shrugged.

"He's not supposed to be talking to you!" Kalia shook her head but had a smile on her face.

I'm dealing. You?

Confused…but happy as hell!

I couldn't help but beam at that response. I knew what he was confused about and I had a feeling everyone else did too, though they pretended they weren't listening.

I'll be seeing you very soon. I love you. I looked to see if they heard and saw the smiles, except for Maia, who was pretending to concentrate on the tiny rhinestones she was expertly gluing on my nails.

I'll be the one in the front with the huge smile on his face. I love you, Lily.

⟨⟩ THIRTEEN ⟨⟩

By nine a.m., my stomach was turning and my hands were shaking to the point that I couldn't hold the photographs we were looking at still. Kalia and Fiore kept laughing at me and calling me the 'blushing bride'. Riley and Beth had already left with Pierce and Raul to go their hotel to get ready for the wedding.

In only two short hours, I would be walking down the aisle to the man of my dreams. Everything was finally going my way. After all that had happened lately, it was still hard to believe things could be this easy. I had made what everyone, including myself, thought of as a mistake. I had committed the ultimate taboo. I had fallen in love with a human. That one simple thing had set off a chain of events that had caused so much violence, but had brought us to a happy ending anyway. Kalia interrupted my thoughts when she came back in the room with a basket full of make-up.

"It's time to start getting you dressed," She set the basket on my vanity table and pulled out the seat. "I want to have you ready before Aaron and I get ready. Maia will be in when she's ready since she'll be receiving the guests."

I made my way to the seat on shaky legs. She smiled and put an arm around me, squeezing me to her side. I took a deep breath and nodded to let her know I was ready.

"It's a really nice thing you know, what you did for Maia. She really means it when she says she's sorry. She doesn't often see the error of her ways so this is really important," Kalia said.

"I can definitely sympathize with her when it comes to her feelings for Ian. He was charming when he wanted something. I fell head over heels for him too. I also know how hard it was to get over him."

"Well, I'm happy for Maia but I'm happiest that you did get over him.

Christian will make you happy for the rest of your days." Her eyes glowed with happiness.

"I do know that. I just hope I can make him happy."

"You already have."

She took her time applying my make-up. If she didn't like a color, she blended a new one on her hand. I guess that's what you do when you're a painter. Once she was satisfied with my face she began taking the rollers out of my hair. The whole time, she had me facing away from the mirror so I couldn't see her progress. She pinned some of my hair on top of my head but left the rest hanging down my back.

"Cover your eyes and don't breathe," she said. "It's time for the hair-spray."

She had to have gone through a whole can of hairspray because I held my breath for quite a while. Every time I thought she was done she'd arrange something else and spray again. I couldn't imagine what it would be like to be a model and have to sit through this daily. No, thank you.

"Now your veil." She expertly placed it on my head, over the tiara she had let me wear as my *something borrowed.* The tiara had been the one her mother had worn when she was married and then Kalia when she married Aaron.

"Do you think I'm doing the right thing?" I asked, suddenly feeling more than nervous – panicked.

"You don't have a choice in the matter," she answered, as she fluffed the veil.

"What do you mean?" I didn't understand her choice of words.

"Fate brought you together. I believe there is someone out there for everyone, someone created just for us. You found yours and this is the logical next step."

"I know he will do everything in his power to make me happy, like you said, but I never really believed in fate or happily-ever-after. I guess maybe I was wrong," I admitted.

"You and Christian are meant to be together. You will be happy, forever. You'll see."

As if on cue, Maia knocked on the door and entered before we gave permission.

"Ready for the dress?" she asked and walked to my closet door.

"We are." Kalia pulled me up from my seat and led me away from the mirror.

I stepped into the dress and they pulled it up. Once they had everything clasped and my veil fluffed to perfection, Kalia stepped away from me. Tears instantly welled in her eyes. Even Maia had a genuine-looking smile on her perfectly made-up face. She looked gorgeous in a shimmering, blue floor length gown and her usually straight dark, blunt hair in curls.

"No crying today, please," I said, feeling like I might join her if she didn't stop.

"You really are the most beautiful bride I've ever seen," she cried. I turned my glance toward Maia in time to see her nod. I heard the front door open and close and my stomach filled with butterflies in anticipation.

"I'm going. Guests are starting to arrive. I have to lead them out back." Maia smiled at me again before she left the room.

"She's trying," Kalia said, obviously hearing my silent question. I nodded. Today was certainly not the day to question Maia's intentions.

"Can I look yet?" I asked, feeling the usual butterfly party in my stomach.

"Oh, of course, I'm sorry!"

She led me to stand in front of the mirror and at first glance I wasn't sure who I was looking at. A beautiful, graceful woman, with cascading curls down her back stared back at me. Her eyes were innocent, trusting, and glowing from happiness.

"Is that really me?" I touched my face, careful not to mess up Kalia's amazing work, to make sure it really was.

"I told you. You are perfect."

"You did it," I told her.

"I only enhanced what you already had," She fluffed my veil some more. "I need to go get ready. Fiore will be in with your bouquet any minute. Some guests are apparently a little early."

"I hope your friends like me," I said nervously. Kalia and Aaron had invited vampire friends of theirs I had never met. Christian and I had had no one to invite. All my human friends were gone and Ian had made sure that I'd had no friends since our separation.

"There's nothing not to like. Besides, once you're with Christian, you'll notice no one else, trust me." She kissed my cheek lightly and rushed out of the room. Fiore came in right after.

"Wow!" she said.

"Wow, yourself," I replied. She looked like someone from the front cover of a romance novel in her sparkly burgundy gown. Her hair was piled high on her head with rhinestone combs on the sides. "You look absolutely gorgeous!"

"Not compared to you," she took a deep breath. "Christian is one lucky man. He better take good care of you."

"We'll take care of each other. It's a promise."

Aaron walked in next. He looked stunning in his tuxedo. There was something so elegant about having the ceremony performed by him dressed like that instead of the typical clergyman.

"Well, it's almost that time already," he kissed my cheek. "You look like an angel."

"Thank you."

"The piano player is ready to go. Everyone is seated. You and Fiore need to get downstairs," he said. He looked almost as nervous as I felt.

"How's Christian doing?" I asked.

"He's been like a little boy on Christmas morning. He hasn't sat still for hours. Are you ready?"

I took a deep breath and swallowed hard. I had a habit of holding my breath when I was nervous and I had no idea when I'd breathe again.

As Fiore and I waited for our cue to start walking down the aisle, we could hear the loud chatter outside. Within moments, Kalia was at my side so I didn't really have time to go into a full panic. Soft music started playing, Fiore's cue to start. She handed me my bouquet and made her way down the back steps toward the tent and the aisle that would lead me to my husband. The aisle was lined with cord draped in white calla lilies and dark green ivy. Everywhere I looked I saw white flowers with a sprinkle of burgundy flowers here and there. The chairs our guests sat in, most of which I didn't recognize, were covered with burgundy silk.

I draped my arm through Kalia's and waited for our turn. She beamed at me. I was overwhelmed with emotions at that moment and fighting hard not to let the tears start.

"I love you…mom."

She looked as shocked as I felt but she quickly recovered and a smile washed over her face. "I love you too, my daughter. Now let's get you to where you belong."

I hadn't even noticed the wedding march started and the guests were on their feet, eyes on us. We started walking down the steps, slowly, my knees shaking with every step I took. It wasn't until we were half way to the front that I finally laid eyes on him. He stood next to Pierce, his eyes sparkling, his smile wide. His blue eyes sparkled like diamonds with his happiness. He took a deep breath and gathered himself but his smile didn't diminish. In fact, the closer I got to him, the wider it grew. When we reached the front, I realized I had no idea who was watching us walk down the aisle since I paid attention to nothing but Christian. Kalia was right. No one else mattered.

She placed my hand in Christian's. Aaron asked, "Who gives this woman to be wed?"

"I do, her mother." Aaron's eyes widened but he became serious again as he prepared for his role. The ceremony was short and simple. We repeated the customary vows, exchanged rings, and lit a unity candle. I looked into his eyes, as we settled in front of Aaron again, and I knew I was home. I was exactly where I wanted to be, now and forever.

When Aaron said Christian could kiss the bride, I threw my arms around his neck and clung to him until he had to force me away. "Lily, I don't think Aaron is finished yet."

Since the guests were also vampires, they heard and erupted into laughter.

"Oops!" I'm glad it was impossible to blush.

He announced us for the first time as Mr. and Mrs. Christian Rexer and the laughter turned to thunderous applause. We made our way back up the aisle, with Pierce and Fiore following, and back into the house. I felt like I was in a daze as we walked into the kitchen. It wasn't until Kalia grabbed me into her arms that I finally took a deep breath. I realized Christian never let go of my hand.

"Take a break for a few minutes and then back outside. I'm so happy for you," she said before releasing me. That's when I finally really looked at my new husband.

Christian stood in front of me, my hand still tightly grasped in his, looking down at me with so much love and happiness in his eyes that I felt like I would melt. A sense of security, very foreign to me, engulfed me. I couldn't believe this tall, perfect man had really chosen to spend eternity with me. He wrapped his arms around me and kissed me so passionately that Fiore and Kalia actually let out an "aw".

Aaron cleared his throat and I couldn't help but giggle as I reluctantly pulled my face away from Christian's.

"That was a beautiful ceremony, Aaron. Thank you," Christian said.

"It was an honor. Thank you for letting me do it." He put his arm around Kalia. "We should go back out. Everyone wants to congratulate the bride and groom and we have pictures to take. Don't forget your flight leaves tonight so you'll want plenty of time."

My husband looked at me with a huge smile and grabbed my hand. Together, as husband and wife, we walked out to greet our guests and celebrate the start of our new life.

⌘ FOURTEEN ⌘

The reception began as soon as we had finished posing for what seemed like a thousand photos. Tables were set up on either side of the wooden platform that would be our dance floor. Vampires sat talking and laughing together. I was passed from one set of arms to another and introduced to so many I couldn't keep their names straight.

The only ones that looked out of place were the humans in the band. They must have been wondering why there was no food at this wedding reception but Kalia had thought to have drinks and snacks for them. When they played the song that was to be our first dance together, the party grew so quiet you could hear a pin drop. Christian took me in his arms and we twirled around the dance floor like we had been dancing together all our lives.

"I didn't know you could dance like this," I whispered, my lips brushing his ear.

"I never had the opportunity to show you. You're pretty amazing yourself, Mrs. Rexer." Butterflies danced in my stomach when he said my new name and I leaned to kiss his lips as we kept dancing. The crowd applauded and cheered.

"I can't seem to find words adequate enough to describe the love I feel for you," he said, breaking away from our kiss first.

"I love you too. I'm so happy. Happy doesn't seem like a good enough word either." He nodded.

The rest of the reception was spent with almost everyone dancing. Kalia danced with Christian and I danced with Aaron. Fiore and Aloysius danced to a few songs together and they made a stunning couple. They even sat together when they weren't dancing. Christian danced to one song with Maia, since I thought it best to include her, hoping she had been sincere in what she'd said about starting over. Soon after, Carlton, a friend of Aaron's, persuaded Maia to one dance. While they twirled on the dance floor, he kept his eyes on her face but she refused to look at him. He didn't seem to care as long as he was dancing with her. I almost felt bad for her – almost.

I threw the bouquet, which a shocked Maia caught, and Christian threw my garter, which to my surprise, Carlton caught. He looked at Maia and she quickly looked away. When he slid the garter up Maia's leg, he looked at her with longing but she paid him no attention. Cameras snapped like crazy but she always turned her face from them.

As the sky streaked in yellows and oranges with the setting sun, Aaron made the announcement that the bride and groom needed to leave for the airport and the party abruptly came to a halt. The band began breaking down their equipment and packing things up. Yet another line formed and we were passed from vampire to vampire, hugged and kissed, and wished much happiness. I took Christian's hand and we made our way back into the house to change our clothes and gather our luggage.

"I can't believe this is actually happening," I said as I wrapped my arms around my husband's neck, pushing our bedroom door closed with my foot.

"It already happened and it's a dream come true. You are forever my wife," His lips brushed mine. "I think you're going to need help getting out of this gown." He smiled.

I nodded and turned my back to him, waiting for him to undo the clasps. His fingers trembled as he did so and the gown fell around my feet. I felt his lips touch my shoulder and a chill ran up my spine.

"We better hurry. We don't want to miss our flight, do we?" I said, wishing our flight wasn't so soon.

"I know, I know. I wish it were later too. I would love some time alone with you." He went to the closet and grabbed the clothes he had already picked out for the trip to Lima. It was spring here, which meant it was autumn in Lima so we both dressed in jeans, sweaters, and sneakers, to be comfortable for the long flight.

"I need to pull all the pins out of my hair," I said and started. He held out his hand to receive them and laughed as I set one after another on his palm.

"I am so glad I'm not a girl. That looks like a lot of work." He placed the pins on my vanity table as I ran my hand through my hair and fluffed it with my fingers the best I could.

"Ready, Mrs. Rexer?" he asked, taking my suitcase.

"Ready, Mr. Rexer," I replied and leaned to kiss his smiling lips.

"Oh, sorry to interrupt," Aaron said but his smile betrayed him. "I came to see if you need help carrying this stuff."

"Sure. That would be great," Christian said and handed over one of the suitcases. "Is Maia coming to the airport?"

"No. Riley and Raul are staying here tonight instead of the hotel and she offered to keep them company." We all started down the stairs.

The front door was already open and we could see all the vampires that attended our reception assembled along the front walk. As we passed through the crowd, rice rained over us and they clapped and cheered. Aaron placed our things in the back of the car as we said our goodbyes. Maia was the last to walk over to us. She held her arms out to me as she drew near. I looked at Christian and he nodded.

"Have a nice honeymoon," she said as she withdrew her arms from around my back. I wasn't sure but it sounded like she spoke through gritted teeth. Another chill ran down my spine as Christian helped me into the car next to Aloysius. Trusting her was going to take some work.

As we went down the driveway, Maia was the only one who didn't wave. I watched as she opened her cell phone without taking her eyes off our departing car. I focused on her thoughts but she had already blocked me.

As much as we looked forward to our honeymoon, it was difficult parting with Kalia and Aaron. We waved to them until they were out of sight as we walked through security with Aloysius leading the way. To my surprise, Christian and I had seats in first class but Aloysius would be seated in coach. He said he didn't need anything special and wanted to give us some privacy, not that we would get much on a crowded airbus.

"Did you notice anything strange as we drove away?" I asked my new husband as we settled in our seats.

"Like what?" He fastened his seatbelt and then took my hand.

"I don't know. Maybe it was nothing," I said and took his hand in mine.

"There's nothing to worry about except you and me now. All we're going to do from this day forward is have fun and love each other, nothing else." He gave my hand a squeeze as the plane took off. I leaned back in my seat so he could look out the window with me.

"You're right. No worries," I said but my stomach turned as the plane sped down the runway. I wanted to trust Maia, believe in her, but there was still something not quite right. Something was nagging at the back of my mind, though I couldn't name what that something was. I guessed there was nothing left to do but wait and see what happened when we returned. I hated waiting.

ᴄᴏ→FIFTEEN ᴄᴏ

Our flight landed in Lima about thirty minutes ahead of schedule. The sun had not made its grand entrance yet but Christian and I covered our skin with light foundation anyway. Once we made it through the long immigration lines in the airport and were standing outside with our luggage, Aloysius hailed a taxi. His Spanish was flawless as he haggled a price with the driver, which was a hard thing to do at the airport because drivers often took advantage of tourists.

"Where is your place, Aloysius?" I asked as I inhaled the familiar aroma of the city. It was a mix of dust from the lack of rain in the coastal desert and car exhaust. Most people might turn their nose up at the scent but to me it was inviting. Of all the places I'd visited, Lima was my favorite and when I left it years ago, I left a piece of my heart in its hands.

"It's a two story apartment in a building on the edge of Miraflores. It overlooks the Pacific. There's a doorman at all times. There's also a pool and a garden on the roof." He sat in the front seat with the driver.

"It sounds lovely," I said. Aloysius smiled.

As we entered heavier traffic, Christian's eyes grew wide. His hands grabbed at the armrest on the door or flew up to grip the ceiling of the old station wagon that should have been junked long ago. "Aren't there any traffic laws in this country?"

Aloysius laughed and remained perfectly relaxed, his hands on his lap. "There are but I think they're optional. Don't worry, the driver knows what he's doing."

"Yeah, but does anyone else?" He gripped the armrest with both hands this time as the car veered around two other cars and squeezed in front of another with a blaring of the horn. Though the road was two lanes wide, someone had figured out that three lanes worked out just as well.

"Think of it as organized chaos. It's almost like Peruvians can read each other's minds. They seem to know the other drivers' moves as well as their own," I explained, prying his fingers from the armrest and holding his hand in mine.

We reached the building and the driver parked in the usual parking space: the sidewalk. Christian released the breath he had been holding for most of the ride and got out to retrieve our luggage. Aloysius paid and led the way into the twenty-some story building. As soon as we reached the door, it was opened before he could grasp the knob.

"Buenos días, Señor Benjamin. Good to see you," a short, dark skinned doorman said in a heavy Spanish accent. His eyes swept over Christian and me.

I extended a hand to him but he looked at Aloysius before taking it. *"Buenos días. Soy Lily y el es mi esposo, Christian."*

Christian looked shocked at my Spanish but also shook his hand. The man didn't flinch from the coldness of our skin. It didn't surprise me, considering Peru was a very superstitious country and their beliefs were diverse.

"This is Pepé. This is my granddaughter and her new husband. It's their honeymoon," Aloysius explained. Pepé looked confused. *"Luna de miel."*

"Ah, *sí*." Pepé smiled. "You need Carmela?" he asked.

"Sí, por favor," Aloysius said and headed to the elevator with us close at his heels.

"Who's Carmela?" I asked.

"She's my housekeeper."

Once inside the elevator, Aloysius took a key off his key ring and handed it to me. I tucked it into my pocket. The doors opened to the twenty-seventh floor and he led the way down the long hallway. Tables with fresh flowers on them lined the hall, along with an occasional, lavishly carved wooden chair with a plush velvet cushion on the seat.

"Even the hallway is beautiful," Christian said as he set our suitcases down and waited for Aloysius to unlock the door. Three beeps sounded but stopped when he punched some numbers into a keypad. "You have an alarm system?"

"It was already here when I bought the apartment," Aloysius explained. "I didn't bother taking it out. I'm seldom here anymore. Remind me to give you the code." Aloysius started taking sheets off all the covered furniture, but when I started helping he shook his head. "You two get settled.

Carmela should be here soon anyway. She'll take care of the rest. Your room is at the top of the stairs."

Christian picked up our suitcases and I led the way up the spiral stairs in the corner of the living room. There were a few doors on that level but I opened the one Aloysius said would be ours. Christian dropped the luggage and whisked me off my feet and into his arms. "You are such a romantic," I said.

"I can't help it. This is a threshold, is it not?" He kissed my lips before I could answer and carried me to the bed. He set me down as if I were a feather. We didn't even look around the room before he was over me, his lips devouring mine.

A light knock on the door brought us back to reality. "Yes?" I yelled.

"I'm going out for a while so make yourselves at home," Aloysius said. "Carmela will be here any minute so let her know if you need anything. Oh, and don't worry about her."

I looked at Christian but I could tell he didn't know what that meant either. "What do you mean?" I asked.

"She knows." I heard his footsteps descending the metal stairs.

"What does he mean, she knows?" Christian moved to sit on the edge of the bed, shrugging. Before we could ask what he meant, we heard the door downstairs close.

"I'm not sure I want to be here when she gets here. Want to go hit the town?" My eyes went to the window to check the weather. It looked gray enough to venture out with no extra cover-ups.

"Sounds good to me. We have all the time in the world to be together." Christian went into the bathroom attached to our room and ran his hands through his hair. He looked like his usual perfect self, even after sitting on a plane for so many hours. "I am totally in your hands in this city. I've been to Peru before but this is a bit more crowded than what I'm used to."

"Where in Peru have you been?" I asked. I was going through the clothes in the suitcase trying to pick something that would help us blend in. From looking out the window, I saw that most were wearing a layer or two. It wasn't that cold.

"I've been here two times. Some digs up north in Trujillo and Chiclayo and then, of course, Machu Picchu. That's something we should do while we're here. It's such a magical place. So, anyway, where are we going?" He came out of the bathroom with his hair looking like it did when he went in.

"I was thinking we could walk through downtown Miraflores and head toward the ocean. I love the cliffs there." I grabbed a windbreaker.

"Sounds like a good plan to me," he replied and took my hand.

The doorman was on the telephone as we passed through the lobby so he raised a hand and waved. As soon as we walked onto the street the smells of the city filled my nostrils. I could also smell the saltiness of the Pacific Ocean so I led us to the left, following my nose. The streets were crowded with people. Some were walking leisurely but most seemed to be in a hurry, some carrying shopping bags and some carrying books and wearing gray school uniforms.

"This city is so alive, even this early," Christian said as he looked at the people walking by. He stood almost a foot taller than most and I saw heads turning to look at him. Two children walked by pointing and I heard the word "gringo" whispered as they passed. I couldn't help but smile at their curiosity and their delight at seeing an American.

"Did they call me what I think they called me?"

"Yes they did. You realize that's not an insult, right?" I asked. I remembered the first time I heard someone say that while pointing to Ian. Christian shrugged. "It's fascinating to them to see someone with your hair and eye color. You're also very tall."

"I do stick out like a sore thumb. I can see over everyone's heads. I remember that from being up north. I swear there were adults only three feet tall there." He smiled.

"You'll see people that short here too. I feel tall for once when they're around. I need to exchange some money," I said and stopped at the curb. Buses went by so full that people were hanging out the doors. Taxis pulled to the curb, beeping their horns and cutting off the traffic behind them. I kept my eyes straight ahead so they would keep going. I felt a tug on the back of my shirt. A young boy, no older than seven, stood behind me. His face was dirty, and his hair was tangled and too long. The wool sweater he wore was much too small and full of holes. "*Señorita, un caramelo por favor*," he pled, still tugging on my shirt.

"What does he want?" Christian asked, noticing the plastic bag the child held in his free hand.

"He's selling candy. I normally wouldn't do this but the children really get to me." I pulled out a dollar bill, since I hadn't exchanged any money to *soles* yet. The boy's eyes lit up and his smile revealed rotten teeth. He pulled three pieces of candy out of his bag and handed them to me.

"*Gracias, señotita. Dios la bendiga.*" He took the dollar and examined it with wide eyes before stuffing it in his pocket.

"Did he say God bless you?" Christian asked as I dragged him across the street as soon as there was an opening in the traffic. "A child like that does tug at your heart."

"I know. I don't like to buy something from every beggar I encounter but the children are a different story. Their parents expect them to make money every day and if they don't, they get in a lot of trouble. I saw a little girl get slapped by her mother when she didn't make enough money. I feel bad for them. Most of them never even step foot inside a school." I headed for the man with the blue vest who was standing on the corner.

"*¿A cuanto está el dolar?*" I asked.

"*Dos ochenta, señorita,*" he answered and then focused his eyes on Christian. I pulled out a bill and handed it to him. He examined the bill closely and then punched some numbers in his calculator, holding it up for me to see. I nodded and he counted the colorful Peruvian bills as he set them in my hand. He looked from Christian to me again before he shuddered and turned to walk to another possible customer.

"What was that all about?" Christian asked as we continued down the crowded sidewalk.

"He could tell something was different about us. These people believe more readily than most. Don't worry about it. See, he's over it already," I said looking back to see the man was busy waving his arms and trying to flag down new customers.

"Those are nice," Christian said as he stopped to point through a shop window. "They would look great on you."

"Which ones? The way-too-high boots or the shiny red heels?" I asked.

"The boots. You should try them on. They are so you," he said with a hopeful smile on his face. "I bet they're real leather."

"They do make great shoes here. They don't look at all practical though," I complained though the more I looked the more I liked them. They were knee-high black boots with a small silver buckle around the ankle and very thin four-inch heels.

"For me?" he begged. I couldn't help but laugh.

"Okay. You don't have to beg." I looked at the other display window in case there was something else I liked before walking in. Cigarette smoke hit my nose before I noticed the man leaning against the trashcan. He nodded in greeting. I opened the door and pulled Christian inside.

"What's wrong?" he asked.

"Nothing. I'll try the boots on for you," I answered. I looked out the window and the man was still there, looking at us as I looked at him. My attention was taken from him as a sales woman came to ask if I wanted to see something. I pointed to the boots, gave her my size in European measurement, and she disappeared behind a curtain.

Moments later, we left the store with the boots in a bag and a satisfied smile on Christian's face. I looked at the trashcan as soon as we were out but no one was standing there. As we neared the intersection to the coastline, I smelled cigarette smoke again. I turned to look behind us as a shadow disappeared into the doorway of a restaurant.

"What's wrong, Lily?" Christian asked, following my eyes.

"I don't know. I feel like we're being followed."

"Why would someone be following us?" he asked.

"I don't know. Let's forget about it. I guess I'm just feeling a little paranoid." I pulled him across the street, zigzagging through traffic and onto a wide sidewalk. I looked around but didn't recognize the park I thought should be on this street.

"You look confused," Christian said as he looked around the crowd, now a bit paranoid himself.

"This is all so different. It used to be a park. Now it's a...mall?" The last time I had been in this district of Lima a park sat here. There were benches, a round, concrete rink where children roller-skated, a fountain, and the bird-like statue. The statue was still here, along with the fountain, but the rest was gone. At the cliff's edge sat a huge, modern shopping center that looked like it was carved right into the cliff.

"Whatever this is, it's beautiful, very modern," Christian said as he took in the sites.

Keeping a tight grip on his hand, I dragged him through the crowd toward the briny scent blowing at our faces. My hair was its usual mass of tangles as the wind blew it to veil my face. Cigarette smoke filled the heavy air around us and I turned to find the source, pulling my hair away with my free hand. A teenage girl stood against the rail, her arm around a boy, the cigarette dangling from her parted lips. The skinny dark-haired boy held a cell phone out in front of them and clicked a photo. She grabbed the phone from his hand and ran toward the stairs, laughing as she dared him to chase her. It wasn't the man who was watching us earlier.

Don't worry about it. Try to relax and enjoy our honeymoon. Christian kept his comment from reaching the happy crowd around us. I nodded and smiled at him. I would do as he wished but I would keep my guard up, just in case.

When we reached the railing on the patio, we both stood against it and looked out at the vastness of the Pacific Ocean. The waves crashed against the shore and the white caps rolled onto the fine, brown sand. Looking closer to where we each had a hand on the orange rail, the cliff unfurled into the nothingness below, or at least it looked like nothingness until my eyes spotted the tiny cars on the road along the beaches.

"This is breathtaking," Christian said and leaned to kiss my cheek. "What is that glow over there?" He pointed to the far left.

I focused my eyes in that direction and could, in fact, see a faint orange glow. It was daylight now but very hazy. The glow was confined to one spot on the sand. "I don't know…maybe, a fire? There must be people on the beach." I tried to focus on any sounds that might be coming from that spot but it was difficult with all the traffic and the beeping horns. The happy chatter of the shoppers around us also drowned out the possibility of hearing that far.

Deciding to forget about the fire, I turned my eyes back to the stairs on my left. The boy that had been chasing the girl down the stairs stood on the bottom step, his hand gripping the railing. He turned his head and a smile spread across his lips. I thought I saw his head nod slightly.

"He wants us to follow him," Christian said, already pulling me away from the railing.

"What? How do you know that?" I asked, not really wanting to move but curious anyway.

"I…I don't know. I feel it, somehow. Come on."

The boy never turned to look at us again. He kept his eyes straight ahead, his pace fast, as we followed behind him without speaking.

⤳ SIXTEEN ⤳

We crossed the street toward the beach but the boy was nowhere to be seen. We had lost sight of him as we waited for a break in traffic and by the time we got across, the only ones left on the beach were the ones sitting around a fire. There were five of them, all in dark clothes, all wearing hoods. They kept their faces low and toward the fire, their features indistinguishable.

"Where did he go?" Christian asked. He turned to scan the beach.

"I don't know. Is he sitting with them?" I nodded toward the hooded figures.

"Go away! We don't want your kind here!" One of the hooded men spoke with a thick accent. Their heads stayed low and I couldn't tell which one had spoken. None of them looked slim enough to be the boy we'd followed.

Christian gripped my hand tighter. "Are you talking to us?"

"Yes. You are not welcome here. Go back to where you came from," the same one spoke again. He was probably the only English speaker in the group.

"What do you mean *our kind?*" Christian asked. I tried to listen to their thoughts but immediately hit a wall. I didn't think humans were capable of blocking and they were definitely human. Their hearts beat like drums in my ears.

"Blood suckers are not welcome in this city. Remove yourselves or we will remove you."

"We mean you no harm. We are merely tourists," I said before Christian could answer.

"Go or we will make you disappear. You will not like our way."

I pulled Christian back toward the street. *Let's get out of here. Maybe*

Aloysius knows who they are.

He nodded but continued looking behind us until we reached the street. None of them had bothered to move. They hadn't even raised their heads to look at us.

We climbed the steps to the mall and exited toward the upper street. I held my arm out to hail a taxi when a hand shoved me hard on the back. I lost my balance and fell off the curb, rolling onto the street. A car swerved around me, its tires screeched, and the horn blared in anger. I jumped to my feet and in one bound was back on the sidewalk next to Christian, rubbing the shoulder that hit the pavement and wiping my hair from my face. Gravel stuck to my shirt. My fangs were bared and I was ready for a fight.

The scent of humans was all I encountered as a small crowd gathered to see what had happened but all kept their distance from Christian. He grabbed my arm and pulled me closer, protectively.

"What the hell happened?" I hissed through my teeth.

"I don't know…it happened so fast…I didn't…" Christian tried to explain but looked as confused as I felt. Still the crowd watched, whispering in rapid Spanish to each other, but did not approach.

"Did you push me?"

"I'm not sure." He pulled me into his arms but my muscles clenched. "I think I might have."

"Why would you do that? I don't understand…" I pulled out of his arms as he lowered his gaze to the sidewalk.

"I don't know. I'm not even sure it was really me but there was no one else here. I lost sight of you for a moment and next thing I know, you were in the street, already getting up." He reached his hand out but I pretended not to notice, my stomach turning into knots.

"What do you mean you lost sight of me?" I kept my voice down only so the crowd would not hear but it was difficult to restrain myself from screaming at him.

"You were there one moment, hailing a taxi, and the next…everything went black."

A small yellow car with only one headlight pulled to a stop next to us, beeping its horn two times.

"Taxi?" the driver asked, leaning toward us.

"*Sí*," I answered and pulled the back door open. I gave him the address and slid as far over as the small plastic seat would allow. Christian slid over to me but I turned my face to the window and kept my hands folded on my lap. My mind tried to deny what happened but the knot in my stomach was a constant reminder; a reminder that the man I loved, and married, tried to push me in front of a car, and on our honeymoon!

"Lily, please look at me," he whispered.

I said nothing as I kept my mind from him by concentrating on the blurring scenery as we sped down the street. Couples walked hand in hand, laughing at some joke only they shared. Teenagers sat on the steps of a well-lit mansion, laughing and swatting at each other playfully, passing a bottle of Inca Kola between them, not a care in the world.

"If I did do it, and I still don't know if I did, I didn't do it on purpose. I would never do anything to hurt you." My lips pressed together and my back stiffened. I refused to look at him while he spoke. "Okay. You won't talk to me right now. I get it. I love you with everything that I am. I swear it." He paused to wait for a reaction from me. I gave him nothing.

He sighed and continued, "At least answer one question, please. Are you hurt?"

I snapped my head toward him and glared. "Of course I'm hurt! My husband tried to kill me! What do you expect?"

To my utter shock, he smiled. "Good. Now that you're talking, first of all, I don't know how or why that happened. Second, I doubt a car could kill you anyway, but that's not what I meant. I meant are you hurt physically?"

"No. I'm not. My shirt is ruined though," I answered. I knew deep down inside that Christian loved me but something else was going on here, something was very wrong. "We really need to talk to Aloysius." I reached for his hand out of habit, before making up my mind on whether or not to stay angry with him.

The taxi pulled up, two tires on the sidewalk, in front of the apartment building. I handed the money to the driver and slid out of the seat and to the sidewalk without waiting for Christian's assistance. The hurt expression on his face was breaking my heart but, then again, so was the fact that he had tried to hurt me.

"Aloysius, are you here?" I called as soon as we had the front door open.

"I'm in my bedroom getting dressed. I suggest you do the same," he yelled from upstairs.

"Why?" I asked as we climbed the stairs to our room. "Are you expecting someone?"

Christian moved a few paces closer to me. I clasped both hands behind my back. I saw his face sink but I turned away.

"No. We're going out. It's your first night here and I'd like to show you a good time. In a few days, I will be heading up to Trujillo and then your honeymoon will be all yours. I hope you don't mind." He stepped out of his bedroom wearing jeans as black as night, a long sleeved white shirt so crisp that it offset his ebony hair. On his feet, he wore black leather dress shoes with a silver buckle. He looked like a man in his early twenties, ready for a night out on the town. The top three buttons on his shirt were undone and I saw how close the color of his skin was to the whiteness of his shirt.

"We ran into some problems tonight and we'd like to talk to you. We thought maybe you'd have some answers," I said.

"Well, we can talk about it on the way if you don't mind." He looked at me so I nodded. "Now, go get dressed, please. There will be dancing so dress appropriately. I have some calls to make before we leave. Just let me know when you're ready." He started down the steps toward the living room without a backward glance.

"What should I wear?" Christian had his suitcase already open on the bed and was shuffling the clothes around. We hadn't even unpacked yet.

"I don't care." I started pulling things out of my own suitcase, trying not to look at him.

I chose a denim mini-skirt, black ruffled sleeveless top, and the new boots. I took my pile and went into the bathroom, closing and locking the door behind me.

"Do you want me to leave the room?" Christian asked from the other side of the door.

"No. That would look really bad. This is supposed to be our honeymoon." Worrying our gracious host was not something I wanted to do right now, especially since he would be leaving us soon. I wanted to talk to him about the people on the beach. I decided I would say nothing about what happened with Christian, not right now anyway.

The look in Christian's eyes when I re-entered the bedroom told me he approved of my outfit but his tight lips told me he was confused about me getting dressed in the bathroom instead of with him. He looked great in his dark jeans and black v-neck sweater, his white tee-shirt sticking out at the top of his chest. I caught myself before I could compliment him.

"I'm not planning to tell Aloysius what happened with us. I just want to know who those people on the beach were." I grabbed my small knitted bag, containing only my lipstick and identification, and slung it over my shoulder. I knew better than to carry anything too important in a purse and my money was already in the front pocket of my skirt. It was too easy to get a purse snatched in Lima, even from a taxi.

Aloysius had a taxi already waiting at the curb in front of the building. He gave the driver directions to downtown Lima, to a popular tourist spot where live music played and dancers entertained the crowd with typical Peruvian dances.

"You said you had a problem today?" Aloysius turned to look at us from the front seat. I took Christian's hand only so we looked like the honeymooners we were supposed to be. He smiled and squeezed my fingers anyway.

I told him what happened with the kid we followed and the group on the beach. Aloysius put his hand up to stop me and glanced at the driver. He was mouthing the words to the Spanish song on the radio and seemed oblivious to our conversation. He most likely didn't speak English or just didn't care what we had to say.

"Let me guess. He told you our kind is not welcome in Lima?" Aloysius smiled, amused.

"You know them?" Christian asked, tightening his grip on my hand.

"Pay no attention to them. They consider themselves vampire hunters. I have yet to hear of one vampire casualty caused by them, however." He laughed and looked at the driver again. He was still singing along to the song on his radio, his head bobbing slightly.

"But they are human, right?" I asked, thinking about how the kid put the idea of following him into Christian's mind.

"As far as I know, yes. They call themselves vampire hunters but will frown upon anything supernatural," he explained. He was taking money out of his pocket so I assumed we were nearing our destination. "They're hypocrites, if you ask me."

"Why do you think that?"

"Well, I haven't seen them in years, but I know a few of them also consider themselves witches. I'm pretty sure that qualifies as supernatural. Here we are then."

We followed him into a crowded vestibule, where happy chatter, in various languages, swallowed anything else I tried to say. That was all the information we would get tonight. Aloysius paid for the three of us and we followed him into a large room to find a seat. A raised stage sat in the front of the room where musicians were setting up their instruments. A lower stage, larger than the first, sat empty below it, the wooden surface shining as if it had just been waxed. Three sides were surrounded by tables and surrounding that was another platform with more tables. He led us to one on the bottom level and at the center of the two stages.

A waiter came over as soon as we were seated and Aloysius ordered three Pisco Sours. Christian leaned toward me and asked, "What are those?"

"Pisco is liquor made from grapes. A Pisco Sour has lime juice in it and foamy egg whites on the top. It looks and smells really good but I've never actually tasted it." Sitting next to him, with the excitement of the crowd, and the sounds of the band warming up, I felt my anger fading away layer by layer. Aloysius smiled at me and I wondered if he sensed my anger and hurt.

"In between dances," he said, "the band will keep playing and give the audience a chance to dance too. I'm hoping your husband won't mind sharing you. I so love dancing."

Christian shook his head. "Not at all. After all, you are family."

Music started and a man's voice filled the room as he introduced the first of the dancers. The crowd hushed and all eyes were on the side of the room where a line of men wearing colorful *chuyos* and playing pan flutes walked in a line toward the stage. The *zampoñistas* played while they danced around a man beating a drum. Christian leaned closer to me, his eyes never leaving the stage. When that act ended and the *zamoñistas* had filed back to what I assumed was the dressing room, the man on the stage invited the audience up to dance and the band started playing something very fast and very Latin.

My feet started tapping under the table without my control and Christian turned a scared face toward me. "What is it?" I asked.

"I never danced to this kind of music before. I might be really bad at it," he said into my ear. "But shall we try anyway?"

"Trust me," Aloysius said. "No one will care. Just have fun. That's the whole point."

I answered by pushing away from the table and leading him by the hand to the dance floor. We worked our way into the crowd and found a spot toward the middle. He might feel a little less self-conscious if we were surrounded by dancers and all eyes were not directed toward us. He looked at me expectantly, not knowing what to do, so I took one of his hands and placed it on my hip and started moving against him. We swayed back and forth, my legs on either side of one of his, his fingers gripping my hip as it moved back and forth against him. Turning on the dance floor, grinding against him, I noticed Christian wasn't breathing. His hand had slid down my hip as I moved to the rhythm of the music and he now gripped my bare thigh. I wondered how much of my body was on display as we danced against each other, but as crowded as the dance floor was, realized no one could see. I also realized that I didn't really care.

His eyes sparkled as our bodies moved to the music and I felt the fluttering in my stomach and the sudden hunger in my soul. *I want you.*

I looked up at him when I heard that but didn't have a chance to respond as his wet mouth crushed mine. My fingers tangled in his hair and I pulled his face against mine, realizing we weren't even moving anymore. I didn't care. *I'm sorry...I'm so sorry I doubted you,* I thought, never taking my mouth away from his. Applause filled the room before he could respond. We parted and looked around, shocked. The music had stopped and the crowd had left the dance floor, leaving us alone, kissing while everyone watched.

They're clapping at us!

I know...what do we do?

Smile and walk back to the table...what else?

Oh, my God! This is so embarrassing. He looked only at the floor as we walked.

I guess we just became part of the entertainment...

As we neared our table, we finally looked up. Aloysius clapped along with the rest of the audience and his amused look confirmed that he'd also enjoyed the show.

"That was quite a show," Aloysius teased when we returned to our seats and hung our heads in embarrassment.

The announcer broke the applause by introducing the next act. As the dancers filed out of the dressing room in their elaborate costumes, the men in colorful costumes and the women in skirts so short you could see their black panties, Christian stiffened and sat straight as a board. "What?"

He didn't need to answer. I saw him too. Leading the line of dancers was the boy that had led us to the beach. His eyes were focused on us and his smile sent chills up my spine.

⌘ SEVENTEEN ⌘

"He's only a boy," I said to Aloysius as he unlocked the front door and we followed him into the apartment. He led us into the living room and we sank into the plush white sofas.

"What does he have to do with the hunters?" Christian asked.

"You're right, Lily. He is only a boy but that has nothing to do with it. It doesn't matter how old you are to have talents and start training in witchcraft. If he is the one that put the idea of following him into your head, Christian, then he most likely is a witch, or at least training to be one," Aloysius explained as he stretched his legs out and rested his feet on the coffee table. "As far as who he is, I don't know. I don't remember seeing anyone that young with the group of hunters in the past, but then again, I'm not here much. It is possible that some of them have children."

"Don't they ever bother you?" I asked, trying to make some sense of this.

"We met many years ago, when I first bought my apartment and started spending extended periods of time here. We seem to have an un- spoken understanding. I don't bother them; they don't bother me. I keep my identity as secret as possible from humans and they like that. I try my best to blend in where ever I go."

"So what are we supposed to do to avoid them?" I asked, thinking about how often Christian, as a new vampire, would need to feed.

"Keep doing what you're doing. Enjoy your honeymoon and be the tourists you're supposed to be. As for feeding, try to stick to La Perla and Rimac, if at all possible," Aloysius advised.

"Why those areas?" I asked.

"Those are areas that need cleaning up, if you catch my drift. No one there will mind a few missing vermin. The police can't even keep up with them. They'd probably be grateful." Aloysius crossed the room and slid the curtain aside, unveiling a floor to ceiling window overlooking the glowing nighttime city with the Pacific as a backdrop. The blackness of the ocean was speckled with a light here and there from what I assumed were ships. It looked as peaceful as a painting.

Both La Perla and Rimac were areas I had heard of in the past but they were places I never ventured into. Since Ian was not opposed to killing innocent people to satisfy his thirst, we hunted in the more populated and tourist areas of the city. We frequented the bars at the most popular hotels, the parks, and the walks along the cliffs that overlooked the beaches. Some nights we even hunted at the theater or the opera. I walked over to stand by Aloysius and made the mistake of leaning toward the open window to get a better look. My head started spinning instantly as I leaned out. Aloysius chuckled and pulled me back with an arm around my waist.

"Afraid of heights, I see." He kept his arm around my waist.

"Believe it or not, she is," Christian answered.

"How then do you manage to fly?" Aloysius asked, raising his eyebrows.

"The times I've flown have all been times when I've had no choice," I answered, thinking of the times Ian grabbed me and flew with me in his arms, like when he gave me the proposition to save Christian's life. Either I leave with him and forget Christian or Christian dies. He flew with me in his arms then from Oregon to New York. When I realized I could actually fly myself, it was purely an accident. I was falling out of a tree. "I flew Christian away from captivity because I had no choice. He was too weak to walk far on his own and I had no access to a car. I can and will fly when I have to, but, believe me, I don't have to like it."

Both men laughed but I ignored them, walking back to the safety of the sofa to sit by Christian.

"It almost feels like they knew we were here. I mean, the boy, he was with a girl and they walked away. He came back after a little while by himself. That's when he told me, in my mind, to follow him." This time, Christian was the one to get up and start wearing circles into the area rug as he paced around the coffee table.

"Do you think it was a coincidence that he was at the club tonight? I mean, what are the chances?" A low rumble under my feet made me yank them up onto the white sofa. Aloysius gripped the frame of the open window as the glass rattled. We looked at each other. Dead silence.

"What the hell was that?" Christian asked. He had stopped walking and stood with his arms out, like a tightrope walker in a circus.

"It was just a very small earthquake, nothing to worry about," Aloysius explained and leaned to look out the open window. "It looks like no one outside even noticed."

"I forgot about those. I felt a few when I was last here but nothing major." I felt vibrations in the front of my body and braced myself for another tremor. Christian stopped pacing again and both men looked at me. "What?"

"That's your cell phone," Christian said with a grin.

"Oh, right…" I reached in the front pocket of my skirt and pulled it out. "Hello?"

"Everything okay?" Aloysius asked when I closed and re-pocketed my phone.

"Yes, of course. Kalia called to make sure we were okay and enjoying ourselves. They send their love," I explained.

"Then why do you look so worried?" Christian asked.

"It's probably nothing, but Maia is gone again. She didn't tell them where she was going." Maia seemed to be trying to make amends before we left for Peru but something inside me screamed that something was still very wrong.

"I wouldn't worry too much about it. She's probably in Europe again, looking for a new man," Christian took my hand and pulled me from the sofa. "Why don't we change and go for some dinner?"

"That's a good idea, and remember what I told you, stick to La Perla and Rimac," He started down the hall toward the spiral stairs. "I'm going to get packed. I have to leave sooner than I thought."

"Why didn't you tell him what actually happened?" Christian stood facing me.

"I didn't think it was important and besides…I couldn't."

"Not important? How can you say that, unless…you don't believe me! That's it, isn't it? You don't trust me."

"Christian, I never said that…where would you…" I walked back to the window and away from him so he couldn't see my face.

"You're doing it again."

"What am I doing? I don't know what you are talking about." I didn't hide my irritation.

"That brick wall that I slammed into in the beginning, the one I finally thought was coming down from around your heart…you've been putting it back up lately, brick by brick."

I spun to look at him. "That's preposterous! I don't have a wall around my heart. If I did, you wouldn't be here."

"You don't see it, do you?" He stood behind me and wrapped his arms around my waist. I stiffened without meaning to. "I'm not Ian. I would never do the things he did. I would never use you or manipulate you and I most certainly would never intentionally hurt you."

I turned in his arms and pushed him back so I could look at his face. "I never said that! I never compared you with Ian."

"You don't have to say it. I'm in tune with your mind, remember? Whatever happened today, it was not my fault. I would never do anything like that. You're my wife," He held a hand out to me. I hesitated for a moment but when I looked at his eyes, the hurt in them melted my dead heart. "We'll figure this out, one way or another."

"I know…you're right. Let's go to dinner."

THE TAXI DRIVER raised his eyebrows when I asked him to take us to La Perla but, wanting to earn the outrageous fare he quoted, didn't object as he shoved his way back into traffic. Though it was very late, Lima's streets were still bustling with people walking arm in arm, their laughter heard as we sped past. Traffic wasn't even that much lighter at this hour but Christian ignored the chaos and relaxed at my side, his fingers intertwined with mine. He glanced down at my ring once in a while as if making sure it was real.

"Right here is fine," I said in Spanish as the driver approached an extra dark corner. His surprise was visible in the rearview mirror but again he did not argue. I handed him the money and slid out of the car.

"We're still close to the ocean, aren't we?" Christian asked as I led him up a dark street that smelled unmistakably like urine.

"Yes. We're not far from the naval academy. On the beach, in La Punta, there is no sand until you get further into the water. It's all smooth rocks that don't really hurt your feet when you walk on them. There are gorgeous old houses along the beach too, where the aristocratic society once lived. Maybe we can go there after we feed," I suggested as I paused to decide in a direction. I listened for voices but heard nothing. "We'll have to come back during the day too so we can take a boat ride."

We continued up the narrow street and turned a corner. Christian yanked my hand and made me stop. "Do you hear that?"

"What?"

"I hear footsteps when we walk and when we stop, they stop." He motioned behind us with his head.

Let's walk again...

We took a few steps and, sure enough, I heard them this time. *Keep walking until we get somewhere where they can't hide...*I didn't know if there was a place like that considering all these old, dilapidated houses had long corridors next to their doors but it was worth a try.

As we rounded another corner, Christian stopped. He leaned forward, both hands clutching his forehead.

What is it?

My head feels like it's going to explode...like when...you know...

I knew all too well. When he was kidnapped and taken to Ireland, the woman who took him kept causing him constant headaches so she could keep feeding him pills and keep him drugged. I didn't think it could happen now that he was not mortal but I guess I was wrong. I helped him to the dusty cement wall of a building so he could lean against it and the footsteps started again, but faster.

"Do not move!" A young man wearing a black jacket with the hood tied tightly around his head, so I couldn't see his hair, aimed a gun at us. A laugh escaped my lips before I could stop it.

"Do you really think a gun is going to help you?" I asked incredulously. I could see the kid's hand shaking as he tried to stand taller to make himself look tougher than he obviously felt.

"She said to shoot him." He motioned to Christian by aiming the gun in his face.

"Who said?" Christian dropped his hands from his forehead and pushed me behind him. The kid said nothing but continued aiming the shaking gun.

"Why him?" I asked, trying to see around Christian who was acting as a shield.

"Because, how do you say? He is new and weak."

"Wrong! He is as strong as I am. Who sent you?" I demanded, making my way out from behind Christian. The kid jerked his hand to aim the gun at me now, his wide eyes darting back and forth between our faces.

"I cannot say the name." The gun was aimed at Christian again but the kid's hand was shaking even worse, as if he was struggling to hold on to the weapon. I looked at Christian and his eyes were locked on the gun, his forehead scrunched. A moment later, the gun floated in the air out of the kid's reach. The kid turned to run but I grabbed the back of his jacket. He snapped back toward me so fast he collided against me and we fell to the sidewalk. Flipping him over and jumping on top, I straddled his waist to keep him down.

Christian grabbed the gun out of the air and knelt next to us. "It's the kid from the beach and the show."

I pushed his hood off his head to reveal greasy black hair. "So it is. You're getting to be a pain in the ass, kid." I shoved his head back to the pavement with a thud. "Who sent you?"

He swallowed hard and tried to turn his head. I grabbed a handful of greasy hair and made him face me. His eyes widened with terror.

"Lily, you're hurting him," Christian said, placing a hand gently on my shoulder. I didn't know how he could stay so calm when all I wanted to do was bash this kid's head on the pavement for all the trouble he was causing.

"Lady, please. I no want to die. She will kill me or they will." His eyes filled with tears.

"She? They? Which is it?" I demanded through clenched teeth. This was supposed to be our honeymoon and already we had nothing but trouble.

"I cannot tell you. Please let me go. I will go away. *Por Dios*," he pleaded.

"God isn't going to help you now!" I shoved my knees into his chest.

"Lily, please. Let's take him with us. Let's try to help him. Maybe he'll talk then," Christian said.

"Why should we help him? He's been nothing but trouble. Why shouldn't I kill him right now?"

"Because I know you better than that. You wouldn't be able to live with yourself if you killed him without reason," he explained, trying to coax me off the boy.

"He pulled a gun on us! That's reason enough for me."

"But he didn't pull the trigger. He had an opportunity and he didn't take it."

He was right. He had the chance to shoot us in the back or shoot Christian when he stood in front of me. He hesitated and that cost him.

"Fine. We take him but we take him unconscious."

What?

A snack…not enough to kill him…just knock him out for the ride.

⤙ EIGHTEEN ⤚

The boy curled up on his side on the guest room bed while I looked through my suitcase for something to tie his wrists and ankles. I had put Christian in a cab before I took to the air with the unconscious boy in my arms. The front door opened and slammed shut as I pulled a scarf out of my bag. It would be best to at least tie his arms up for now.

"What the hell are you doing?" Christian threw the bedroom door open, letting it slam against the wall.

"What are you talking about?"

"Do you realize we are now kidnappers? What were you thinking, Lily? I said *help* him, not tie him up like some prisoner!" His voice was harsher than ever and I froze on the spot.

"It's not like we kidnapped some innocent! This kid has been following us around since we got here: first, on the street when we were walking to the mall, then at the mall, at the beach, at the show, and now this. Do you honestly mean to tell me what I'm doing is wrong? As soon as he's conscious he'll run. I won't let that happen until I get answers." I went to work tying his wrists. He groaned a bit but didn't open his eyes.

"It is wrong, Lily. Someone's going to be looking for him. He's just a boy. He must have family," Christian sat on the bed next to him to examine his neck. "Is he going to be okay?"

"Of course, he is. We didn't take much. He'll sleep it off for a while."

"We need to get him out of here before he wakes up. That's best, I think."

"No! I want to know who he is. I want to know who sent him. He's not going anywhere until he talks."

"Is it that important? Are you willing to get in trouble over this?" He came to stand behind me and wrapped his arms around my waist.

I pushed him away and turned. "I'm tired of this, Christian. I wanted normal! This isn't normal! We're on our honeymoon and we're being pursued. Why does it always have to be us?"

"Maybe they're after us for money. They can clearly see we're tourists. If they know anything about Aloysius then they know he has money, plenty of it," he reasoned. I shook my head.

"Then why not wait until we're out and rob us? Why go to all this trouble to follow us everywhere we go? That kid was not only spying on us, but he even admitted he was sent to kill you. Why?"

"I don't know." He sat on the edge of the bed and looked at the sleeping boy's face. "I guess we will have to wait to get our answers."

"Christian," I sat next to him, took his hand, and stared at my lap. "I'm sorry I'm so on edge, but I wanted this trip to be perfect and it's been nothing but problems."

His hand, gentle on my chin, drew my face toward his. "It is perfect. You're my wife for all eternity now. What more could I ask?"

"I guess you're right. We've dealt with worse already, haven't we? I'm really worried about something, though."

"What's that?"

I swallowed hard, exaggerating my point. "What will Aloysius say when he gets home to find we have a tied-up teenager in his apartment?"

"I don't even want to think about it. Hopefully we'll have him out of here before he gets back."

WE WATCHED THE boy sleep, tossing and turning, and listened to him mumble unintelligibly. Though we listened intently, we could not make out what language he was mumbling in. After about three hours of our vigil on him and the front door, though we both knew Aloysius would not be back so soon, the boy finally tried to open his eyes. I ran over to sit by his side.

"*Agua...agua...*"

"I know that one. He wants water," Christian jumped up from the foot of the bed and went toward the door. "Is that okay?"

"Of course. We're not torturing him; at least, I hope we don't have to." Christian shook his head and left the room.

"Can you hear me? Do you speak enough English to talk to me?" I started talking as soon as Christian left so he wouldn't go back to sleep.

"Yes, but go slow, please," he replied with a heavy accent through dry lips.

"Good. We have questions – lots of questions. I'll wait until you've had a drink first." After all, I wasn't completely heartless.

Christian hurried in with a glass of water and handed it to me. He slipped his arm behind the boy's head and I tilted the glass to his lips. He kept drinking until he had emptied half of it and then turned his head, his eyes fluttering, trying to focus on the room. I grabbed a tissue from the nightstand and wiped his wet chin.

"Where are we?" he asked.

"Don't worry about it. You are somewhere safe," I answered.

"What is your name?" Christian asked with a gentle tone.

"Jose Luis. Where did you bring me?" he insisted.

"Don't worry about that right now. You're in no danger. We only need to talk to you," I explained.

"Why are you following us?" Christian asked. He propped Jose Luis's head against a pillow. His head lolled to the side as he struggled to hold it up. Christian looked at me with fear. *Did we take too much?* I shook my head hoping I was right.

"I cannot tell you."

"Why not? Did someone send you?"

"I cannot say. I be dead if I say." His eyes widened.

"That's not going to happen while you are with us, but we need to know why you are following us."

He shook his head and closed his eyes. I grabbed his shoulders and shook him but Christian placed his hands on my shoulders and shook his head.

He's obviously afraid…working for someone…what if we offer him protection – long-term?

Are you kidding me? Protect this little rat? I clenched my hands on my lap, fighting the urge to shake Jose Luis to his senses.

I looked at Christian's eyes and saw his desperation to protect this kid. It was so like him to want to protect someone no matter what. Always thinking of others first. I nodded.

"We won't tell anyone we spoke with you. That's a promise," I told Jose Luis, who had opened his eyes and was staring at me.

"You are pretty."

"Um…thank you…" I answered. I looked at Christian but he just smiled. "So, who sent you?"

"I cannot…she will know."

"Again *she*? Who is she?" Christian's tone was much gentler than mine would have been so I let him continue the questioning. I wanted a chance to get answers my way.

"I cannot. Please. She will kill me."

As soon as I tried to invade the boy's mind, it was like slamming my head against a brick wall at full speed. I grabbed my forehead as I felt the physical pain. How could he do that when he should be weakened from blood loss and also human?

"Stay out of my brain." He tried to sit up but didn't make it far before flopping back on the pillows. "What did you do to me?"

"Don't worry about it. It was nothing life-threatening. You'll be back to normal soon enough," Christian explained.

"If you tell us who *she* is, we'll tell you what happened," I urged. Christian looked at me and shrugged. I guess he wasn't going to argue my methods. "After that, we'll give you exactly what you need to get better."

"If I say, then I have to leave here. I cannot stay here and not be dead."

I can't wait to hear this. What does he need to get better? I shrugged and took Christian's hand. He would have to wait too.

"We will find you a safe place to go. We promise. We won't let whoever she is near you."

He sat up against the pillows again. He licked his dry lips and looked nervously from Christian to me. "Her name is Melinda."

I looked at Christian who looked as confused as I felt. He shrugged.

"What is her last name? What does she look like?"

"Melinda. That is all I know. I not know what she looks like. We only spoke on the telephone," Jose Luis said and held his bound hands toward the glass of water. Christian held it to his lips and Jose Luis drank greedily.

"I'll get you more. Are you hungry?" Christian asked from the doorway.

"No! He gets no food, just water for now," I answered, not wanting Jose Luis to get too much from us before we could get what we needed from him.

"Who were the people you led us to on the beach?" I asked as soon as Christian was gone.

Jose Luis closed his eyes and turned his face away from me. Christian came back with the water but Jose Luis did not move.

"Please, tell us something. We won't hurt you. We already promised you safety."

He turned back to us with tears rolling down his face, his hair hanging in his eyes. Christian set the glass down and sat next to him, gently wiping the hair from his face, trying to give him the encouragement and comfort I couldn't give.

"They are my family now. I live with them, on the mountain. They are all I have." He swallowed back more tears before turning his eyes to me. "Please, no hurt them."

"We will let them live if they leave us alone," I said avoiding Christian's face. I knew he didn't agree with my methods – much too hard.

"I want to sleep," Jose Luis said as he sniffled and dried his eyes with the scarf around his wrists. "I need...bath."

"You need a bath?"

"No. I need..."

"Oh, bathroom?" Christian asked.

He nodded. I looked at Christian. *That's all you.*

We helped the boy stand on wobbly legs and then walked him to the bathroom, one of us on either side. Once there, I let Christian take him in while I went to the living room to check my phone. I had the sudden urge to call Kalia and Aaron. I realized at that moment how much I was starting to rely on them and it brought an unexpected smile to my lips.

Christian joined me after tucking Jose Luis into bed and closing the bedroom door.

"As soon as he wakes up, I want to know who all those people are," I said.

"Aloysius said they're the hunters. If that's true, why are they sending the youngest and obviously newest member to deal with us? It doesn't make any sense." Christian sat on the sofa, draping his arm around me and squeezing me to his side. I let my head drop on his shoulder, letting his comfort envelop me and take my worries away, at least for a little while.

"And who the hell is Melinda?" I asked, closing my eyes to shut the room out.

"I have no idea. By the way, what is it that he needs to recover from the blood loss?"

I opened my eyes and lifted my head so I could see his face. "Um...a very rare and bloody steak."

"Is that all? I thought it was some deep, dark secret, some magic potion or something." Christian's eyes crinkled with amusement.

"The problem is, I have to go out and get one. Aloysius won't have such a thing in his refrigerator, I'm sure. I won't be long." I wrapped my arms around him to kiss him goodbye.

Be careful, my love.

"I promise. I will always come back to you." I kissed him once more and left.

BEFORE THE KEY fully turned in the lock, the door was yanked open and it pulled me forward. "I was so worried," Christian whispered into my hair as he held me in his arms, forcing me to drop the bag.

"I'm sorry it took me longer than I expected. I think I was being followed," I mumbled against his quiet chest. He moved to arm's length and looked at me.

"The one doing all the following is here, still asleep."

"I know. That's what is so weird. No matter how hard I tried, I didn't catch even a small glimpse of who it was. He or she kept a good distance and a blocked mind," I picked the bag up off the floor and walked to the kitchen with him close on my heels. "So I took a long way to the store, up and down streets, hoping to see something or maybe just lose the person."

A spine-chilling scream made me drop the frying pan on the tile floor. Christian crouched, ready to attack. "It's Jose Luis!" I said, already running for the bedroom.

It took a moment for my eyes to adjust to the blackness of the room before I saw Jose Luis curled up in a ball on his side, his body rising and falling from his strain to breathe. He screamed again. "What is it?" I yelled as Christian turned on the lamp and inspected the room and the adjoining bathroom. From where I stood, I could see that the windows were tightly shut.

"*Mi cabeza...mi cabeza va a explotar...*" he moaned between sobs.

"What did he say?" Christian asked.

"His head is going to explode. What the hell does that mean?" I bent over his curled up body and tried to get a look at his face.

"Maia! She can do that, remember?" Christian offered.

"Yeah, but it happened to you too, when you were taken. Maia was nowhere near you."

"Right...so she's not the only one with that talent, unless...there really is something wrong with him," His face filled with worry. "He looks so helpless."

"No matter what is going on with him, I still can't get into his mind. I can't get past his wall." Jose Luis's body went totally still. I jumped, thinking he was dead, but his heart still beat weakly.

"Jose Luis?" Christian asked, sitting on the other side of the bed. "Are you okay?"

"Yes, I think," he responded and I breathed a sigh of relief at hearing his calm voice. "I sleep but I am tired still."

"We have some food for you. I have to cook it and then I will feed it to you," I informed him.

"Please let go my hands," he whispered. "I will be good."

I looked at Christian and he nodded without hesitating. *What makes you think he won't run?*

"I promise I will not."

"Great! He can hear us."

I nodded to Christian and he started loosening the scarves. My body stiffened, waiting for some kind of a fight from Jose Luis as soon as he was free to use his arms but it didn't come. I didn't know if it was from his weakened state or if he truly wanted our help. Regardless, it was best if Aloysius didn't come home to find him tied up in the bedroom.

Jose Luis sat at the dining room table and devoured his undercooked steak without taking a breath. It was a good thing I had picked up a few more things while I was at the store, remembering that a human would need more to sustain him than one piece of meat.

"It is good," he said with a mouthful.

"Thanks for saying that but it's not. I'm an awful cook." I confessed.

Both of them laughed and I couldn't help but laugh with them. "Do you want more of this stuff?" Christian held the empty glass.

"It's *chicha morada*, juice of purple corn," Jose Luis explained with a mouth-full.

"I remember it. I just didn't remember what it was called. I had it years ago. It was really good," Christian said as he poured him more out of the bottle I had put in the refrigerator. As I sat at the table across from the boy, I was surprised to realize that I was curious about him, not only because of what he was doing, but about him in general.

"Where are your parents?" I asked.

"They are gone. I was ten when it happen." He swallowed a gulp of his drink and wiped his mouth on his sleeve. "Bus crash."

"I'm sorry," I said and reached for his hand before I realized what I was doing. He shivered at my touch and I yanked my hand away.

"I am sorry. I never touch vampire before," he explained and smiled. His teeth were shockingly white against his deep tan.

"It's okay. How old are you now?" I couldn't say why but I wanted him to relax. Christian beamed at me and settled into a chair next to me.

"Fifteen."

My face must have shown my surprise because he laughed. "I thought you were older. How did you end up with the hunters?"

"I was living in a house that was…how you say…nobody?"

"Abandoned?" Christian offered. Jose Luis nodded.

"I get money from people of buses and streets, from pockets. One day, I steal from wrong pocket and when I wake up I was with them, their house. They wanted me to stay with them because of what I can do and because I speak English."

"Where did you learn to speak English so well? I mean, classes are expensive," I asked.

"I had books from when I was in school and I learn some on the street from the tourists. I hear it one time and I know it."

"That's impressive," Christian said. "Are there a lot of English-speaking vampires in the city?"

"Sometimes, from the US, England, the islands. Some are German." He ate the last of the food on his plate and leaned back on his seat. "Thank you for the food."

"How do you feel now?" I asked and took his plate to the sink.

"Okay, I think. Not so tired."

"So what is it that you can do?" Christian asked, not giving the conversation a chance to die.

"Vampires listen to brains. They cannot listen to mine but I can listen to theirs and talk to them that way."

"Yes, I clearly remember," Christian said but he smiled, encouraging him to open up.

"Have you met many American vampires?"

"No. I see them sometimes, listen to them. But I am too young to sit in meetings with them and the elders."

I raised my eyebrows at Christian. Why would vampires need to meet with the hunters?

Jose Luis heard my silent question and continued. "They must have permission from the elders to hunt in the city, sometimes to stay in the city. They cannot hunt innocent people. They must meet with the elders when they come and when they are going to leave. We must know who is here all the time."

Christian stiffened in his seat. "What is it?" I asked looking at him. He was clenching his hands into such a tight ball on the table that I thought he should be bleeding from his fingernails digging into his flesh.

"Uhh...nothing. Why?"

"You look uncomfortable," I said. Jose Luis backed his chair away from the table but stayed seated. He looked back and forth between us, his eyes growing wide, his Adam's apple sliding against his throat from swallowing so hard. Christian pushed his chair away also. "Do you hear something I don't?"

Christian shook his head slowly, not taking his eyes from the boy's neck. It was at that moment that I realized what was happening, but I wasn't fast enough to react.

⤫ NINETEEN ⤫

Christian leapt across the table, the empty vase and dishes flying to the tile floor with a crash. Jose Luis's body flew to the other end of the room with Christian's heavier mass on top of him, making both look like rag dolls easily thrown in the air. In an instant, I was on top of Christian, trying to pry his fangs from the boy's neck, pulling his head away by his hair. Jose Luis struggled under him but to no avail. With one fist still gripping hair, I grabbed Christian's chin and turned his face toward mine. His eyes clouded over and his expression looked like that of a sleepwalker.

"Christian, look at me. Focus! Focus on my face!" He made no attempt to breathe or blink. Jose Luis finally went limp under Christian's weight. Since neither was moving, I took that opportunity to jump into Christian's mind. I heard his anguish. "I am so sorry, Christian. I wasn't thinking."

The metallic smell reached my nose as Christian's shoulders slumped in defeat. He blinked and shook his head. The scent was mouth-watering to me so I could just imagine what it was doing to Christian. The fact that he was trying to focus on my face showed me he had more self-control than I did at his age.

"Oh, God. What did I do?" he whispered, turning away from me to look at Jose Luis's pale, terrified face. "Did I?"

I nodded. "It was not enough to cause any serious damage. See? He's fine."

"I didn't mean to. I don't know what happened."

"It's my fault, baby. I should've known better. You haven't fed," I caressed his cheek with my fingertips, still holding his head up with the other hand.

"Why do you always take responsibility for my actions?" he snapped. "I'm a grown man."

"I know. But this whole thing is new to you and it is up to me to teach you and take care of you until you adjust." Though his tone of voice hurt, I knew I shouldn't take it to heart. It was his hunger speaking. "Come on, get up with me."

He let me pull his shaking body up, stepping away from Jose Luis in unison. The boy sat up and backed against the wall, wrapping his arms around himself, ignoring the trickle of blood running down his neck. "*No me maten, por favor,*" he pleaded with a weak voice.

"*No te vamos a matar. Te lo prometo,*" I responded without taking my eyes off Christian. "Christian, listen to me. This is not your fault. You're a newborn vampire. You needed to feed."

"It's not your responsibility to take care of me," he said, his voice sounding a little stronger than I expected. "I should've gotten up and walked away instead of doing this."

"But it is my responsibility. I made you what you are. I am responsible for you."

"Um…excuse me," Jose Luis interrupted. "What about this?" He motioned toward his bleeding neck.

"In a minute," I answered. He slumped back against the wall. I wasn't finished with Christian yet.

"No. I did this, I will fix it," Christian said and before I could stop him, he moved to kneel at Jose Luis's side. The boy slid away from him, keeping his body tight against the wall. "I am truly sorry, Jose Luis. Please forgive me."

Jose Luis looked at me for guidance and I nodded. He didn't reply but didn't move away when Christian approached him again. "I've seen you do this, Lily," he assured me. He bit the tip of his tongue and then leaned toward Jose Luis's neck. The boy stiffened and his eyes bulged.

"It's okay, Jose Luis. He won't hurt you again. He's going to make it better. Please trust him," I encouraged. Christian rubbed the blood over Jose Luis's puncture wounds, exactly as I would have done. The bite marks closed before our eyes. Jose Luis's body finally relaxed and he took a deep breath.

"You need to feed, Christian." I looked at Jose Luis. "But we'll have to either tie him up or take him with us."

"Leave the boy to me." We all jumped as Aloysius appeared behind me. "Go feed. We will talk when you return."

"How much trouble do you think we're in?" Christian asked as we walked back to a well-lit street in search of a taxi. We had fed and were fully sated, but nervous about facing Aloysius. We walked slower than normal, trying to delay going back to the apartment for as long as we could.

"I have no idea. He didn't sound too angry but then again, he's always composed. The calmness of his manner actually makes me a little nervous."

"I know what you mean. Is that your phone?" Christian asked as we settled in the back seat of a run-down car that smelled like it had been used as a toilet.

I grabbed the phone out of my pocket and opened the text message to read it. "Fiore's in Miami. She's on her way here!"

"What? What is it about 'you're my wife' that she doesn't get?" Christian looked out the window with his back tense.

"What is that supposed to mean?" I had seen his jealousy before, but I still didn't know why. Was he seeing something I wasn't when it came to Fiore?

"Nothing…forget about it. Why is she coming?"

"She doesn't say."

The taxi turned down a dark road that I didn't recognize. We bounced in our seats before we were thrown back as the taxi started to climb a steep, winding hill.

"Where are we going?" I asked the driver in Spanish. The only response was his eyes in the rearview mirror, looking back and forth between us.

"Something wrong?" Christian asked, looking out the window at the cliff that dropped off to what looked like a black hole.

"We're going the wrong way. This is nowhere near the apartment building," I answered.

"We're not even on a real road, are we? It's nothing but dirt. I don't like this either," Christian took my hand and squeezed it. *We should get out…*

As he transmitted that thought to me, the car came to a stop. "*Bajen!*" the driver commanded. I didn't argue and we got out. While Christian and I stood to the side, the car backed up, turned around, and sped away, raising a cloud of dust that made us cough.

"What the hell was that all about?" Christian yelled, waving his hands to clear the dust.

"I don't know. They usually bring people up here to rob them. He didn't," I explained. The cross stood in front of us, aglow in white lights, and the ocean to the left. "The planetarium is up here." The wind pushed my hair in front of my face, making it hard to see. I reached in my pocket for a hair tie.

"Is this some kind of joke? 'Let's see if the tourists can find their way back?' Hey," Christian took my hand to stop my advance. "Not only did he not rob us, but he didn't even let us pay him."

"That's really not good. Someone is waiting for us up here. I'm sure of it." We stood still for a moment, deciding on which way to go. "We need to get off this mountain."

"Which way?" he asked.

"The fastest way possible, you on my back and off the edge of that wall," I answered, walking toward it.

"Did you hear that?" He grabbed my hand again.

"What? The wind?"

"No. It was a laugh – a woman. I'm almost positive."

I listened more closely but heard nothing. I started walking again when suddenly I heard someone clear a throat. "Where are you going? Don't want to play?" It was a woman's voice, one I didn't recognize. I caught the light scent of a flowery perfume.

We spun around, raising more dust. "Who's there?" I yelled.

"So you are playing? I'm so glad," the voice yelled back. I looked at Christian. He motioned for me to remain quiet.

"Do you hear an accent?" I whispered to Christian. He shook his head.

"What are we playing and who are we playing with?" he asked with a strong commanding voice.

"I ask the questions. Let's begin, shall we? First question, what have you done with the boy?" The voice sounded even closer, yet we saw no one.

"The boy is alive. That's all you need to know." Christian started to usher me behind him. I stiffened, refusing to let him shield me. "Are you Melinda?"

She hesitated before she spoke again. "I can be whoever you want me to be. I want the boy back."

"What do you want with him?" I asked before Christian could take over again.

"That is not your problem. Your only job is to bring me the boy and I will trade him for someone you will want." Her voice seemed to surround us.

Chills went through my body when I heard that. Fiore? Could she have Fiore?

"Perhaps." She laughed.

So she was reading my thoughts. Communicating secretly with Christian would be futile. "Where?" I asked. Christian looked at me with shock on his face.

"I thought you'd see things my way," she said with a laugh. "Tomorrow at midnight, right here."

"Fine. We'll be here," Christian answered.

"No! Just her and the boy. If you bring any others, your little friend dies. You got that?"

"Are you crazy?" Christian blurted.

"Agreed," I answered.

"Good girl. I knew you were smart. Him, not so much," she laughed. "Until tomorrow then. I can't wait." I heard the rustling of clothing before I saw the dust her departure created.

"I will never allow it. You realize that, don't you?" Christian whispered as we headed to the edge of the mountain.

"What other choice is there? You heard what she said. Besides, I can take care of myself. I've been doing it for almost a century," I explained as he climbed on my back and wrapped his arms around my neck.

"I seriously wish you'd start seeing me for what I am: an immortal, just like you."

"Sure. We'll talk later. Right now, let's get the hell out of here." We plunged off the wall, screaming all the way.

ᗌ TWENTY ᗌ

As the elevator climbed, we fidgeted, unlike vampires, anticipating Aloysius' wrath. "Did you even hear Aloysius enter the apartment?" I asked trying to break the silence and ease the tension.

"No. It's like he appeared out of thin air."

"I don't think that's possible. At least, I've never seen it before but with him, who knows? I feel a lot of power coming from him. He's a little intimidating, don't you think?"

"That's an understatement," Christian replied as the doors slid open.

We walked in hand-in-hand and with our heads held high. No matter what Aloysius thought, we had a good reason to do what we did. I was prepared to defend us.

"Is he okay?" Christian asked.

"Yes. This time, but that was much too close. Lily, you should have known better," Aloysius turned his face toward me. "What do you have to say for yourself?"

"I…don't know. I was worried about what to do with Jose Luis and wasn't thinking about what was going on with Christian. I won't let it happen again." So much for defending us.

"Excuse me, but don't I have any responsibility here? I'm not a child. Everyone seems to be treating me as if I am." Christian released my hand and went to stand directly in front of Aloysius.

"In our world you are considered a child, a newborn. You need to be taught. Lily of all people should know that," Aloysius explained, softening his voice. "I'm sure she doesn't want you to have to learn everything for yourself, the way she did."

I shook my head. Christian relaxed a bit and went to sit on the sofa. We followed.

"That's neither here nor there right now. It seems we have a situation on our hands. What are we going to do about it?" Aloysius asked calmly as he sat back and crossed his legs.

"I don't think Jose Luis is our first priority right now. We ran into some other trouble tonight."

"Oh?" Aloysius asked as Jose Luis walked into the living room. He looked around the room and decided to sit cross-legged on the floor.

"Get up boy! You're not a servant here. Sit in a chair," Aloysius commanded. Jose Luis jumped to his feet and rushed to the other armchair. Once he was seated, Christian explained what happened as we were returning from feeding.

"I think they have Fiore," I said.

"How is that possible? Isn't she supposed to be on a plane right now?" Aloysius looked at Jose Luis who was fidgeting in his seat. He nodded to him and the boy's hand stopped and his shoulders slumped a bit. I wondered what was passing between them.

"Whoever was talking to us said she would exchange Jose Luis for our friend. Who else could it be?"

"I don't know," Aloysius crinkled his forehead. "Still, she's supposed to be on a plane."

"Maybe that's only what they wanted us to think. How do we know they don't have her and used her cell phone? They could have already had her in their custody and either sent the message themselves or forced her to send it. That's very possible, don't you think?" I said, looking from Aloysius to Christian. They nodded.

"Regardless, I do know we need to come up with a plan. They will expect us to comply with their wishes. They will expect only you and the boy tomorrow night." Aloysius looked at Jose Luis, who still sat quietly, his hands folded neatly in his lap. "They really want you back." Jose Luis said nothing.

"That's not going to happen. I will never let her go alone!" Christian jumped to his feet and started pacing.

"I can assure you I don't plan on it either, but we have to figure out how we're going to keep them from seeing or sensing us," Aloysius explained.

"I can help with that," Jose Luis said. We all turned toward him.

"How exactly do you plan to do that?" I asked.

Christian sat back down.

"I can cover them," He motioned toward Christian and Aloysius. "The problem is I have to be with them to do it."

"I can do that too but you won't be with them. You'll be with me." How was it possible that this human child possessed so many vampire qualities?

"Wait a second. What do you mean you can cover us?" Christian didn't hide his impatience.

"With my brain. I can make myself part of the shadows and if I am touching you, you too."

"What do you mean part of the shadows? Oh, you mean blend?" I asked. Jose Luis nodded. "Well that's a new one for a human." My temper was starting to flare but I didn't care. What if the person they had was Maia? I didn't want Aloysius or Christian hurt and I wasn't willing to exchange Jose Luis for Maia, if it did happen to be her and not Fiore. If Aaron and Kalia didn't love her, I'd gladly turn down their offer of an exchange.

"Um, Lily?" Christian had his hand in front of his mouth, trying not to laugh.

"What?" I snapped, making Jose Luis jump in his seat.

"We can all hear you, remember?" he asked.

"Oh, right. But it's true. I have no use for Maia. They can gladly keep her and she can slowly kill them all by driving them crazy! But that's not the point right now. What does he mean he can do that? He shouldn't be able to do any of the things he does."

I looked at Aloysius, hoping they wouldn't question the part about not wanting to give up Jose Luis since I really had no explanation for my sudden feelings.

"I have seen that done before. There are vampires who have that ability, like you, Lily, but I've never seen it done by a human either, unless, he's not totally human…" He turned to Jose Luis, who was now slinking in his chair, and raised his eyebrows. Jose Luis offered no explanation, and before anyone could say anything, Aloysius continued. "Thank you for that offer but Lily is right, you'll be with her. I think I may be of more use in this matter."

"How is that? She specifically said no one else was to be with them," Christian squeezed my hand and I snuggled into his side, sharing his fear. In the past, I tried as hard as possible to avoid trouble but had no problem facing it when it found me. Now, I felt like a scared child who was always chased by trouble.

"I don't know if you noticed that I didn't use the door tonight." We both nodded. "I appeared instead. Maybe we can do that."

Christian and I exchanged a knowing look. "How long have you been able to do that?" I asked. This was a gift I'd heard of before, but had never met anyone that could actually do it. Though it had been explained to me by Ian, I still didn't understand how it was possible to disappear and materialize somewhere else, but then again, science had never been my favorite subject and his explanation had been purely scientific.

"Ever since I was turned. It was my special gift I guess. It happened by accident one day and scared the hell out of me. I was in a store fitting room and I was thinking about getting something to eat, you know what I mean, at the bar on the corner and, poof; I was there, in my boxer shorts. That caused quite a stir."

We couldn't help but laugh and, though he looked embarrassed at first, Aloysius joined us. We all felt more relaxed and knew he was more interested in solving the problem at hand than in lecturing further about my mistake with the 'new-born' Christian.

"So, here's the basic plan I have in mind." He leaned back in his seat again. "When the opportunity arrives when I can be of help, call me mentally, Lily. I will be close but not close enough that they can sense me."

"Wait a damn minute." Christian was on his feet again. "I'm tired of being left out of anything important. I understand why Lily did it when I was human but I'm not anymore. I have powers of my own that may help."

"Fine," Aloysius said with a smile. "You'll be with me but you may not like the experience of traveling that way."

"I don't care. I'm going." Christian sat back down but didn't look at me. He didn't want to see the disapproval on my face. "Can you do that with me?"

"All I have to do is grip your arm and you'll go with me."

"What do I do?" Jose Luis asked.

"You do whatever Lily tells you to do. I'm sure she will have a plan of her own," Aloysius said as he stood. "I am going to call Carmela, have her stock the kitchen with some food for the boy and prepare rooms for him and Fiore." And with that said, he left the room.

Christian and I smiled at Jose Luis, reassuring him and ourselves. Aloysius wouldn't be calling her at this time if he weren't sure we would return with Jose Luis. I wanted to believe that too but there was still the matter of whether or not Jose Luis wanted to stay once we walked away. Christian looked at me. I turned away and stood. It was going to be very difficult to keep any secrets from him. I knew he would question me about it as soon as we were alone and I honestly didn't know what I would say. The thought of keeping Jose Luis with us had not really entered my mind until now. Aloysius seemed certain that we wouldn't be parting with Jose Luis any time soon.

"I want to go out," I said suddenly feeling restless. "I don't really want to be here when Carmela arrives. This is our honeymoon and I think we deserve to have some fun, at least until tomorrow night."

"You're right. There's nothing we can do for now so we might as well. What about him?" Christian looked at Jose Luis.

"No worries, *Señor* Christian. I will stay with *Señor* Al and wait for food and my room," Jose Luis offered. Since when did we call Aloysius *Al*?

"As long as you promise to stay put."

"Stay *put*?" Jose Luis looked at me and shrugged.

"Stay put means stay here, as in don't you dare try to leave," I explained. I felt like I was talking to a grounded child.

"*Lo prometo,*" he assured us. "Things are open very late in Miraflores. Go. Have fun. I will eat and then sleep."

"Right. Sleep is what you need most right now to build up your strength. Okay, we'll back before sunrise," I assured Jose Luis.

Christian and I went down the hall to let Aloysius know we were going out. He was happy that we were going to try to have some fun on this trip. I wondered how many people had to deal with pissed off vampires while on their honeymoons. Christian laughed and grasped my hand as we walked out the door.

"Do you think Jose Luis will be there when we get back?" he asked as we entered the empty elevator. He leaned against the glass wall while I stayed on the other side. My eyes settled on the tallest of the buildings, all lit up like a Christmas tree. I didn't want to think about how that must feel during an earthquake. It had to be at least sixty stories.

"I don't think he's too anxious to get back to the people he runs with. I get the impression they just use him for his talents. They don't really care about him."

"But you do?" His eyes found mine and an uneasy feeling settled in my stomach.

"He's not much younger than I was when I was left to fend for myself. I can tell how scared he really is, no matter how tough he tries to act." I took my eyes from his and looked at the street as the elevator reached the ground floor. "He's a kid. He deserves a childhood."

"Right." Christian led the way out and toward the front door where a new doorman was awaiting to open it for us. It must be Pepé's night off. "Where are we going, by the way?"

"Oh, I don't know. Let's follow our instincts, and the noise, and see where it takes us. This is a happening city at night."

"I leave it totally up to you. You've been here before," he said and draped an arm across my shoulder.

"I'm not sure I would know my way around anymore. It's been a long time and things have changed," I explained as we turned the corner and the voices grew louder as did the sounds of pan flutes and *cajones*. Even back then I had been left alone most of the time, only sporadically having the privilege of being escorted through the unfamiliar city. It seemed the only time Ian really wanted me around, even then, was when he needed to talk to someone and my ability to speak Spanish was of use to him.

His long stride was difficult to keep up with and I found myself almost running to keep up. "I don't understand why you need me to escort you to the store. You're the one who speaks Spanish, remember?" his gruff voice sounded from a few feet ahead of me. "You can't buy shampoo by yourself? You're not a child, Lily!"

"I'm sorry, Ian. I thought maybe we could spend a little time together tonight. You just came back and I missed you. How long are we staying here anyway?"

He stopped suddenly and I almost passed him before I noticed. He smiled at me, like a father at a stubborn child. "I just got back and I don't yet know what we are doing next. I'm here now and that's all that matters and if I have to hold your hand to buy a bottle of shampoo, so be it."

I swallowed hard, gathering the courage to say what I wanted. "You spent more time with me before you made me into this…thing that I am. If you didn't want me like this, why did you do it?" He stiffened and turned away.

"Lily?" Christian whispered and hugged me closer to him. "Where did you go?"

"What?" I looked at his face and it took a few seconds for his features to change from Ian's to Christian's.

"You were…remembering, I think." His voice sounded a little shaky but his smile was soft.

"I'm sorry. I don't know what happened."

"It's perfectly understandable. It must be the place. But it's okay now. You're with me," he assured me. "I have an idea. When we get all this straightened out, let's take another trip. Just the two of us."

"That sounds like a really good plan. Somewhere where there are no other vampires."

We both laughed at that idea and continued toward Miraflores Park or Parque Kennedy as it was more commonly known. It was pretty bad that we felt we needed a vacation from our honeymoon.

❧ TWENTY–ONE ❧

"What are we doing about Fiore?" Christian asked as cars whizzed past us while we waited to cross. We could see vendors were still in the rotunda at the park and young lovers strolled by hand in hand.

"She hasn't answered any of the texts I sent. That may just be because she's perfectly safe on the plane though. Anyway, we have a few hours before she should arrive. I told Aloysius we'd take a cab to the airport and wait." I grabbed his hand at the first opportunity and dragged him across the street. "I have no details on her flight but we can look at the board when we get there." I knew it was wishful thinking that she would be arriving, but it was worth a shot.

"I guess that's all we can do." We reached the curb without being run over.

"Where's your money?" I asked

"In my back pocket. Why?"

"Switch it to the front, some in each pocket."

"Oh, right…pickpockets. I guess this is the perfect place for that. It's a good thing I fed, so many people." His eyes smiled but his lips didn't show it. How could I make him understand that what happened with Jose Luis wasn't his fault?

"Let's go look at what they're selling and please let me do the talking. Actually, try not to talk at all or they will take advantage and charge us double for everything," I advised, as I had learned all those years ago. He nodded and tightened his grasp on my hand as I led the way into the middle of the happily chatting masses.

We stopped at a stand where a young man was selling silver jewelry. I made my way between two women but Christian could see right over my head. That was an advantage I never had.

Those hoop earrings would look good on you…

Really? Aren't they too big?

The medium ones then. They'd look great when you wear your hair up…
ask how much?

Even though I usually kept my jewelry very simple, I humored him and haggled my way to a reasonable price. When I told him how much, he didn't hesitate a moment and handed the money over to the smiling Peruvian. Glad he was spending our money instead of just thinking of it as mine, I let him pay. I took the earrings before the man could put them in a bag.

"I'll wear them now," I told Christian as I put them in my ears. I needed more than anything to see his smile and to remember, at least for the next ten hours or so, the reason we were here: our honeymoon. Once the earrings were safely clasped, I wrapped my arms around his neck and planted one on his lips. His hands went up my back to the nape of my neck where his fingers tightened possessively. His kiss took my breath again and for a brief moment erased everything and everyone around us. It wasn't until I felt a tug on my shirt that I finally withdrew.

"*¿Un caramelo, señorita?*" A young boy, no more than ten years old, was tugging on the back of my shirt. His dirt smeared face lit up as he looked to us with hope. His parents, no doubt, were nearby, also peddling their wares in order to buy their next meal. I knew that if they were watching, and he failed to sell me his little, plastic wrapped candy, there would be hell to pay when he was alone with them. I took a *Sol* coin out of my pocket and handed it to him. He smiled broadly as his little dirty fingers closed around the coin.

"*Gracias, señorita y…señor.*" His neck bent all the way back as he looked up at Christian with wide eyes. "*El señor es gringo.*"

"*Sí. Es americano. Buenas noches,*" I answered and steered Christian away from the still smiling and wondering boy. Christian, with his blue eyes and light hair, was definitely on display here.

"The earrings look great on you," Christian said. "But I'm not the only one who thinks so."

"What do you mean?" I turned to follow his gaze. A man was sitting on a bench; a newspaper rolled in his left hand while he held a bottle of Inca Kola in the other. He sipped it through a straw and set it down on the bench between sips. He was very obviously watching us and didn't turn away while we watched him. "That can't be good. Let's walk away. If he gets up too, then we've got a problem." I took his hand again and walked toward the other end of the park. As I feared, the man stood but didn't follow. He took out a cell phone instead and held it to his ear.

"He's not speaking English," Christian said.

"Or Spanish," I added. "I don't know what he's speaking but we're leaving anyway."

"Don't look now but he's coming our way." Christian tightened his grip on my hand.

"You've got to be kidding me. Come on," I said pulling him toward the curb. "We can lose him.

We ran across the street, zigzagging and dodging the cars whose angry drivers lay on their horns. We made it to the other side and started down a crowded street full of pizza restaurants. The people in Lima called it Pizza Street for a good reason. Waiters and waitresses called to us as we passed, trying to convince us their restaurant was best by waving menus in our faces. One waiter actually grabbed Christian's arm and he shook him off. The waiter lost his balance and fell on his butt on the ground. He screamed at Christian as I pulled him back onto his feet. A crowd had gathered to watch, shielding us from view.

The waiter wiped the back of his pants with his hands, never taking his wide eyes from my face. I listened to his mind while he stared into my eyes, his pulse speeding and his heart drumming in my ears. The crowd whispered around us and I shut them out, concentrating on the image I was sending to the man's mind. I felt Christian's hand on my shoulder but did not acknowledge the touch.

"Come with me," the waiter said as the crowd parted to give us room. I followed him into the restaurant holding Christian's hand again.

"Lily, what are we doing?" Christian whispered as we filed past tables full of laughing teenagers.

"He's helping us out. Just follow," I answered.

The waiter led us through a kitchen, where cooks in black pants and white shirts were busy at a counter. Some were rolling out dough, and some placed toppings on dough on pans, readying them for the oven. It was at least twenty degrees hotter in there. He led us to the other end of the small kitchen and to an open door where a waitress stood with a cigarette dangling from her lips. She counted wrinkled bills with her other hand. She raised her eyes for a moment, nodded and smiled, and went back to counting money without a second thought.

We stepped out onto the alley behind the restaurant and stopped. The waiter reached into his pocket and produced a set of keys, which he held up for me to take. "Thank you," I said as I took them, careful not to touch his fingers.

He pointed to a set of stairs to the side of the building. I nodded and turned, leading Christian to the steps. As I turned the key in the lock of the only door at the top of the landing, I looked below before pushing the door open. A woman pushing a child in a stroller walked down the darkened street, keeping her eyes straight ahead as she murmured to her passenger. No one else seemed to be there so I pushed the door and stepped in, Christian at my side.

"What in the world just happened?" he asked as I searched for a light switch or at least a table lamp.

"I asked that man if they had a back door or some place we could hide. He gave me the keys so I guessed that meant yes." I switched on a lamp that was on an end table next to a love seat. It had no shade so the light bulb threw out more light than usual, distorting our shadows on the wall.

"Incredible. I didn't know you could get people to do what you want like that," he said as he looked around the one room apartment. A beaded curtain separated this room from a closet-like room that contained a toilet and a small sink, but no shower.

"Yeah, but it's never been something I like. I feel like I'm manipulating people." I pulled the curtain aside and looked out the window. A man stood below, his hands in his pockets, as he looked up and down the street. I closed the curtain and sat down on the dirty love seat. "He's down there. I doubt he knows we're here, but I say we wait a while before we try to leave."

Christian nodded and sat next to me. "That's a pretty good power you have. I would love to be able to get people to do what I want."

"No, you wouldn't. I don't like controlling people. It's not my place to do that," I explained.

"I can understand what you mean, but it could come in handy sometimes. Have you always been able to do that? I mean, I know you can make people see things, but this is different."

Trying to avert his eyes, I played with my fingernails. "Well, I knew I could make people see what I wanted them to see, but I didn't know I could actually suggest things to them until Fiore did it." I continued looking at my fingers.

"I should've known. So I take it this is the first time you've tried it then?" He took one of my hands and held it. I raised my eyes to his.

"Um, not exactly. I tried it once with you, in the cabin. It was nothing major."

He stood and walked toward the window then decided against pulling the curtain open. "And you never bothered to tell me?"

"I just wanted to see if I really could, that's all. I suggested that you drop the subject, I forget what it even was really, and you did. I made a vow to myself to never use it on you, and I haven't. I won't. It just really seemed necessary tonight so I decided to try again." I stood and walked toward him, keeping a slight distance for now. "Are you mad at me?"

He turned with a shocked expression and closed the gap between us. "Of course not. I'm just a little surprised, but I'm not mad at you. I could never be mad at you." He kissed the top of my head and let his lips linger, inhaling the scent of my hair. I backed away from him enough to grasp his hand and lead him back to the sofa.

"So, what do we do while we wait?" he asked.

"I'm sure we can think of something," I said as I leaned toward him. My lips found his and I kissed him fiercely, as if it would be the last time our lips ever met. His hands reached up and his fingers entwined in my hair, his chest pressing against mine as I turned slightly to meet his body. He moaned into my mouth.

"Are you sure about this?" he asked, panting for breath to get the words out of his mouth.

I grabbed a fistful of his shirt and pulled him closer again, my fingers fumbling to undo the buttons. "We have time to kill." I draped a leg over his as I finally got the last button open. "Take this off."

"What if the waiter comes up and catches us?" Christian asked though he slid the shirt off his shoulders, revealing his perfect chest.

"What if he does? I have the keys." I trailed my lips along the top of his chest as he sighed. His hands pushed the back of my head against him.

"Right, I forgot."

᎛ TWENTY-TWO ᎛

"**I** want to get to the airport. I can't relax until I see Fiore safe and sound." I said as I pulled the back door to the restaurant closed. We had just returned the waiter's keys. He asked no questions when he put them back in his pocket.

Leaving the excitement of Pizza Street, we walked down a darkened side street in search of a taxi. "If she does show up, then that could mean we're rescuing Maia."

"I guess so," I said with a sigh. Car lights lit up the street and I waved my hand in the air, hoping it was a taxi. The driver pulled over and I told him where to take us. One way or another, we were rescuing someone.

"Where to now?" Christian asked as I paid the driver. The airport was bustling with people, even at this hour.

"We can look at the arriving flights and see what's coming in from Miami. That's where she was when I last heard from her. It's only about a five-hour flight from there to here. I guess we could have called Aaron but, with all that was going on, I didn't think of it. He probably knew her itinerary." That would've been the easier thing to do anyway.

"Yeah, but this is more like an adventure."

"Aren't you tired of adventure by now? That's all we seem to have." I couldn't help but laugh at his easiness.

"That's what it's like with you, always an adventure, and I wouldn't trade it for the world. Not as long as I have you, anyway. Just think of how bored we'd be if things were normal all the time."

"Normal would be just fine with me," I said.

We walked into the airport and headed right to the arriving and departing flights displays. "Llegadas Internacionales, that's the one. You take that one and I'll take this one." I pointed to the two arrivals boards.

"Here. I see one," Christian said.

"When?" I asked.

"Wow, military time. We have," he looked at his watch. "Two and a half hours yet. Then two more flights after that. One isn't until 4:30 AM."

"Let's hope it's one of the earlier ones then. This could get boring. Oh, we have to remember the gates. " I went back to look at his board.

"Trust me, it's never boring with you," he said.

"I don't know whether that's a compliment or an insult." I smiled anyway.

"Never an insult. Hey, there's a souvenir shop over there. It's still open." He pointed to the shop enclosed in glass walls.

"I was planning on going shopping for Kalia and Aaron anyway. We might as well start here."

We walked into the shop and started browsing. A man was looking at an intricately painted mirror and raised his eyes to mine. He smiled and went back to the mirror. A woman held a leather-covered bottle of Pisco in her hands and also raised her eyes to mine. I nodded a greeting and tried to look interested in the painted glass jewelry boxes we were standing in front of.

I feel like we're being watched...

Me too...you think?

I don't know but I don't want to be in here anymore...

Christian took my hand and we exited the store without buying anything.

"We can't go anywhere or do anything. Do you think they were really watching us?" he asked.

I turned to look as we walked away. They were both looking at us and diverted their eyes awkwardly. "They still are. Who the hell are they and how do they know where we are every second?"

"I don't know. I think maybe we're just being paranoid now. Regardless, that second honeymoon is sounding better and better. I wish we could just hop on a plane right now and start all over again."

"Yeah, me too. But we have someone to rescue and Jose Luis to deal with. Besides, we don't have our passports with us."

"Oh, I know. It was just wishful thinking." There was always unfinished business to take of, it seemed. When would it ever end?

"Let's go sit outside somewhere and wait. It won't be long until the first flight comes in," Christian suggested.

"That sounds good." I glanced back once more to make sure the couple wasn't following us before leaving the airport. They weren't. Maybe we were just being paranoid. We sat on a bench and watched the traffic on the street. There was also plenty of entertainment from all the passengers coming and going from the airport and Christian and I made a game of it. We tried to figure out why people were here without listening to their minds, making up all sorts of crazy stories. One woman, who traveled with a little girl, who to us became a midget in disguise, was a spy for a Colombian drug cartel. She was here to gather information on possible competition. We made up many more stories, laughing at some of our more outrageous inventions. Finally, the first arriving flight was announced and we went to find our way to the gate.

We stood among the crowd of awaiting friends and family, bodies crushed against us as the crowd grew larger and larger. After what seemed like an eternity, the first of the arrivals walked through the doors to the happy shouts of the children in the front row.

"Papi, Papi!" they shouted as they jumped up and down. The man made his way through the crowd to gather them both in his arms. One after another the passengers walked out to their awaiting friends and family. I listened to the thoughts of the room past the automatic doors but it was no use. The noise was too loud and specific thoughts were difficult to distinguish.

"Maybe she will be on the next one," Christian said and squeezed my shoulder.

"Yeah, maybe…there! There she is! She's coming!" I all but jumped over the barrier separating us from the arriving passengers. "Fiore!" Christian dropped his arm from my shoulders.

"Lily! Christian! What are you doing here? I would've taken a taxi." She rushed us out past the crowd before she threw her arms around me. To my surprise, she did the same with Christian.

"What are you doing here? I sent you a message but you didn't answer." Christian and I carried her bags and led her outside to get a taxi.

"Yes, sorry, my battery's dead. I left in a hurry because Maia left again," she explained as we slid into the back of a station wagon. "She refused to say where she was going and she and Kalia actually got into an argument about it. It wasn't pretty at all."

"Really? She always came and went as she pleased and they didn't seem to think much of it. What did Aaron say?" I gave the driver the address and leaned forward so I could see Fiore past Christian.

"Not a whole lot. He seemed to want to stay out of it. Maia and Kalia were actually yelling at each other. Maia ran upstairs and came back down with a suitcase. Next thing I know the front door slams and Kalia is crying in Aaron's arms," Fiore explained. "I didn't get to hear all of it because I tried to stay in my room. I didn't want to interfere but Maia was acting a little too secretive for my taste so I told them I would check on you. I'm supposed to call them after we talk."

"She didn't tell them where she was going?" I asked.

"No, she refused. I thought that was pretty rotten considering Kalia and Aaron are the ones paying for all her escapades," Fiore told us. "Had that been me and my parents, I would not have been allowed to put a foot outside the house if I'd talked to them like that."

Maia's comings and goings seemed a little strange to me from the beginning but I hadn't thought about the money issue until now. Maia didn't work so it was only logical that Kalia and Aaron paid her way for everything. How ungrateful could someone be?

"I would really rather not involve them if we don't have to. They've done enough already," Christian said and looked at me. I nodded in agreement. They, along with Fiore, had bought us this trip and it was supposed to be a happy event. The last thing I wanted was to make them regret it.

"I don't think this is anything we can't handle." I filled Fiore in on everything that had happened up until her arrival. With Aloysius and Fiore as backup, we should be able to figure it out and resolve it before Kalia and Aaron became too worried; at least that's what I hoped.

"So I guess I can tell them you're both fine and having a good time, but you invited me to stay for a little while since I came all this way. The good thing is there are four of us to take care of this now," she explained, which made Christian smile. Fiore was counting him as part of the group without hesitation. "So we figure out what each of our roles is tomorrow night and then we go kick ass."

Christian and I laughed. "I'm glad somebody has confidence enough for all of us," I said, but four against one really were pretty good odds.

"I appreciate what you're doing but you really didn't have to come all the way down here. You could've called," Christian said. I gave him a sharp look but he didn't notice.

"Would you really have told me the truth?" Fiore raised her eyebrows. Neither of us responded so she continued. "Besides, we're friends and that's what friends do."

"Well, thank you." I looked at Christian but he was looking out the window.

When we returned to the apartment, Aloysius was waiting for us in the living room. He detailed the plan for Fiore and then showed her to her room so she could unpack and freshen up. Jose Luis, as promised, had eaten and then gone to his room to get some sleep. That left Christian and I alone.

"Why do you seem so uncomfortable with Fiore?" I finally asked what I had been keeping quiet for so long.

"I'm not uncomfortable with her. It's just that, well, she doesn't need to come to our rescue all the time." He paused to pick up the crystal bowl Aloysius kept on the coffee table and fiddled with it. "She did it when we were at the cabin, showed up without being asked, and she's doing it again."

"Is it wrong for her to want to help?" I tried to contain my frustration at what seemed like neverending tension between them.

"Of course it's not wrong. It's just she assumes she's needed even when she's not."

"Higher numbers for us means better odds, like what happened at the cabin," I explained.

"You're right. I kind of feel…I don't know," he said and put the bowl back on the table. He turned to look at me. "I feel a little threatened by her."

I laughed. "That's ridiculous! Why would you say that?"

"Guess I'm done for now. I ran out of hangers," Fiore said as she walked into the room, interrupting our conversation before I could get an answer.

"We have some extras in our closet," I offered and stood to go get them.

"No hurry," she paused before the armchair. I nodded so she sat. "Am I interrupting something?"

"Just our honeymoon," Christian said.

"Stop it, Christian. She didn't come here to get in our way. She came to help," I said.

"I understand why you're angry, Christian, but she's right. If there weren't a problem, I wouldn't be here," Fiore said in a gentle tone.

"We could've handled it. It's not like we don't have help already. We have Aloysius on our side," Christian argued.

"And you also have a bunch of vampire hunters to deal with. Who knows how many there are? For some reason, they're working with a vampire to get the kid back. She said for Lily and Jose Luis to come alone but I highly doubt she'll be alone. You're dealing with the unknown," she said as she moved sideways in her seat to drape her long legs over the arm.

"I'm not human anymore, remember? And we do have a plan," Christian said.

"She doesn't mean *you're* dealing with the unknown. She means all of us. I've never heard of hunters working with a vampire and I'm sure they are. I doubt that vampire wants Jose Luis for herself," I explained to him, trying to ease the tension. "The last thing any of us needs to have you two fighting with each other. There will be plenty of that tonight."

Christian and Fiore both looked at me. I turned toward the window. Christian sighed.

"I'm sorry," he said.

"Me too," Fiore responded. I continued to stare out the window. How I wished we were out there, enjoying the pulse of the nighttime city instead of making battle plans, yet again.

⤞ TWENTY-THREE ⤝

It was decided that Jose Luis and I would take a taxi to the exchange location. Fiore, Christian, and Aloysius would make their way to the bottom of the mountain on their own. It was best if Jose Luis and I didn't know their exact location, that way we had no way to give their arrival away in case someone tried to read our thoughts.

"I don't want to go back to them," Jose Luis said as he looked out the car window at the blurring scenery on our way through town.

"I really don't want that to happen either. We'll have an opportunity to take you both, you'll see," I assured him, though I didn't know if I could keep my word. We had no idea how many vampires or hunters we were facing tonight. It wasn't even definite that there would be hunters but we couldn't rule them out since Jose Luis was one of theirs.

The driver stopped about half way up the mountain as I had suggested. Jose Luis and I stepped out and he surprised me by reaching for my hand. I smiled at him but my fear must have been obvious because he squeezed my fingers.

*Christian, if you can hear me, I love you…*I thought. Jose Luis smiled but didn't say anything.

"There's much wind up here," he said as he wiped hair from his face.

"It was like this the last time we were up here too. I'm pretty sure we have to go to the top. I'm just hoping we don't have to deal with any thieves on the way, we have enough to worry about."

He nodded and held his head high. His determination showed and I couldn't help but share the feeling as we continued forward on the dirt road. I lit the way with a flashlight for his sake. My boots were already covered in dust, small bits of the black leather showing through here and there. Some strands of my hair escaped my braid and fell in my eyes but

I had no free hand to fix it. Jose Luis appeared unwilling to let go as he squeezed my fingers tighter and tighter with every few steps we took.

"You live up here?" I asked, remembering what he had said.

"Not here. Another mountain, San Cristobal, by the river," he explained.

"Oh. When you had said mountain, I assumed you meant this one." That mountain, where he lived, was considered to be one of the poorest sections of the city. Regardless of the living conditions on the mountain however, tourist buses made the trip to the top daily because of the amazing view of the city. On a clear day, one could see almost the whole city of Lima and San Lorenzo Island.

"How far do we go?" he asked, a little out of breath.

"We're almost there. See the cross? That's where we were when we heard her." I swallowed hard and pictured Christian's face. I needed to hang on to him to make it through this trial and his image was all I had.

You listen well...

"*Ay, Dios...*" Jose Luis whispered. He hid behind me and tightened his grip on my hand.

"Shh...don't panic. It will be okay," I reassured him.

Are you going to show your face this time or are you too scared? That may have made things worse but I was sick of playing games.

"All in good time. Let me see the boy," she demanded.

"Let me see my 'friend'," I countered.

"All you need to do is look up."

Jose Luis gasped, knowing what she meant before he even looked. I raised my head to look at the scaffolding that created the cross at the edge of the mountain. Way at the top, blowing in the wind, was white cloth and what looked like hair.

"You have got to be kidding me! I brought what you wanted and I came alone as you demanded."

From either side of the base of the cross, two black-cloaked figures appeared. They were at our sides before I could even release Jose Luis's hand and drop the flashlight. One man grabbed Jose Luis's arm and pulled him from me. The other held my arm, keeping me in place. Jose Luis and the other man disappeared from view, leaving behind nothing but a cloud of dirt.

"This is not fair!" I screamed. "You have what you wanted and I have to work for mine?"

"Nothing is fair in this world, little girl. Especially not losing your mate because some stubborn girl doesn't want to be with her maker anymore, don't you agree?" she said. Her voice sounded too calm.

"Ryanne?" I asked. The hand gripping my arm was starting to dig into my skin, though I wasn't making any attempt to move.

"Not quite." She came from the shadows surrounding the base of the cross, from the same place the men had appeared. Her long, blond hair blew freely in the wind, as did her long black dress with the billowing sleeves. She looked more like a witch out of a storybook than a vampire; not ugly, but scary all the same.

"Who the hell are you?"

"Ryanne is my little sister. What you did to her was wrong and I won't stand for it." She advanced toward me, never taking her eyes from mine. She looked familiar but that was probably because she resembled her sister.

"Killing Fergus was not personal. They were trying to kill us. It was self defense," I explained, knowing it probably wouldn't do any good.

"It doesn't matter. My sister loved him more than anything in this world." She stood in front of me, her green eyes boring into mine, her lips a thin, tight line of anger. "You want your sister, go get her."

I wanted to say that Maia was not my sister but bit my lip instead. The only reason I was even up here, on this mountain, with this vampire, and the two humans, was for Kalia and Aaron. I swallowed hard and looked to the top of the cross, where Maia was tied up as if she, herself, had been crucified. It was really high.

"Arturo, walk her to the base and release her. Stay on the ground but watch her," she commanded her minion.

"*Sí, señorita*," Arturo replied and started shoving me to the cross. His grip on my arm was vise-like. My feet shuffled along on the dirt. I tripped over stones and it only made his grip tighter, angrier.

"You're hurting me," I spat without looking at him.

"I *haf* orders. Walk! Fast!" he said. His pronunciation made me want to laugh but I contained it.

Once we reached the bottom of the cross, he released my arm but turned me to face the base. "Go," he commanded.

The bottoms of the four legs holding up the steel cross were surrounded by white concrete. I either had to jump to get up there or get a boost. Arturo seemed to sense my predicament and knelt on the dirt, cupping his hands and, to my surprise, offering them to me. I hesitated before putting my foot into his hands. His teeth showed, glowing white against the contrast of his black hooded cape, as he gave me the push I needed to reach where I could start climbing.

Gripping the steel beams as tightly as I could, I found a place to put my feet. I continued higher and higher that way, trying desperately not to look down. If I did, my climb would be over. Where are you Christian? Why aren't you here yet? About half way to the top, I heard a commotion below and made the mistake of looking down. The ground started spinning instantly. I hugged the closest steel beam. Jose Luis was being shoved into a car.

"Where are you taking him?" I screamed.

Of course, no one answered me. There was nothing much I could do until I retrieved Maia and got back on the ground, so I continued my climb. The wind was much harsher at this altitude and more of my hair fell out, blinding me with each gust, and forcing me to stop until I could see again. When I was close enough to touch her feet, I paused to take a deep breath. I would need my hands to untie her and was not looking forward to letting go with even one. From my vantage point, it looked like she was right at the horizontal part of the cross, which may work to my advantage.

As I suspected, the horizontal part of the cross was much tighter in its construction than the base. I made my way to a section where I could spread my legs for balance and lean against a beam for back support. That freed my hands but if I lost my balance, I'd fall. I'd have to start climbing all over again. It would've been much easier if I could fly from level ground. That was definitely something I would need to learn in the future.

"Maia, can you hear me?" I asked as I worked to untie the knot at her feet. The rope they used wasn't very strong and it practically fell apart when I tugged.

"Lily? Is that you?" she asked in a weak voice. Her head lolled to the side so I couldn't see her face.

"Yes. I'm getting you out of here," I worked my way to the rope around her waist. Her shirt had gone over the rope and her skin was red and raw under the twine. She flinched when I tugged on the knot. "Sorry about that. I'm almost done." Despite the fact that I really didn't want to be up here, rescuing her, I still didn't want to see her in pain.

"Feels like I have no skin left on my stomach."

"Yes, it's pretty raw, but it will heal. When I untie your hands, I'm going to press my body against yours, to keep you steady," I explained. "I want you to wrap your arms around me as soon as they're free and hold on tight. Think you can do that?"

"Uh, huh. I think so."

She turned her face toward me when I reached her. Bruises surrounded her left eye and her right eye was swollen to a slit. Blood was smeared on her jaw. I couldn't tell if it was hers or not. They must have beaten her right before they tied her up; otherwise, the bruises would be healed by now, or at least yellowing. Untying her hands was easier but trickier. I had to wedge my body against hers and I didn't particularly like being that close to her.

"Okay, now! We're going down!" I commanded and then turned my body with hers pressed against me, her face buried in my chest, and almost fell backward. I grabbed the beam in front of me to steady us. "I have to bend to get on the other side of this beam so we don't go straight down. Just relax your body. Move with me but hold on."

"Holy shit! We're flying! We're really flying!" she screamed as we launched off the beam and toward the ground that seemed so far, but not for long.

"Wrap your legs around my waist or we'll fall when we land," I said. We'd most likely fall anyway. Landing was something I hadn't yet mastered.

My feet hit the ground hard and I ran a few steps but the weight of her body pulled me down anyway. She hit the ground with me on top of her. "You okay?"

"I don't know. You're on top of me," she said with her usual cocky attitude. So much for gratitude.

A hand gripped my shoulder and yanked me off her. I spun to swing at whoever it was but a hand caught my wrist before my fist made contact.

"It's me, Lily. Are you okay?"

"Christian!" I threw my arms around his neck. "Where are the others?"

"Right here," Aloysius said. I hadn't even noticed he'd been standing behind Christian. "Fiore is following the car that took Jose Luis."

"How's Maia?" Christian asked.

"I'm just lovely. Can't you see my face? See what they did to me?" Maia answered.

"Same as usual," I said. "Where did the woman go?"

"She ran that way." Aloysius pointed downhill.

"Let's go then," I said. There was no time to waste. If she was here to avenge her sister's mate then Ryanne was probably here too.

"No need." We spun to look at the woman who had come up behind us while we were busy with Maia.

"Samantha?" Christian said. He backed away a few paces.

"Who?" I looked between them and saw the recognition on Christian's face.

"My name is Melinda, not Samantha. That's just one of my passports. Did you miss me, my love?" She laughed.

"What are you saying? Christian, is this the woman who kidnapped you? Oh my God!" I covered my mouth with my hands before I could scream.

"What, Lily?" Aloysius asked, stepping closer to my side. Maia was slowly backing away but I couldn't stop staring at Melinda long enough to stop her.

"This is the woman who took Christian's money. She's the one in the picture with him. His supposed wife who didn't want a divorce," I cried.

A car roared up. A dust cloud so big developed as the tires screeched when the car came to a stop about ten feet away, that it blinded us. Men poured out of the open doors.

"Party time!" Melinda announced. "And you're the guest of honor, Lily."

∽ TWENTY-FOUR ∽

Christian grabbed my arm and pulled me behind him. Aloysius tried to grab Maia but she jumped out of his reach. She ran away screaming into the darkness. One of the men punched Christian in the jaw, his head slamming into my face. My nose burned but I saw no blood when I took my hand away. Christian's foot made contact with that man and pushed him into another. Both of the men hit the ground.

"Find Maia and get her to safety," Aloysius yelled over the other voices. "Go, Lily. We can handle things here. We'll get there as soon as we can." His fist connected with the nose of a large man, who fell to the ground as if he suddenly had no bones to hold him up. Blood poured from his nose onto the ground.

"I'm not leaving you," I yelled.

"Go, Lily. We're okay here. They're human. Piece of cake," Christian insisted.

I turned to look for Maia and Melinda but both had disappeared. Melinda must be chasing after Maia. Aloysius and Christian didn't seem to notice my hesitation. They were both too busy fighting.

Running downhill, I could still hear the commotion Aloysius and Christian were causing. All the screams and grunts told me they were causing a lot of damage and that made it easier for me to leave Christian. As I rounded a corner, a faint light glowed in the distance. I squinted to get a better look and made out the shape of a small building. Looking around and seeing no sign of Maia, I decided to try the building.

"Hello! Is anyone here?" No one answered. It was the remains of an old stone building. It had four walls but lacked a roof and a door. The windows were openings where glass had once been, like large, hollowed-out eyes. The odd thing was that this was the only place on the mountain where I saw any green. Weeds almost as tall as my waist filled the inside of the ruins. Candlelight flickered faintly in the corner, casting dancing shadows in the corner above it. I peered inside from the door opening. On a small cot, a body lay curled up on its side. Dark hair covered the face, but I could tell by the hair and the slight shape it was a female. Why would there even be a bed in this structure?

I poked my head further in and the smell of urine overwhelmed me. I held my hand to my nose and stepped in. "Hello? I'm sorry to bother you but…"

The person on the cot rolled over. Maia smiled as she looked at me through one eye. A fist crashed into my back and I hit the ground face first. Rolling onto my back, I kicked out with both legs and made contact with Melinda's stomach. She screamed and flew right through the absent door.

"How easy it was to convince the others to leave you alone," she said as she stood and wiped the dirt off her clothes with both hands. She tucked a strand of hair behind her ear. "Those idiot hunters are keeping them busy. It turns out they are good for something after all."

"Maia, get out of here!" I screamed, not taking my eyes off Melinda.

She sat up on the cot and placed her bare feet on the ground, her legs swallowed up by the weeds. "I'm afraid. I'd rather stay with you," she said.

"Why are you even here? Go, now!" She sat still, looking at me through her good eye.

"She's not going anywhere, but you are," Melinda said as she walked toward me.

I jumped and kicked her again but she was a little too far away. I only succeeded in angering her more. She stumbled, gained her composure, and came at me with more ferocity. She bared her fangs and her eyes glowed red with rage.

"You killed my sister's mate! You killed Maia's mate! It's your turn to die!" she screamed.

I ducked just in time to avoid her fist on my face but it came down on my back instead, knocking the air out of my lungs. I fell flat on my face outside the ruins with her on top of me. I tasted mud and blood, strong and metallic. Her weight didn't keep me down long and I managed to push her off. This time, my fist connected with her jaw and I jumped away. Blood spattered on dry soil. Maia screamed and ran to the side of the building as Melinda wiped her bloody mouth with her sleeve.

"He was my maker!" I screamed as I ran at her like a bull at a matador. Pain exploded in my head as it connected with her stomach. I landed on top of her, slamming my head into the stone wall in the process. Maia screamed again. Melinda took that opportunity to grab a handful of my hair and yank my head back. She brought her knee up fast and I landed on my back again, not sure which hurt worse, my stomach or my head. She smiled. Maia smiled above her.

"Maia, why?" I asked as I realized what was happening. Maia was not in danger. Melinda had had her chance to take her, but she continued to pursue me instead.

"What do you mean? I'm her prisoner, right? I'm not to blame here," she said.

"No, you're not. You're lying!" I screamed as I tried to wriggle myself free of Melinda but with no success.

Maia's smile did not waver and it was eerie with that swollen eye. She took something out from behind her back. It was a piece of wood.

"What are you doing?" I asked but I knew exactly what they planned. "Christian!" I screamed. Melinda clamped a dirty hand over my mouth. It smelled of mud and blood.

"Let's see, you took my sister's mate. You took Maia's family and her mate. You took Fiore away from Ian. That's a lot of taking, don't you think?" She laughed when I tried to answer but couldn't. "Ian loved you. I have no idea why but he did. I never understood it, though I did question him. He just said he loved you and refused anything more. And even though he loved you and wanted you back, you chose to kill him rather than return to him. That's never a good thing, right Maia? I taught you that." Maia said nothing.

"What business is it of yours anyway?" I mumbled through the gaps in her fingers. "What do you care who he loved or who he wanted?"

"I don't give a damn what he wanted. The only thing that matters to me is enforcing the law and that law says that we do not kill our makers," she turned to look at Maia, who stood without expression, watching. "And, you took him away from this poor child, even though you didn't want him. I'd call that selfishness, don't you think?"

"I didn't take him away from anybody. He came after me. And, I didn't take Maia's family. She still has them," I insisted, getting the words through her gaping fingers.

"It doesn't matter anyway. She was happier before you came along. It's high time you pay for all the damage you've caused."

Maia nodded. Her smile faded a bit as she held the stake out to Melinda's outstretched hand. So this was it? This was how I was going to die, after finally finding happiness. *I love you, Christian.*

Lily? Where are you? Christian was trying to find me. Hope stopped my tears.

Melinda's eyes widened. "Oh, no you don't. Enough of that! Answer him and he dies with you," she snapped.

Maia's eye grew wide as a shuffling noise came from around the corner of the building. Christian and Aloysius must have found me. Any minute now they would yank her off me and we would go home.

Melinda's teeth gleamed as she smiled, raising the stake above her head in both hands. I wriggled under her but she had me pinned with her legs. The stake came toward me in slow motion, or so it seemed. I heard a scream right before the pain in my chest took control of my mind. Then another scream rang in my ears but faded, echoing. My chest was on fire but at least my hands were free again. I clutched at the wood protruding from my chest. My fingers found something wet and sticky. Water. I needed water to put out the flames, not this sticky stuff.

*Water...fire...Oh, God...*I couldn't make my mouth work. The earth spun and my eyes blurred as I realized what I was actually touching. *Help me...*Everything went black.

⤳ TWENTY-FIVE ⤳

"I can't transport her that way now. It's too dangerous. She's too weak and I don't know what it would do to her," Aloysius said. His voice was so close but I couldn't see him.

"Then what the hell are we supposed to do?" Christian asked.

"Here, take my coat. Wrap her up in it. We'll have to take a taxi. We don't have another option."

"A taxi will take so much longer," Christian argued.

"I know, but I won't take the risk of something worse happening to her because of the transport."

"This is insane! I want to pull the stake out," Christian argued.

My body bounced a little and my head felt too heavy to lift. Someone carried me but I couldn't see who it was. I wanted to see but couldn't force my eyes open. Nothing on my body seemed to work.

"I told you we have to wait until we get her back to the apartment. It's too dangerous out here. We could be interrupted," Aloysius explained. "I know how you feel, but trust me, this is only temporary. Melinda missed her heart when you grabbed her. She will live."

"It doesn't matter. She's in pain and I can't stand it. We were too late!"

"No, we weren't. We were just in time. Had we arrived a second later, she would've killed her."

Why couldn't I open my eyes? I couldn't even answer them. I couldn't tell them that my whole body was on fire, but they had to know. Someone was carrying me. They had to see and feel the flames. Why weren't they getting burned? All I wanted to do was jump in a pool or soak in a cold bath but I had no way to tell them.

"But we lost her anyway," Christian said. A hand touched my head softly as I continued to bounce in someone's arms. It must have been

145

Christian caressing my head. Aloysius's voice was closest so he must have been carrying me.

"That is only temporary. Our first priority is Lily. We'll find Melinda. I promise you I will personally hunt her down if that is what it comes down to."

"Where the hell is Fiore?" Christian sounded angry.

I wanted to tell him not to fight with her, how tired I was of hearing them bicker. A car horn beeped twice and I was handed over to Christian. Aloysius gave the driver the address. He must have looked suspicious because Aloysius explained to him that I was sick.

The talking stopped, as did the movement of the taxi. I smelled Pepé but he didn't say a word. Instead, I heard him run ahead of us and summon the elevator. Once we exited the elevator, the running started.

"She's losing too much blood," Christian said.

"I know. We'll pull the stake out as soon as we get her settled."

Oh, God, pull out the stake? It's still there? My uncooperative arms prevented me from checking. The burning had spread from my chest to my arms, and now my legs. All I wanted was water but I couldn't tell them. Why weren't they hearing my thoughts? Why couldn't I hear theirs?

"Set her down gently," Aloysius instructed. "Don't worry about the sheets. I have plenty more."

"I can't believe this happened. I should've been with her. I should've never left her," Christian said as he propped my head on the pillows. "Why the hell isn't Fiore here yet?"

A door opened and closed and heels clicked on the tile floor.

"She's here now. I'll go talk to her. Stay with Lily and keep her calm. Do nothing else. I'll be right back," Aloysius said and the bedroom door closed.

"I'm so sorry, Lily. I never should've told you to go without me," Christian said as he took my hand. I tried to squeeze but couldn't. I had no strength. This wasn't his fault and I couldn't tell him.

The door opened again and two sets of footsteps followed.

"Oh, God, Lily," Fiore said from somewhere near my face. A hand stroked my hair. "How could she do this?"

"We will find her! But first things first, Fiore, stand here with the towel ready. As soon as it's out, cover the wound and put pressure on it. Don't worry about it hurting her. We need to stop the blood flow. Christian, I will hold her shoulders down, you'll pull it out."

"I don't know if I can do this," Christian said with a shaky voice.

"You won't be causing more pain than she's already in. You have to do this. Grab hold, I'll keep her arm out of the way, and one fast yank should do it," Aloysius explained. "Are you ready?" They must have nodded because I heard nothing. No one bothered to ask if I was ready.

"You'll find the strength, Christian. Trust me," Fiore said.

Someone pulled me further down the bed by my ankles. I felt Aloysius climb on the bed and position himself behind my head, hands on my shoulders, pushing me down into the hard mattress. Christian must be the one who climbed on my torso and straddled my legs. Everyone was ready except me.

"On the count of three…" Aloysius said.

I'm not ready! I wanted to scream but it was useless. My mouth didn't work, my arms didn't work, nothing worked.

"One, two, three!"

A scream so loud escaped my lips it scared even me. My body was splitting in half and they didn't notice. The pressure on my chest fueled the fire instead of extinguishing it. I wanted everyone off me. Why were they doing this to me?

"There's so much…blood," Christian said. He sounded like he was going to be sick.

"Of course there is. What did you expect?" Fiore snapped.

Please don't fight now…can't you see I'm dying?

"Excuse me if it bothers me. She's my wife!"

"No kidding, Romeo. She's also my friend!"

"Both of you stop it. This is not helping her," Aloysius said. "As soon as we get the bleeding under control, she's going to need blood."

"I'll do that," Christian said.

"We'll have to take turns. She'll need quite a bit after all this…blood, everywhere," Aloysius explained. "A little at a time and she should be good as new in a couple of days."

That long, really? I can't take this pain much longer. How much blood could there possibly be?

"She's in for a long couple of days," Fiore said. Her pressure on my chest felt a little lighter as she spoke, but only for a moment.

"I'm going to call Aaron. He'll be really upset with me if I keep this from him," Aloysius said.

"Do you have a mop?" Fiore asked. "I don't want her to see all this blood when she gets up."

"Of course, come with me. I'll get you a sponge and a bucket for the headboard, too."

How much blood did I lose if they were cleaning the bed and the floor? The pressure on my chest started again after Fiore left so Christian must have taken over. *Can you hear me?*

Guess not. It was probably best that he didn't know how excruciating this pain was. I wished I could stop Aloysius from calling Aaron. He and Kalia would probably be on the next flight and they had suffered enough already because of me. What difference did it make anyway when I was just going to die?

"If I could take your place, I would," Christian whispered. "I promise I will never let something like this happen again. I will never leave your side. I will protect you from now on. I should have all along, vampire or not."

This wasn't your fault. I could've fought harder but...Maia. I wanted her out of there. She's...

"I'll clean the floor if you'll do the wood," Fiore said.

"You start. I want to stay here for a while."

Fiore sighed. "You know none of this was your fault, right?"

"How can you say that? She's my wife. I'm supposed to protect her."

I heard water swishing in the bucket and then it plopped on the floor. "She's been alone most of her life. She's used to taking care of herself. She expects that."

"How do you even know that?" Christian asked with anger in his voice.

"When she was in Ireland, Ian trusted her to be out of the cottage only with me. We took a lot of walks together. We talked, compared stories. That's how we became friends. We opened up to each other."

"But it's not like that anymore. She's not alone anymore," Christian snapped. I wished they'd stop treating each other like enemies. We had enough of those.

"Christian," Fiore's voice was soft, almost a whisper. "It's not going to be an easy habit for her to break, but she's a lot stronger than you think. She won't blame you for any of this; you'll see."

"It's just that..." he took a deep breath. "I wanted to show her that I could protect her now. I'm strong enough. I don't want her to think she has to fight alone, ever."

"She won't. Just keep loving her the way you do. Only a blind man would question your love." Fiore talked while she continued mopping.

Her breathing was more labored, as if she was having difficulty getting the blood off the floor. How much could there possibly be? Maybe that was the reason the room seemed to be spinning so much. A soft knock on the door halted her mopping.

"I think it's safe to take the pressure off now," Aloysius said. "I'll take my turn first since I have to leave."

"Where are you going?" Christian asked.

"I have to talk to some of the vampires in the area, see why the hunters are working with Melinda. Maybe they know something we don't."

"Maybe you can find out why the boy is being used as a bargaining tool," Fiore suggested.

"I'll try. Now, if you'll excuse me, Christian?" Aloysius stood by until Christian moved. Once he did, Aloysius sat on the bed beside me. He raised his wrist to his mouth, I heard the sound of tearing flesh, and then he placed it over my mouth, propping my head with his other arm. I clung to his wrist using my mouth like a suction cup.

The delicious, warm, bittersweet blood poured down my throat and took all the pain away, for a little while. I felt the blood flow down my throat and through my burning veins. My breathing came faster and a thumping sound started in my ears. If I'd had the energy to grab his wrist with my hands and keep it at my mouth I would have, but he pulled away before I was even close to satisfied. "Now, now, just a little."

The burning in my body seemed to intensify instead of dissipate. How long did I have to endure this pain? How long was I going to lay around completely useless?

"Wait a few hours and then give her some more, but not too much. That stake caused a lot of damage and it will take time for her body to repair itself. Don't weaken yourselves by giving her too much." Aloysius said. "I'll be back as soon as I can."

The door closed again. I wanted to turn my head to look but it felt like a pile of bricks laid on my forehead. All I could do was stare at the white ceiling.

Time seemed to crawl. Seconds felt like minutes and minutes like hours. I had no idea how long I lay still until light danced through the slatted blinds. I'd been this way for at least six hours. How many more? Sometime during the night, Fiore and Christian had argued over who would feed me next. I wanted to scream at them to stop but still had no power over my body. The burning had stopped and been replaced with complete numbness. I don't know which was worse.

Finally, the argument was settled and Fiore's blood is what I tasted next. Again the feeding stopped before my thirst was sated. Christian took her place on the bed and rubbed my forehead for what felt like hours. They chatted about unimportant things until...

"Christian, why do you hate me so much?"

My body jerked and Christian jumped from the bed. "What the hell was that?"

⊶ TWENTY-SIX ⊷

"Lily? Can you move? Can you hear me?" Fiore asked. I tried to move my hand but it felt like it didn't even exist.

"I don't think that movement was voluntary," Christian said and rubbed my forehead again.

"I guess not. It might be too soon," Fiore moved to stand at the end of the bed. "Now, about my question…"

"You are serious, aren't you?" he asked. She must have nodded. "What makes you think I hate you?"

Fiore's heels clicked against the marble floor as she paced. "You seem disgusted that I'm here. You always look uncomfortable around me. You give me looks that could kill, need I say more?"

"Not once did I ever say I hated you! Why would you even ask me that now, while she's like this?"

"When else can I talk to you? You're always with her."

"She is my wife. This is supposed to be our honeymoon. Where else would I be?" He stood. I stopped breathing.

"That's not the point! I want to know what I did to make you hate me so much. Is that such a tough question?"

Please don't do this…

"I don't hate you!" Christian yelled. "I never hated you."

"Really? You could've fooled me!"

"You're being childish, Fiore. Now is not the time for this."

"Tell me, when would be better for you?" She stood at the other side of the bed now. They were yelling right over me and I could do nothing to stop them.

"I don't hate you. I never said that!"

"I'm having a hard time believing that."

"I'm sorry if you are, but that is your problem, not mine. There is one thing I hold against you, though," Christian said.

"What is that?"

"You helped Ian kidnap us. You helped him keep her in Ireland against her will. You knew about me all along and you still went along with his crazy scheme."

"Yes, I did help him at first. Remember I loved Ian? At the time, I was willing to do whatever it took to keep him by my side, even if I had to share him with someone he loved more than me, but then Lily and I became friends. It became harder to do what Ian wanted then."

"How can you even say he loved her? I would not call kidnapping and blackmail love."

"You may find this hard to believe but Ian did love her, in his own way. He didn't know how to take 'no' for an answer and he didn't know when to let go, but he did love her."

"I'm sorry but that still makes no sense to me. I was taught that when you love someone, you take care of that person, and you do whatever is in your power to make that person happy, even if that means letting that person go."

"Unfortunately, not everyone was raised the way you were. Did you know Ian grew up in an orphanage?"

"No, I didn't," Christian said and I felt him sit up straighter. "I guess that could explain his skewed way of showing love."

"It does. Once Ian had something he wanted, he was determined to hang on to it at any cost. He grew up with so little. It didn't matter to him that he left her. He expected her to be there for him when he decided to return, no matter how many years it took or how many other women he loved. He couldn't stand the fact that she could possibly love someone other than him. She never fell in love with anyone else. It was only Ian, until she met you. It was tearing him apart and I had to deal with that. I had to watch him as he became crazed with jealousy. He was bitter and depressed. Nothing I tried to do for him helped. That's why I went along with his plan, to make him happy again."

"I guess it's not up to me to understand his crazy mind. Hell, Lily spent years with him and still didn't understand him."

"I honestly don't think Ian understood himself. Not only did he have nothing as a child, but he was physically and mentally abused in that orphanage. Ian couldn't stand to be in his own head. That's why he never truly let anyone else in. He may have been a tough vampire on the outside, but on the inside, he was just a scared little boy."

"That doesn't make a difference to me now. He caused a lot of damage and I'm glad he's gone," Christian said and took a deep breath. "To get back to your question, I do not hate you."

"Then what is it? I know you don't want me here, or anywhere near you."

"It's not me I don't want you near," Christian said, his voice quieter. "It's her."

"What?"

"I don't want you near her."

"What is that supposed to mean?" By the sounds of it, she started pacing again.

"You think I'm stupid? You think I don't see the way you look at her? The way you come running every time she's even remotely in danger? The way you say her name, as if it was your favorite word?" Christian said.

"That's ridiculous. She's my friend!"

"But you'd rather that weren't the case. Am I wrong?"

Christian, that's insane...she's my friend...

It was silent for far too long and I could do absolutely nothing. I couldn't even see their faces. *Please don't get physical because I can't stop you. I don't want you hurting each other.*

"No!" Fiore yelled. "You're not wrong. Are you happy now?"

No, no, no! What are you saying?

"Of course I'm not happy, but I needed to finally hear you say it," Christian said.

Fiore took a deep breath but her voice still sounded shaky. "I'm in love with her! There, I said it. Is that what you wanted?"

"Thank you for finally telling me the truth. At least now I know I'm not crazy, that I didn't imagine it."

"It doesn't matter anyway. It doesn't change anything, at least not for me. She loves you. She married you. I'm just her friend and I know I will never be more."

"I know she married me. That was the happiest day of my life. But I also know she loves you. Maybe as a friend, maybe more, but you're right. She married me. Still, I'm not sure I like how connected she is to you." Christian sat back down next to me. He draped his arm over my chest.

"What do you mean?" Fiore asked.

"I'm not sure. I get the feeling that there is something deep passing between you sometimes. Like you know what each other is feeling."

"That's because she has my blood running through her veins," Fiore said and started her nervous pacing again.

"I know. I watched you feed her, remember?"

"No. Not just now." She took a deep breath. "It happened in the cabin. I gave her my blood to make her stronger for the fight."

"What? Where the hell was I?"

"You had fallen asleep on the sofa."

"Both of you went behind my back? What else happened?"

"Nothing! She had no idea what I was doing until I did it. I didn't want to take any chances so I made her stronger. That is all, I swear."

"I wish you would've told me."

"You were human then. I guess we didn't think you'd understand," Fiore said.

"So you've been connected that long? I guess I should be thankful because she was strong enough to fight Ian, but I can't help but feel a little uncomfortable with it."

"Well, don't. Because of our connection, I can feel how much she loves you, not me."

Fiore sighed and sat on my other side. She sniffled as if she was crying. Christian's hand moved on my chest and he leaned farther over me. I lowered my eyes as best I could. Across my chest, Christian's hand was wrapped around Fiore's. *So this is what it took to get them to stop fighting? Me dying?*

I had known Christian was uncomfortable with Fiore but I had no idea why. The reason was clear now, but how did I face Fiore because of it? How could I go back to the way it had been, knowing how she felt? I wished I hadn't heard any of that argument.

"Do you think she heard all that?" Fiore asked.

"I have a feeling she did. She's kept her eyes open the whole time."

"So now what?"

"I don't know. I guess we just take it one day at a time. We have to deal with this mess."

"Do you want me to leave when this is all over?"

No! Don't even think that!

"I want Lily to be happy. If you leave, she won't be happy." He planted a kiss as soft as a feather on my forehead. "I think we can be adult about this. After all, I can't blame you for falling in love with her. Look how hard I fell."

"I will do my best to stay out of your way."

"That's not going to happen. We live together. I don't know if anyone else noticed what I did so there's really no reason for you to act any different, just keep being her friend. She needs that," Christian said.

Needles suddenly poked my feet. My legs felt like they wanted to leave the room without me. The poking started in my fingertips next. Was this a good sign?

"Thank you, Christian, for being so understanding. I guess I expected worse."

"I was raised this way," Christian said. He stood looking down at me. My breaths came faster and faster as my body started feeling like a human pincushion.

"Well, your parents did a great job. You're a great man, did you know that?"

Christian laughed. "I never thought of myself that way, but thank you."

"You'll be a great husband to her. I know she'll always be happy as long as she has you."

"I want to get her out of these bloody clothes," Christian said as he stood.

"I can help you. Which dresser has her clothes?"

"I'm afraid I will need help," Christian said. "I don't want to hurt her. Hers is the one by the window."

Drawers opened and closed as Christian gingerly unbuttoned my shirt. His eyes never left my face. His pained expression made me want to wrap my arms around him but they felt like lead. Was it possible to prick lead with needles?

"These flannel pants should be more comfortable for her. Do you have a loose cotton shirt?"

"Check the closet. I'll get this one off. I hope she wasn't too attached to this outfit. I don't think it's salvageable." Christian lifted my head and slid the shirt down my back. He pulled my jeans down my legs and slid them off. "I need help getting the shirt on. I don't want to move her more than I have to."

"Okay," Fiore said as she came to my side. It was nice to know they were working together for once instead of against each other.

"What are you looking at?" Christian snapped.

"Just…um…her wound. It's closing nicely."

"Yeah…" He slid the shirt over my head as she waited, then pulled my arms into the sleeves. Fiore pulled the new shirt down as Christian held me up, and then lay me back down on the soft pillow. "I can do the pants myself."

"Nonsense. Nice underwear," Fiore said with a laugh.

"Don't push it!"

"Women notice these things."

The pants slid up to my waist, making it feel like someone was pushing the needles deeper into my skin. I groaned.

∽ TWENTY-SEVEN ∾

"Lily?" Christian rushed to stand by my face. "How do you feel?" My voice refused to work and I tried to blink but couldn't. *I can't talk...*

"I heard her." Fiore rushed to my other side.

"Me too. Thank God!"

"You watch her, look after her. I'm going to go get flowers or something, something to make the room nice for her," Fiore said as she went to the door. "Need anything?"

"I'm good. If you see Aloysius, see what's keeping him."

"Will do," she said before she stepped out. I heard her heels clicking down the hall.

I don't know which pain was worse: the horrible burning or the pins and needles poking my whole body. The feeling spread to my face and I could do nothing to stop it. Not being in control over my own body was disconcerting.

I need you, Christian. Please make this stop...

"What can I do? Please tell me. I want to help. This is killing me!"

"Fff...bb..." *Oh, forget it! Blood. I need your blood.*

"Yes, of course." He got on the bed on his knees and leaned over me. "Think you can do it or should I?" His neck was already at my mouth and I inhaled his sweet, warm scent, the scent that attracted me to him and kept me hooked since the first time I laid eyes on him.

*Me...I think I can...let me try...*My lips caressed the tender flesh where his neck joined his shoulder. My face tingled even more. He leaned in closer, pushing against my mouth. My fangs made a painful descent through my gums and punctured his flesh without hesitation. I didn't even need to think about it. The warm sweetness poured into my mouth and down my throat, making my head spin. No other blood had ever had that powerful of an effect on me as his did. It awakened all of my senses. I grabbed his head, tangling my fingers in his silky hair. He moaned. His body relaxed against mine as his blood filled my veins and repaired my wounded body. The tingling was subsiding in my limbs but increasing in my chest, face, and head. I grabbed his head harder and pushed him to me, trying to melt into his body. *Lily, Aloysius said not too much...though...*

Please, don't...I need this...I need you...all of you...

He pushed his hands under my back and held me tightly as I continued to drink and run my fingers through his hair. "I love you, Lily."

"I love you too," I said as I dropped my head to the pillow and gasped for air. Of all the times for my body to decide it wanted to breathe again.

"You're talking," He backed off me to look at my face, his hand covering the still-oozing wound on his neck. "Thank God!"

"What's going on?" Fiore entered the bedroom, her arms full of something with an overpowering, but beautiful scent.

"She's talking...and moving, sort of," Christian explained.

"Really? What did you do?" she asked and set the bundle down on the nightstand. I turned my head toward the wonderful fragrance.

"Nothing. I just fed her and she put her fingers in my hair, now she's talking."

"What happened? Can someone help me sit up?" I said.

They both ran to either side of the bed. Christian held me up and Fiore moved the pillows, fluffing them, so I could lean against them. The tingling in my body was gone but replaced by a feeling of heaviness, as if my limbs were made of lead. Christian pulled the sheet up to my waist and placed my hands on my lap.

"Melinda tried to stab you in the heart with a stake. I grabbed her and she missed your heart but got you pretty good anyway," Christian explained, taking a hold of my hand.

"Not that part. I remember all that. I meant, what happened with Maia?" I asked, trying not to look at Fiore.

"We don't know. We were too worried about trying to help you. We lost track of her. Fiore lost Jose Luis since they were in a car and she was on foot. Melinda disappeared too, after I ripped her off you."

"Don't worry, we'll find Maia. I don't think they will kill her. They still need her," Fiore said. I finally turned to look at her, met her eyes for a second, but this time it was she who looked away.

"I think she's been with them all along," I explained.

"What do you mean?" Christian asked.

"I think she's working with them. I think her kidnapping was just a trap."

"What makes you think that?" Fiore asked. She kept her eyes on Christian and I knew both were wondering if I'd really heard their argument.

"My memories are hazy, but I think she handed Melinda the stake."

"That can't be right," Christian said and squeezed my hand. "It looked more like a real kidnapping to me."

Great. Now they don't believe me. It didn't matter. Until we found her, and Jose Luis, our questions would remain unanswered. I felt too tired to argue. "What is that wonderful smell?" I asked to drop the subject for the time being.

"Oh," Fiore jumped up to grab the vase. "Aren't they wonderful? They call them *floripondio*."

"I've heard of these," Christian said as he inhaled the sweet fragrance. "Datura in English, I think. Aren't they supposed to be poisonous?"

"Hmm…beautiful and poisonous? I know someone like that," I said then regretted it.

"What do you mean?" Fiore asked, still holding the vase.

"Never mind. I highly doubt the flowers will hurt us since we're not human. Where is Aloysius?" I asked.

"He went to see if he can find out why the hunters and vampires are working together, but that was a long time ago. I wonder what's keeping him." Christian said and took the vase from Fiore, placing it gently on the nightstand next to me. "These are gorgeous."

"Yeah." Just like Maia, I thought.

"I don't know but I have a bad feeling about it," I said and took Christian's hand. "He should've returned by now."

"I know. Oh, I almost forgot, Kalia and Aaron are on their way. Aaron called while I was out," Fiore announced.

"What did you tell them?" I didn't want them to have to run to my rescue again.

"The truth," Fiore said.

"We don't even know what the truth is!" I sat up straighter, happy that I could move on my own again, even though I felt clumsy.

"Fiore, can you please give us a minute?" Christian reached out and squeezed her shoulder. I'd never expected affection between them but it was better than the constant anger.

"Sure. I'll be in the living room if you need me."

"Are you okay? I mean, aside from being…" Christian kept his voice down.

"No, I'm not okay. I'm fed up! I'm tired of the constant chaos!" I pulled my hand away from his.

"I know. We'll get all this straightened out, you'll see."

"I just wanted a normal honeymoon, or at least something close to normal. Is that too much to ask for?" I folded my arms over my chest and realized how childish I must look.

"I know, me too, and I promised you another honeymoon and that's exactly what we're going to do." He leaned in and brushed his lips against mine.

"About Fiore," I started.

He put a finger to my lips. "Shh…We don't need to talk about that right now. I just needed to understand her."

I nodded. He was right; we had too many more urgent problems. They seemed to have come to some kind of understand between them without any help from me.

"Help me get up, please." I pushed the sheet off my legs.

"You need to rest for a while yet. You've been through too much."

"I feel fine," I argued, trying to get my legs to the floor, though they felt too heavy to move.

"You are one stubborn woman." He laughed.

"I know. I've heard that before. I can't just sit around here and do nothing, especially not when it's time to kick some ass!"

He shook his head but his smile contradicted the motion. "You'll never change, will you?" He helped me to my feet. "No, don't answer that. I wouldn't want you any other way."

"Are you sure about that?" I asked as he picked up off the bed.

"I'm positive. What would I be doing if I hadn't met you? Teaching a bunch of teenagers, going home by myself every night, doing it all over again the next day? No, this is much more exciting."

"You're nuts, you know that?"

"I have heard that before."

∽ TWENTY-EIGHT ∽

"What are you doing out of bed?" Fiore jumped up from the sofa, giving Christian a look of disapproval.

"You know she's not going to listen to anything we say. Besides, a change of scenery might do her some good."

"Why are you talking about me like I'm not standing here?" Not that I was standing very well. My head spun and my legs felt like rubber so Christian supported most of my weight. I looked at both of them with resign. "Okay, so I'm not quite strong enough to kick ass yet."

"I'm glad you know that. Besides, Kalia and Aaron will be here tomorrow afternoon. I told them we'd meet them," Fiore said as she and Christian led me to the sofa.

"We're going shopping then, as soon as my head stops spinning."

"Do you need more blood?" Christian asked.

"I don't think so. It should pass once I'm moving around."

"Ooh, shopping! I love shopping, but what are we shopping for?" Fiore asked.

"Weapons," I said and both raised their eyebrows.

"What kind of weapons are we talking about?" Fiore asked.

"Whatever we can get our hands on: knives, guns, swords, stakes, I don't care if we have to use baseball bats. Wait, do they even play baseball here?"

"I don't think so…soccer. Would soccer balls make good weapons?" Fiore laughed.

"Where do you propose we get weapons?" Christian asked.

"The same place we feed. If we're dealing with hunters, they'll have weapons; hell, Melinda and Maia used one." I leaned my head back on the sofa and closed my eyes. The room spun faster. I opened them. "We have humans and vampires to deal with. Who knows how many? I'd rather not show up empty handed."

"I can understand that, but do you really think we'll be able to buy those things?" Fiore asked and sat next to me. Christian rushed to sit on my other side.

"When money talks, I'm sure we can get anything we want. I really don't care what we get as long as we have something. I don't even care if we gather piles of rocks." They both laughed.

"Do you even know how to shoot a gun?" he asked.

"Of course I do." Both looked shocked.

"Jesus Christ!" Christian yelled. "Why they hell do you do that?"

Aloysius stood in front of us, his shirt torn and smeared with blood. "Sorry 'bout that. I didn't mean to scare you. I did not expect you to be out here. I didn't expect Lily to be up and about yet."

Fiore ran to his side. "What happened to you?"

"Don't worry, Fiore. It's not my blood." He unbuttoned his shirt and pulled it off, tossing it on the chair. My eyes scanned his chest and stomach but found no injuries.

"Whose is it then?" Fiore asked, her eyes glued to his muscular chest and flat stomach. I couldn't help but smile at her staring like a high school girl. She caught my look and dropped her gaze to the floor.

"I followed one of the hunters for a while but she didn't lead me anywhere special. I think she was actually just shopping. She carried a basket," he explained.

"She? I thought the hunters were all male." I stood slowly to make sure I could but Christian took my elbow anyway.

"That is not actually true. Remember that they are also witches. From what I've seen in the past, females are more powerful than males, in terms of magic. This woman definitely was." Aloysius walked to the armchair across from the sofa and sat down. Fiore's eyes followed his every move. "That's probably why they are welcomed into the group."

"So what happened? Where'd the blood on your clothes come from?" Christian asked.

"I cornered her when we reached a dark alley. She knew I was behind her all along and she led me there. It turned into a fight, of course. She shot lightning, or something like it, out of her fingertips. I spent most of the time dodging them. A group of kids walking by distracted her for a moment and that's when I managed to grab her. Her mind was closed to me so I figured if I fed from her, her guard would come down and I'd be able to get some information out of her. So that's what I did. I fed briefly but when a car beeped and startled me she pulled out of my arms and ran. That's how her blood smeared all over me." He reached up and pulled his hair tie out, shaking his ebony hair out. I looked at Fiore's reaction but she turned away, taking a deep breath. "I'm going to take a shower."

"Wait," I said. "Who was in the car?"

"It was just a taxi."

"We're going out for a while," Christian said before he could leave the room.

"Now? Why?" Aloysius paused before reaching the hallway.

"We need to get weapons."

"You don't have to do that. I'll make a call. I have a guy," Aloysius said and climbed the stairs, carrying his bloody shirt.

"Of course he does," Fiore said still watching him as he disappeared up the stairs.

"See something you like?" I asked. Christian laughed but cut it short when Fiore glared at him.

"Well, he is kind of beautiful," she said without meeting my eyes.

"I guess," I said, turning toward the window, my fists clenched. Why would that bother me? She had every right to admire him; after all, he was young and powerful, turned just two years after Aaron's grandmother, his daughter, was born.

"Look, Lily, I just want to say…" she started.

I held my hand up to stop her. "You don't have to say anything. That conversation was between you and Christian."

She turned her gaze to Christian and he nodded. He knew better than to force me to discuss something. Maybe Ian was right when he accused me of not voicing what was on my mind. Regardless, what Fiore felt was none of my business. At least, I tried to convince myself of that.

Christian's face scrunched and I knew he was listening to my thoughts. There was enough tension in the air without discussing Fiore's and my feelings. "So, where do you want to go on our second honeymoon?" I asked to change the subject.

"Anywhere you want," Christian said.

"I wonder if we can rent an island somewhere, so there's no chance of anyone else causing trouble," I suggested.

"I'm sure you can. Movie stars and the rich and famous do it all the time. I can look into it for you," Fiore suggested. "Mediterranean or Caribbean?"

"Who cares? As long as we're alone," Christian said. "This means, you're not going."

"No kidding!"

"I made the call," Aloysius said as he entered the room wearing black jeans and a black shirt, his wet hair falling around his shoulders like a veil. Fiore sighed as he neared. "Carmela will be making the delivery as soon as it's ready."

"Carmela? Why her?" I asked.

"Because I trust her," Aloysius looked at Fiore and then slid a chair closer to her. Christian took my hand as my back tensed. Why was her sudden crush bothering me? "She's been working for me for a long time."

"So she goes to your man, picks up weapons, and brings them here, no questions asked?" Christian asked.

"She knows about me and she knows about the hunters. She minds her business and that's why I keep her around. She takes care of my apartment even when I'm not here. She has full access to everything I own in this country." He ran his fingers through his damp hair. His shampoo smelled like lavender.

"What exactly do you own?" I asked, curious as to what her 'full access' entitled.

"Properties I rent out, downtown, at several beaches, and three up north, in Trujillo. I cash the checks; she does everything else," he explained.

"Wow. So that's how you earn a living?" Christian asked.

I knew he felt badly about losing everything and not being able to work since becoming a vampire. He felt guilty about letting me support him but I didn't mind. My parents weren't rich, but they left me something. I invested it wisely. Ian had left me plenty to live off of for the next couple hundred years. That was the only good thing he had done every time he left me. He'd place an envelope full of money somewhere I'd find it and then I'd invest that too. It was easier to get money from my victims in the beginning because most carried cash. It was a rarity now that most people carried plastic.

"Listen, you two," Aloysius said looking at Christian and me. "There's nothing we can do until we have the weapons and Aaron and Kalia are here. Why don't you go out for a while, enjoy yourselves? It might do Lily some good to get out. I can call a driver for you."

I looked at Christian and he was smiling. Getting away, even for a little while, sounded like a good idea to me, but not something doable. "Thanks for the offer, but I think it's best that we stay here with you."

"Nonsense. Go, enjoy yourselves for a while. I can take care of myself. Besides, it's not me they want," Aloysius insisted.

Christian nodded to me and I knew they were both trying to distract me for a while. I hesitated but nodded to Aloysius, knowing there would be no arguing with him, just as there was no arguing with Aaron.

"Great," Aloysius smiled. "I'll call a car for you." He headed toward the phone.

"No thanks. I've done enough lying around lately. I could use the exercise. I guess I should get dressed."

Christian helped me get up and then let me walk down the hall unassisted, though he stayed close. "You seem much better, steadier on your feet," he said after closing the door.

I pulled the shirt over my head and stood in front of the mirror to examine the wound. He stood behind me, still protective. "It's pretty ugly."

"But it looks like it's almost completely healed," he said, wrapping his arms around me and brushing my neck with his soft lips. "You're still perfect."

The skin surrounding my wound was red and puckered, almost raw looking, but it wasn't overly sensitive anymore. A shudder ran through me as I brushed my index finger over it and realized it was actually numb. Seeing my finger there but not feeling it was a little too creepy even for me. Covering it up with clothing as soon as possible was best.

"It really does look fine," Christian assured me. "It probably won't even leave a scar."

"It doesn't matter. I'll always remember it." Dressed and wanting to escape reality for a while, we left the building and walked toward Kennedy Park. There was always something going on there.

As we neared the park, the sounds of pan flutes, *charangos*, and laughter grew louder. People were dancing, talking, and laughing as if nothing at all was strange about their city. It must be nice to be totally oblivious to the existence of the supernatural, or at least not care about it. It must be nice to only worry about pickpockets and common thieves when venturing out in the night. My life could've been that way too, if only I'd never set eyes on Ian. Would I have been married, had children, and been remembered for something special?

"Stop beating yourself up like this, please," Christian said. "None of this is your fault. How could you have known?"

"How could I not have known? I knew from the beginning that he wasn't normal. I didn't listen to what my brain was telling me. I let my silly heart lead me around and look what happened."

"You met me, married me, and will live happily ever after. That's what happened. We can deal with everything else together. I think we've done alright so far." His smile took my breath away. Maybe he was right. Maybe living happily ever after with him by my side was possible, as soon as we took care of this mess. He was absolutely right about one thing; meeting Ian led me to him. Something I would have completely missed.

"Let's dance," I suggested, leading us to the middle of the happy group. I placed both his hands on my hips and started swaying with the music. Keeping my eyes locked on his, I let the music and the movements of our bodies melt away the frustration of the last couple days. This was our honeymoon and I was determined to enjoy my new husband any way that I could, even if it was only for moments at a time. It wasn't long before his lips found mine, his tongue parting them, and tangling with mine. His hands left my hips and found the back of my head, pushing me even closer, our breathing ragged and shallow. *Let's get out of here!* My mind screamed at him.

He backed his face away from mine, his eyes sparkling in the darkness. His lips were swollen, wet, and red. He grasped my hand and pulled me from the center of the dancing crowd. "Which way?" he asked.

"That way." I pointed to a street I knew led to the beach below. Passing other couples shielded by darkness, we ran hand in hand down the cobble-stoned street and down to the beach. It was a moonless night and the extra darkness was especially welcome. An abandoned building stood close to the ocean, its darkness and cover calling to us. We stopped behind it and I kicked my sandals off. Our feet sank in the wet sand, and he pushed me up against the wall. Carried away by our passion and the fact that we were finally alone, we made love, standing behind the looming ghost of what had once been a popular restaurant.

Laughing at ourselves for acting like this on a public beach, exhausted, and trying to catch our breath, we sank to the sand and leaned against the cool cement. We didn't bother moving out of the way as the water nipped our toes. "I hope nobody heard us."

"Who cares," he said, his thumb caressing the hand he held. "I love the way you sound."

"I guess it really doesn't matter. Did you see all the couples on our way down?"

"Lots of passion in the air tonight," he said and leaned to kiss my lips. My hand made a fist in his hair and my fangs extended, nipping his bottom lip as he moaned into my mouth.

"Don't you two think you've had enough?"

I jerked away from him and crouched into a fighting stance. "Maia?" I called.

"You should be arrested for this public display," she said with a laugh. "But do go on. That was quite…educational. Don't let me interrupt."

"What the hell do you want?" I screamed, though I couldn't see her.

"I just want what should be rightfully mine. You took Ian away from me, permanently. I think it's only fair I get Christian."

"Christian is not yours!"

"Oh, no? We'll just see about that."

Our eyes searched the darkness and settled on a distant shape further down the beach. Christian pointed toward it. Just as I nodded to let him know I saw her too, her body lifted in the air, large wings fluttering as her shape drifted higher and higher into the moonless, black sky, and disappeared from view.

∽ TWENTY-NINE ∽

"I'm telling you, she had wings!" I paced the living room while Aloysius and Fiore watched me from the sofa. Christian stood by the window.

"Wings, Lily? Are you sure?" Aloysius looked at me with concern in his eyes.

"But I saw them with my own eyes. They were definitely wings!" I argued.

"That's not possible, Lily," Fiore said but didn't look away from Aloysius. "Think about it for a minute. How could Maia have suddenly grown wings?"

"You're right, Fiore. It does sound impossible," Christian interjected as he moved to my side. "But it doesn't change what we saw. Maia was carried into the sky by wings, whether hers or someone else's, we don't know. It was too dark and it happened too fast."

"And she's obviously not being held captive anywhere, is she?" I stopped pacing and stood close to Christian. "She's safe and sound and free as a bird, no pun intended."

"Tell me exactly where you were, what you saw, and what you heard," Aloysius said.

"We were, uh, behind an abandoned restaurant on the beach, just below Larco Mar. We were sitting on the sand when we heard her voice. She was standing down the beach, didn't really say much, except that I took Ian and she wants Christian now." I looked at Christian to see if he had anything to add. When he didn't, I continued. "She also teased a little about what she saw us...doing. Then huge black wings carried her away."

Fiore smiled and looked at Aloysius. She knew exactly what we had been doing. I looked at the floor. "What about a parasail? Could she have been using one of those?" she asked.

"You can't go straight up in one of those and that's exactly what she did. She didn't run. She didn't jump. She just went straight up. Besides, I heard flapping."

"What about a shapeshifter?" Fiore asked.

"There's no such thing," I answered. Aloysius and Fiore looked shocked. "What? Please don't tell me I'm wrong."

"I'm sorry but you are wrong on this one, Lily," Aloysius replied.

"Of course I am. Why wouldn't I be wrong? Why am I always the last to know anything?" I moved closer to Christian, looking for his mental support.

"You weren't kidding when you said Ian taught you nothing." Aloysius stood and came to my side.

"Of course I wasn't. Does that shock you? He did it on purpose. The more naïve he kept me, the more dependent I had to be on him."

"I believe that. Though it's not too common, there are some that have acquired the ability to shift. It takes a lot of power and strength and can't be done for extended periods of time, but it is possible."

"Why haven't I seen this before though? It's not like I wasn't surrounded by vampires at one point or another in my years with him," I said through gritted teeth.

"I'd say Ian kept you away from powerful vampires so you wouldn't learn how to do these things. If you'd experimented more, and acquired new gifts or talents, you wouldn't have been as helpless as he wanted you to be," Aloysius suggested.

"I wish he was still alive," I announced, my hands in fists at my sides.

"Why?" Christian asked with a frown.

"So I can kill him again!"

Everyone laughed and I relaxed my hands. Thinking about him wasn't doing anything to solve our problems and besides, the three vampires in the room had a way about making me relax.

"I think you'd have to share that privilege with me and Christian," Fiore said, making me laugh.

"Okay, kids," Aloysius said with an amused grin. "Let's focus. This happened in sight of the mountain. I have a feeling that's where they are."

"I thought it was just for the last meeting but I think you may be right. That's their meeting place. They live on San Cristobal, at least that's what Jose Luis said. They must not want to attract more trouble to their home.

No one lives where they meet, right?" I asked.

"Nobody that I know of, except the woman who takes care of the chapel. She lives there with her children; at least, she did before Melinda got here. Who knows what she's done since?" Aloysius returned to Fiore's side on the sofa.

"If the humans are still on the mountain, is there any way we can get them out of there before they get hurt?" I couldn't fight knowing there were children up there.

"We'll figure out a way," Aloysius assured me.

My stomach knotted at the thought of Jose Luis being caught in the middle of a battle that wasn't even his. Was he a prisoner, being tortured? Was he even still alive? Would he fight on their side or ours? I had no way of knowing, though I wanted to believe he would side with us.

"We'll get him back, Lily. I promise," Christian assured me.

"You honestly believe that, don't you?"

"I do."

"Now, how do we convince Kalia and Aaron that Maia isn't innocent in all this?" I asked, looking at all three faces. Fiore looked at Aloysius, who then looked at Christian. "Am I missing something?"

"Lily, why are you so sure she's not innocent?" Fiore asked, her gentle voice infuriating me anyway.

"You're kidding. Please tell me you're kidding!" My hands curled into fists and I walked away from Christian so I could look at all three of them. The shock on their faces told me what I needed.

"Just consider the possibilities for a moment. She wasn't alone on that beach. You said yourself that wings carried her away. What if she is being used as bait, against her will?" Fiore's voice was so soft, I strained to hear her.

"It is possible, Lily," Aloysius said and came closer to me. I backed away.

"Why do you all insist on taking her side?"

Christian approached with caution. He knew my temper by now.

"No one is taking her side. How could you even think that?" He stood in front of me, his hands at his sides. "We're dealing with the repercussions of Ian's death. Melinda is obviously very powerful, and don't forget Ryanne wants revenge for Fergus' death, too. It is possible that Maia is their prisoner and is doing what she's doing out of fear or because of some promise they made that they'll never keep."

"She could also be brainwashed," Fiore suggested.

I laughed as they all still looked on in shock. "You are all so freaking stupid!"

I slammed the front door behind me and sped past the elevator. Yanking the door open to the stairwell, I took three or four steps at a time, not bothering to even look as I leapt. Pepé called an unreturned greeting as I ran past him. Not bothering to look for traffic, I ran across the street and around the corner. Running at full speed, not caring who saw, I ran in no particular direction, but the wind felt good on my face. As always seemed to be the case, I was headed in the direction of the beach. Once I reached it, I continued straight into the icy water, letting its salty coldness completely submerge my body and my thoughts. It didn't matter how long I stayed under. I straightened my legs and allowed myself to float, waves washing over my face.

How could they be so blind? I could excuse Fiore and Aloysius for believing that Maia was a victim in all this, but Christian? How could he? He knew Maia had brought Ian back into my life, into my home.

"*Miren. Hay una mujer en el agua,*" a man's voice yelled somewhere on the beach.

Planting my feet back on the sand, I swept my head under once more to push my hair back, and wiped the water from my eyes. Four dark figures stood on the shore, one of them pointing in my direction. Great! Just what I needed! Instead of swimming away, which would have been best, I decided to turn back toward them and walk out. In hindsight, it would've been much easier to swim away. So much easier.

∽ THIRTY ∽

As I neared the shore, I realized my white t-shirt was soaked and clinging to my body, same as my jeans. It was no wonder their eyes were glued to my chest. They whistled, but I kept walking, keeping my eyes straight ahead as I tried to walk past them. The larger of the two stepped in front of me and waved a beer bottle at me.

"*Oye, chiquita, no te vayas tan rápido,*" he slurred, waving the bottle in front of my face, trying to hand it to me.

He smiled as I finally wrapped my fingers around it, grazing his hand slightly, and took it. He pulled his hand away and rubbed it. I brought the beer bottle to my face, sniffed it, and threw it behind me into the water.

"*Oye, esa chela es mia,*" he complained. He shouldn't have handed it to me if he didn't want to lose it.

"Look assholes, I'm not in the mood for this! Get out of my way!" I threatened. My anger wasn't allowing my brain to switch to Spanish.

"American *chiquita,*" he said. The four laughed and swayed on their feet. "We like gringas. They are fun."

"Come here, *gringita,*" one of the men said. He grabbed my arm to pull me to him. I raised my knee to my chest and kicked, my foot connecting with his jaw. He landed on his back as a wave crashed to shore and rolled over him.

"*Bruja!*" the larger man yelled. He wrapped his arms around me from behind as his friend stood facing me. "Not nice. We want fun." He whispered in my ear, his stale breath lingering even after he moved his head back to laugh. I tried to kick behind me but he was so close I had no room to move. His friend slapped me across the face, the sting bringing tears to my eyes. He didn't even notice. This wasn't going to work. It wasn't going to be as easy as I'd hoped. All I'd wanted was some peace and quiet while

I tried to get over my anger with Christian, Fiore, and Aloysius. As usual, trouble found me.

The other man helped his drunken friend to his feet and out of the water. He seemed to be the drunkest of the four. He immediately dropped to his butt on the sand even though his friend tried to hold him upright. His friend gave up and stepped aside.

"You want money?" I asked, still in his arms. "I have money for you."

"Maybe after we have fun," he said with a heavy accent. I was a bit impressed that, even this drunk, he still spoke English.

"What kind of fun are we talking about?" I teased. This short man was surprisingly strong as he held me still.

He loosened his grip just enough to turn my face toward his. His mouth, reeking of alcohol, found mine. I parted my lips and closed my eyes, losing myself in the moment, acting out the part for our spectators. A moan escaped him and his friends cheered as he slobbered into my mouth. I fought to keep from gagging.

"Now me," begged the one seated on the sand.

"*Todavia, idiota*! I am not finished," my companion yelled and came back for more.

His slobber made my stomach turn but I forced myself to deal with it. My hands fought out of his grasp and I fisted them in his hair, pulling his head back slightly as his friends continued to cheer, awaiting their turns. One of his hands was trailing up my thigh, getting dangerously close. Every once in a while his fingers gripped my leg hard enough to make me flinch. His other hand kept me pushed against him. My lips traveled from his collarbone to his neck as I left a trail on his already damp, salty flesh. As I sank my fangs into his vein, he pushed himself tighter against me and moaned, bringing on more clapping and hollering from his drunken friends who no doubt thought he was having the time of his life. I smiled in spite of the fact that blood was flowing into my mouth and wrapped my arms around him as his body relaxed. I enjoyed every drop of his alcohol-drenched blood. Once his heart stopped beating, I released my grasp and let his body slump to the sand.

His friends clapped and cheered until they saw the blood I seductively licked off my lips. The clapping slowed and their eyes grew wide but all stayed frozen.

"*Ave Maria Purísima, un vampiro!*" the drunk on the ground screamed. He struggled to stand but it was useless. He was too drunk. Funny, these guys didn't strike me as the religious types.

I turned and looked behind me. "A vampire? Where?" I teased as I searched the beach with my eyes. "I don't see it. I've always wanted to see one."

I approached the one on the sand next, slowly. He stumbled as he tried to get to his feet again, but I grabbed him by the collar, lifting him over my head as he screamed. The front of his pants suddenly darkened as he relieved himself. I laughed. "Aw…are you scared of the little *gringa*? Such a big man like you shouldn't be scared of little ol' me. Let me give you a piece of advice, though. You have to be careful with the *gringas*, especially the undead *gringas*. They don't take crap from scum like you," I advised as I tossed him back into the water, much further this time. The other two ran in the opposite direction, not even caring about their friends, one of which was dead, the other, about to drown his drunken self.

"Where are you boys going? I'm not finished yet!" I caught one by the back of his shirt and pulled him against me. "I thought you wanted your turn. We're going to have fun, remember?"

He nodded but stayed quiet. His eyes were huge and bulging, his heart beat like a freight train in my ears.

"I guess I was too much for your other friends, but you? You look like you could handle me."

His elbow caught me in the ribs and I dropped to my knees, coughing as the air was knocked out of my lungs. He started walking away but I managed to get up. I dove and caught his ankles, toppling him to the ground. I jumped on top, flipped him over, and straddled him, keeping my thighs wrapped around him. "I'm ready for you now."

I leaned down to his neck as he screamed. He brought his knees up fast, pushing me over his head. Rage coursed through my veins and I threw myself headfirst into his stomach, landing on top again. "Please, lady, I have a wife," he begged, his eyes bulging with fear. "I have children." He suddenly spoke English.

"You didn't care about any of that when you wanted me, remember? What is so different now? We're just having fun. I promise I won't tell your wife." I kissed his lips and brushed my fangs against them. His body shook between my thighs. Even so, he brought his hands up and cupped the back of my head, trying to bring me closer as his body arched beneath me. I felt just how much he wanted me. He truly thought he was going to get what he desired. I turned his head gently, trailing my tongue against his salty skin. He moaned and arched more beneath me as his hands trailed down my back and to the top of my jeans. I laughed and he froze again.

As I sank my teeth into his neck, he grabbed a handful of hair and yanked my head painfully back. My hands grabbed his head and twisted, breaking his neck with a blood-chilling crunch. His eyes, wide and glazed over, stared forever at the star filled sky.

Brushing the sand off my wet clothes, I stood and wrung out my wet hair. I looked toward the water but saw no signs of the man I'd thrown. My heart told me to go look for him, save him if I had the chance, but my mind told me to forget about him. My steps unsteady, I made my way back to the street and to the stairs that would take me back to civilization. I saw no sign of the fourth man who ran like a coward, leaving his friends to die alone.

∽ THIRTY-ONE ∽

"Lily, please let me in," Christian pleaded from the other side of the door. I sat on the bed in a robe, having just stepped out of the shower. Letting the hot water run over my body only washed away the dirt and blood, not the horror of what I had just done. "I'm your husband. I just want to help."

Swallowing my self-hatred for the moment, I unlocked the door and went back to the bed. He stood at the foot, his eyes scanning my body for signs of injury. "I'm fine," I said.

"Do you want to talk?" he asked, sitting at my side and taking my hand.

"There's nothing to talk about. I'm sorry I ran out. I was angry. I just needed to calm down," I explained though I knew he didn't really buy it. He was too in tune with my mind and soul for that.

"I don't think it worked. You came in soaking wet and locked yourself in here without a word to anyone. We were all worried about you. Please tell me what happened to you." His eyes showed his pain. I had hurt him just by leaving. He had no idea of the rest.

"Now is not the time, really. I'm fine." I leaned in and brushed his lips with mine. His body stiffened. "What?"

"Um, were you...drinking?" he asked leaning away from me.

I stood from the bed and opened the bedroom door. "Come on," I said and headed for the living room with him following. "Sit please." I motioned the sofa and Christian did as I asked. His brow furrowed with worry. Aloysius and Fiore stopped mid conversation and looked at me.

"I messed up," I said as I paced in front of them, averting my eyes. "I did something really bad."

"What? You drank beer?" Christian asked.

"Of course I didn't. The alcohol was from someone else's mouth."

"What are you talking about? You kissed someone?" Christian jumped to his feet.

"No! It wasn't like that!"

"Then what was it like?" He made no effort to hide his anger this time.

"Please calm down, Christian. Let her explain," Aloysius said. Christian hesitated a moment but sat again. He crossed his arms over his chest.

"I ran down to the beach and straight into the water. Being in the water was helping me calm down, clearing my mind, but when I came out, four guys were standing on the shore," I explained, still not looking at them. "They were drinking and acting stupid. One of them grabbed me."

"Are you hurt?" Fiore asked. I shook my head.

"They wanted to…have fun, as they put it," I said.

"So you kissed one?" Christian asked.

"I had no choice. He had his arms around me and I couldn't get loose. I had to distract him somehow. The point is I drained him. I killed him while his friends stood there and watched," I stopped pacing and finally looked at Christian's expressionless face. "I broke another one's neck and threw the really drunk one into the ocean."

"That only makes three," Aloysius pointed out. "What happened to the other guy?"

"I don't know where he went. I was too busy with the others and I let him get away."

"That's really not good," Aloysius stood. "Did he get a good look at you?"

I nodded. "I don't know if the one I threw got out of the water or not. I should have looked for him but I left instead. I didn't even bother to read their minds. I just killed them. The one whose neck I broke told me he has a wife and children when he was pleading for his life."

"So what, Lily? What did that matter? You did the right thing," Fiore said.

"How can you say that? I killed three innocents. They were only acting stupid because they were drunk!" I argued.

"I'm sorry, Lily, but how can you say they were innocents?" Christian asked. "They were far from innocent!"

"They committed no crime that I know of. I didn't read their minds at all. I didn't bother."

"Since when is rape not a crime?" Fiore asked.

"Who said anything about rape?" I looked at her angry face.

"They were going to rape my wife." Christian stood and came to my side, wrapping his arms around me. I pushed him away.

"That was the alcohol talking. They wouldn't have done that. I killed three men tonight!" I repeated. I couldn't believe what they were saying.

"What do you think they meant by 'fun'?" Aloysius asked, raising my face with his fingers on my chin. "They were going to rape you and only God knows what else. You defended yourself."

I looked at Christian. His expression changed from anger to worry. "What about the one that got away? What if he goes to the police?" he asked.

"That could be a problem," Aloysius said. "Regardless, he wouldn't know where to look for you. They didn't know your name, right?"

"No. They know nothing about me, except, one did say vampire," I recalled.

Aloysius and Fiore laughed. "I doubt he would mention that to the police," Fiore said.

"Yeah, I guess you're right."

"You did nothing wrong," Aloysius reassured me.

"I should not have been there in the first place," I said looking at Christian. "I shouldn't have walked out like I did. I'm really sorry."

"Please remember, I'm your husband. Don't shut me out. You are not alone in any of this," he explained.

"And we're here too," Aloysius said. "We're not siding with Maia. We're just trying to look at all the possibilities before we act. It will be especially hard on my great-grandson if you're right about her. It would devastate him if he lost Maia."

"I do know how much they love her."

"Yes. And until we know something for sure, I'd rather not break their hearts," Aloysius said and then looked at Fiore, who smiled at me before turning back to him. "Shall we?"

Fiore shocked me by placing her hand delicately in his and rising from the sofa. "We're going to go feed. We'll be back soon to go to the airport. Oh, and they're right. You did the right thing by defending yourself, Lily."

Before I could say anything, they disappeared.

"What was that all about?" Christian asked as he put his arms around me and I felt his lips on the top of my head.

"I think Fiore may be more than a little interested in him, don't you think?"

"Umm…is that a good thing?" He moved away to look me in the eyes. I hesitated a moment and he smiled. "Isn't that better than her pining away after a married woman?"

"Of course it is, but if he feels the same, that probably means she'll leave with him." That was a thought I didn't like. How I felt or didn't feel about what she had confessed to Christian while I lay in that bed didn't matter. She was the closest thing I had to a true friend and I didn't want to lose that, as selfish as that was.

WE LEFT FOR the airport as soon as Aloysius and Fiore returned. Finding the correct gate on the arrivals board, we rushed to await Aaron and Kalia. As passengers started pouring out of the doors, I watched for my loved ones. To my surprise, Pierce was the first to exit, followed by Beth, Riley, Raul, Kalia, and Aaron.

"They all came?" I said looking at Christian whose mouth hung open.

"Over here," Aloysius called waving his arms over the crowd.

Kalia wrapped me in her arms as soon as she reached us, my feet leaving the floor for a moment. "I missed you so much."

"I missed you too, Mom," I said as I squeezed her back. She hugged Christian next.

"Let's get out of here, shall we? It's way too crowded." Aloysius took Kalia's suitcase and began pushing his way to the exit. The rest of us followed without a word. "I guess we'll need more drivers."

"Wait here," Fiore said as we exited the airport and set everything down on the sidewalk. "Pierce and I will go rent cars. That should make things a little easier." She and Pierce walked back into the airport before anyone could argue.

"Why are you all here?" I asked as Aaron released me from his embrace and shook hands with Christian.

"We wanted to help, and besides, we could use some time away from the cold," Riley looked at Raul and he nodded and smiled. "Alaska can get a little gloomy after a while."

"You can bring us up to speed when we get to the apartment," Aaron said and nodded toward the exit. "Here they come."

"All set," she said and tossed a set of keys to Aloysius. "We got us two minivans."

"Umm." Aloysius looked confused.

"What is it?" Fiore asked, looking at Aaron's amused expression.

"I don't know how to drive." Aloysius handed the keys to Aaron.

"What?" several voices asked in unison.

"What do you mean you don't know how to drive? Everybody drives," Fiore said, looking at Aloysius with shock.

"I have the ability to disappear and materialize anywhere I want. Why would I need to drive?" Everyone laughed.

"I guess I just assumed," Fiore shrugged and smiled at him, her eyes shining. "Okay, then. You'll ride with me and Aaron can follow us."

We loaded the luggage into the two vehicles and settled in for the scary ride. I grasped Christian's hand in the third row and tried to focus my attention on the conversation, happy I wasn't asked to drive.

THIRTY-TWO

"So these are all the weapons we have?" Aaron asked as he rummaged through the boxes. He had pulled the boxes from the hallway into the living room and was kneeling in front of one, examining the contents and placing them on the floor.

"Between all of us, we shouldn't need much more than our combined powers. The weapons are merely an added sense of security," Aloysius explained. "Besides, we have Pierce and his magic with us now."

Pierce started going through the contents of another box. "I will think of something that will help. We also have Raul's expertise to aid us. He's fought hunters before," he said as he looked at the array of knives and swords Carmela had delivered. He felt the tip of each blade as he also lined them up on the floor.

Raul sat on an armchair, paying no attention to the display of weapons. His brow furrowed like he was deep in thought, but his mind was shielded by a concrete wall, completely impenetrable. Riley's green eyes fixed on him for a moment and she sighed. She turned her gaze back to the rest of the group.

"My poor Maia," Kalia said. All eyes turned to her, even Raul's. "Ian dragged her into this mess and now he's gone. She should have been left alone." My stomach turned.

"Kalia, we will solve this problem. I promise," I said and took her hand. She turned her trusting gaze on me and forced a smile, nodding.

"We've dealt with hunters before. They should be easy enough to beat, or at least subdue. It's the vampires and witches that are more of a concern. We don't know any of them and don't know their powers." Beth walked over to examine the blades Pierce had set out. She took one in her hands and slashed through the air with it, testing it out. "Any idea how many we're dealing with?"

"No, and I don't think they're all Peruvian, either. I think the Irish are here too," Aloysius explained.

"We're dealing with vampires, hunters, witches, and possibly a shape-shifter?" Riley asked.

"It looks that way," I said. "If that's what Christian and I saw last night, then that makes things more difficult, right?"

"Not necessarily. If it is a shapeshifter as you described, it's a bird. What is a bird going to do against a bunch of vampires? Besides, the shift would take too much energy for whomever it is to shift back to vampire and be effective in a battle. It will need to feed and recover right after. It won't have much time or privacy to do that. That's something we will have to make sure of. We'll do whatever we have to do to get Maia back in one piece," Aaron said, squeezing Kalia to his side to reassure her.

"And Jose Luis," I added. Aaron narrowed his eyes and a lump formed in my throat.

"Do you think Aaron has a problem with Jose Luis?" Christian asked once we were in the privacy of our own room.

"I think it's just that he probably thinks I want to make him a vampire or something."

He narrowed his eyes at me. "Do you?"

I spun to face him. "Of course not! I just want a better life for him; however I can help."

"Are you sure that's really it?" He patted the mattress next to him, inviting me to sit.

Setting down the clothes I was mindlessly folding, I sat next to him and turned to look into his eyes. "I just want something better for him. He's too young to be wrapped up in all the craziness. He deserves a chance to be a kid, a chance to have friends, a chance to go to school, and fall in love, like any other kid his age. Is that so wrong?"

"No, but do you think we can offer him that, being what we are?" he asked, his tone gentle.

"It's not like he doesn't know what we are, but I'm not sure. I just know anything has to be better than how he's living now. You didn't see the way the hunters treated him, the way they shoved him into that car like he was just a piece of property. They don't care one bit about him." Jose Luis was an innocent orphan who was trapped in the life of a vampire hunter with the promise of not starving to death. It wasn't fair. They were using him.

"And you do?"

"What?" I asked, though I knew what he meant.

"You care about him?" he asked.

"I guess I do. It's not fair that he has to submit to being used just to have food in his belly and clothes on his back, a roof over his head. None of what happened to him was his fault. He didn't become an orphan by choice."

"Speaking of orphans, did you know Ian was one?"

"Yes, I did. He never gave away too many details about his past but I did know that much. That's one of the reasons I want a better life for Jose Luis. Look what it did to Ian."

"So true," Christian said.

"And if that Arturo guy is any indication of how the rest of the hunters act, that's not very reassuring. He was really mean."

Christian laughed. "Well, it's not me you have to worry about. I have complete confidence in your judgment. As long as we can get him out of Peru, and if he's willing, I am all for taking care of him, trying to give him the kind of life he deserves." He smiled. I threw my arms around him and buried my face in the crook of his neck.

"Thank you so much! I promise you won't regret it," I kissed his lips before getting to my feet. "I will take full responsibility for him."

"Lily, he's not a pet. We will take care of him together. Besides, at his age, he needs a male influence around; you know, a strong masculine role model such as myself." He winked. "There will be things he'll be more comfortable discussing with me than with you, if you know what I mean."

I rolled my eyes. "We need to be ready to leave at nightfall."

"Right," Christian said as he stood and went to the dresser. "It's a good thing we're doing this at night, when it's less likely there will be tourists on the mountain. I guess it's a good idea to wear black, right?"

"It's a good idea to blend, for whatever that's worth," I said and pulled a black shirt over my head.

"You sound a bit worried. Are you?" Christian zipped his black jeans and looked through his drawer for a shirt.

"A little," I admitted. "I don't know what's really happening with Maia. I have no idea how to deal with a shifter, and no idea what kind of powers Melinda possesses."

"Oh, good, because I thought you were worried about having to protect me," he said. I paused and looked at him, trying to smile. He lifted my face with his fingers to look at my eyes. "Please tell me that's not it."

I tried to look at the floor but he wouldn't release my chin. "Well, you are new to this whole thing. I just think maybe it would be best if…"

"Lily, please don't. You are not going to leave me waiting on the side-lines again. I am not human anymore. I have powers of my own. I can fight this time." His eyes bore into mine.

I swallowed hard before answering. "I can't help it. I love you and I'm afraid."

"What exactly are you afraid of?"

"I'm afraid to lose you."

"You will never lose me. Don't waste a single moment thinking like that. I'm not even a little bit scared or worried that we won't succeed. I believe in us, all of us. Doesn't that count for something?"

I nodded. He wrapped his arms around my waist and leaned his chin on my head. "I guess it does," I said.

"Don't be afraid. I've learned a lot from you. Trust me to fight at your side from this day forward."

"You're right. But at the first sign of…"

"Oh, no you don't." He held his index finger up to my lips to stop me. "Let's just leave it at I'm right."

I laughed and nodded. I hoped he was right. Things would be much easier if I didn't have to watch his back the whole time and could actually use my powers to try put an end to this mess. A soft knock on the door pulled us apart. "Are you ready?" Fiore called from the other side.

"We'll be right out," I called. I laced my black hiking boots and looked at Christian. His eyes showed the fear he said he did not feel but his smile tried to convince me otherwise. "Let's do this." He nodded.

The ride to the base of the mountain was quiet and uneventful, except for the loading of guns and strapping of sheaths for the assorted knives we'd be carrying. No one spoke but everyone seemed busy with something. I'm not sure who Aloysius' connections were but they were definitely into some heavy stuff. I was grateful that it had been so easy to get what we needed. I armed myself with a gun and a short sword, but Christian wanted to wait until everyone had what they wanted before choosing his weapons.

"What good does a bullet do with a vampire?" he asked as we pulled the car over to the side of the road at the base of the mountain. We planned to walk the rest of the way under the cloak of night so we wouldn't alert them of our arrival with the roaring motors – at least, that was our hope.

"They're loaded with wooden bullets," Fiore answered from the front seat.

"That's ingenious. What about the hunters then? They're human." He placed a gun in the holster at his side and tried the swords on for size. He decided on a long one, much like the one we had used in the cabin to kill Ian. "Who took the bow and arrows?"

"That would be Aloysius' weapon of choice," Aaron said as he approached the back our vehicle, already armed.

"To answer your other question, I don't think it will much matter what kind of bullets the humans get hit with as long as they go down," I explained. "It will hurt just as much."

When the ten of us had gathered at the car, checked our weapons, and wished each other luck, Aaron said, "Get Maia and the kid, if possible, and get out. Do not engage them if they don't attack first. The last thing we need is for innocent humans to be hurt in all this, or even learn of our existence. We should be able to avoid the woman and the children who live here. I'm pretty sure the hunters would protect them, not harm them."

We nodded in agreement and after a lot of hugging and back-patting, split into pairs to start our climb to the top. It was likely they were using this mountain as a gathering place and would be somewhere near the ruins where I'd fought Melinda previously.

Christian took my hand as we rounded a corner and found a somewhat clear path up the mountain. We communicated mentally when we needed to but kept as quiet as possible, cloaking ourselves and trying to blend with the shadows in the night. The element of surprise would hopefully work to our advantage.

Trust me, Lily. I'm not helpless anymore. Please remember that. Christian reassured me one last time. I squeezed his hand to show him I understood. He was my equal now, not my responsibility. He smiled broadly as he heard my silent thought.

I want to check the ruins first...

Straight ahead if I remember correctly.

I nodded. We continued up the path, the wind blowing dirt in our faces. Our steps displaced stones, sending them rolling down the hill, making us cringe. As we neared, I listened for any signs of movement or beating hearts, but heard nothing except the wind and the distant crash of the waves below. It was way too quiet up here, eerily quiet.

Christian pulled me to a stop as a dark shadow crossed our path and disappeared. *What the hell was that?*

I have no idea but it went that way. I pointed toward the darkened shell of what once might have been a lovely home, or maybe an office. Now it looked like an eerie skeleton looming from the ground. We drew our knives and held them, ready to defend ourselves. The sky was moonless again tonight but our eyes had adjusted to the darkness as we sidled to the opening of the ruins. I held my breath and listened. Someone was humming softly.

"Maia, is that you? Are you here?" I asked, still in a hushed voice. If that was her, she was close enough to hear me. Christian squinted in the darkness, trying to make some sense of the shapes flickering in the candlelight just inside the entrance.

"Why don't you come closer and see?" she taunted, her voice squeaky and childish.

Christian looked at me and it was clear he was restraining a laugh. Maia wasn't very good at disguising her voice. "I don't think so. You come out and face me," I demanded, the blade clutched tightly in my hand. Christian released my other hand and pulled his gun out, a soft click telling me he cocked it. "Stop being a coward for once and show yourself!"

She appeared in front of us so fast, had I not heard the rustling of dry weeds, I would've thought she possessed Aloysius's abilities. Her eye was completely healed and the bruises had disappeared, leaving her skin as white and unmarred as porcelain.

"You're not a prisoner at all. I knew it," I said as I scowled at her. "What kind of game are you playing?"

"It's no game, sis. It's called revenge." She bared her fangs at us, trying to look menacing. Neither of us moved. "You took Ian away from me. You need to pay for that." She made no attempt to move yet so I held my hand up to stop Christian, who aimed his gun at her head and seemed prepared to shoot. I wasn't ready for that yet.

"I did no such thing. He came to me, remember? And besides, Ian didn't love you," I growled. "He didn't love me either. He didn't even love Fiore. He was only ever in love with himself."

"That is not true! He loved me. He told me so," she said as she backed away a few steps.

"Okay, but even if he did, it doesn't matter. He's gone now. He is not coming back. Ever! Think of how much you'll hurt Aaron and Kalia if you do this." I hoped the mention of the vampires she considered her parents would make her snap back to her senses. Instead, she threw her head back and laughed.

THIRTY-THREE

"I doubt Kalia will care who Christian is with, me or you. I think it's only fair you give me what I want."

"What makes you think I'd even consider that?" I asked, too shocked to even raise my voice.

"And what makes you think I'd even have anything to do with you?" Christian asked.

"Oh, please. Don't act like you don't find me attractive. I know you were admiring me at your own wedding, drooling over how I looked in that dress."

Christian advanced toward her, aiming the gun straight at her forehead with a steady hand.

"Christian, please," I urged.

"I've had just about all I can take of her, Lily," He turned his face back to her. "You are nothing but a spoiled, rotten little brat. You're a child. You'll never even be half the woman Lily is. The only reason I have ever been civil toward you was to make her and your parents happy."

"That's bullshit," Maia said, but the look in her eyes showed that she wasn't too sure. "I could make you just as happy, even happier, if you'd let me."

"Read my lips, Maia. I do not want you, not now, not ever!"

"Then you need to die with her, since you love her so much. That's the least you can do."

I stepped forward a few steps now. "Don't you care at all about what you're doing to your parents? They honestly believe you're innocent in all of this. They believe you were really kidnapped."

"I do feel a little bad for Kalia. Her big heart will one day be the end of her," Maia said, her arms crossed over her chest. "Mark my words."

"What are you talking about, Maia?" I stood next to Christian now.

"How do you think it was that I came to live with them? You don't hon-estly think she turned a perfectly normal and happy girl into a vampire, do you? No, Aaron and Kalia are too noble for that. Too perfect. They are the perfect models of what a self-respecting vampire should be like. Don't make other vampires, don't kill poor innocent people, and don't harm a hair on a human's head, please! Pretty damn boring, if you ask me."

"I still have no idea what you're talking about and you're really starting to piss me off. Get to the point already or I'll just have to give my husband permission to blast your head off!"

Both Christian and Maia's eyes grew with shock.

"Kalia thought she was saving a terminally ill girl from an untimely death: leukemia. That's what I told her when we met in the grocery store. I even cried, real tears and slobber and all that. Shaving my head was easy. I knew it would grow back as soon as I was reborn." She smiled but didn't move.

"Why would you do that to Kalia?"

"Because stupid Ian wouldn't do it, why else? Something about not feeling right about turning a minor. That's why I had to convince Kalia to do it."

"Eighteen doesn't exactly qualify you as a minor," I explained.

"You're right, but I'm pretty sure sixteen does." She smiled, satisfied with herself.

"You lied to them?"

"I had to. It was the only way I could be with Ian, the only way to make him really love me…until you interfered."

Christian aimed the gun at her chest now, but I shook my head. I wasn't done with her yet. "So you knew Ian before that trip to Europe? You lied to everybody about that too?"

"I met him about three years before that. He took care of me when I left home. I was only thirteen then. He was all I had." She stuck out her bottom lip and pouted. I laughed and Christian grabbed my hand, signal-ing me to calm down this time.

"Thirteen?" I didn't even try to hide my shock.

She nodded. "I loved him from the first time I set eyes on him."

I certainly remembered what that had felt like. "He wouldn't turn you so you tricked Kalia and Aaron into doing it?" Though I understood better now, my mind wasn't quite grasping the immensity of her deception.

"I ran away from home. My stepfather was a drunk and my mother a useless puppet who jumped at his every command, even when he was using me as a punching bag. She always stuck up for him, saying that if I hadn't opened my mouth, he wouldn't have been so angry. It was always my fault, no matter what I did. I finally got sick of it. I figured they'd be better off without me. When I met Ian, he promised to take care of me and keep me safe, only, he wouldn't turn me. No matter how much I tried, and believe me I tried, he wouldn't even touch me." Well, that was one thing he'd done right. Catching my thought, she sneered at me before continuing.

"I'm originally from Oregon so I went back and searched for another vampire that would do the job," Maia continued. "Living on the streets and being depressed because of my ordeal, I had lost a lot of weight. Kalia was easily fooled by my shaved head and the rest of my appearance. I told her I'd been sick for a long time and the treatments weren't working anymore. The doctors had given me a year, tops, to live. When she asked where my parents were, I told her the truth. She couldn't stand the thought of anyone hurting me." She took a couple steps toward me. I was too stunned to move on my own so Christian forced me back.

"Feeling sorry for me, she convinced Aaron to let her turn me, and keep me, like a little lost puppy." She looked up to the sky and sighed.

"What about your parents? Didn't they look for you?" I asked.

"Of course they didn't! They were worthless. I was just one less mouth to feed. So, eventually, I got rid of them." She said as if it were nothing.

"You killed your parents?" I couldn't believe what I was hearing.

"Like you wouldn't have done the same thing if you were being abused."

"Of course not. I loved my parents. I could never have taken their lives," I shouted.

"And yet, you weren't there when they did die, were you? You didn't even go to their funerals."

"That was not my choice and you know it! Ian seems to have shared my history with you so you should know." I tried to advance again but Christian held me back.

"You could have gone. It was your choice. If you loved them like you say, then Ian should not have come first."

"Why didn't you just stay with Ian after you were turned? Why did you bother to keep coming back to Astoria?"

"Ian was great and all, especially in bed, but...oh right, what am I saying? I'm sure you know that. Anyway, he kept leaving and not saying where he was going or even when he was coming back. I'd get bored. Besides, Aaron and Kalia gave me everything I wanted. I wasn't about to miss out on that opportunity."

Anger made my blood boil and my ears ring. "You lied to Kalia and Aaron. You used them. That is completely inexcusable!" I screamed as I lunged at her with my blade aimed at her heart. Christian lost his grip on my arm and fell backward. Maia jumped away and I missed, nearly falling on my face but catching myself.

"It's not going to be that easy to get rid me. I still have plans for you," she announced as she looked up at the sky again, this time raising her arms.

My eyes widened as the largest condor I'd ever seen hovered above her. Maia gripped the condor's talons and was lifted straight into the air, disappearing from sight as the condor flapped its gigantic black wings.

∽ THIRTY-FOUR ∽

"Acondor? Really?" Christian yelled as we ran after it. Of course, it was no use unless I took to the air, something I had not yet attempted from level ground. I realized the important thing at that moment was to find Kalia and Aaron and tell them the truth. They needed to know Maia could not be trusted. She had just led us all into a trap.

"Apparently that's our shapeshifter. I'm not flying after it yet." I sheathed my sword and grabbed his hand. "We need to find the others and warn them. Maia is definitely not on our side. Someone could get killed trying to protect her. I'm not about to let that happen."

"I know you won't. You already knew she was against us. I'm so sorry we doubted your feelings," Christian said as we ran in the direction of the cross. We could hear voices in the distance.

"Not so fast!"

We came to an abrupt stop and spun around to face a man also dressed in all black, hood tied tightly around his neck. He held a gun pointed at me, but looked at Christian with narrowed eyes. "You are new, *señor*. No?"

"What difference does that make to you? It's really none of your business," I said. This man had no heart beat. He was definitely a vampire.

"It is my business. I was ordered to kill him," he replied in perfect English.

"We seriously don't have time for this. Christian, disarm him!" I commanded never taking my eyes off the vampire.

"As you wish," Christian replied. He narrowed his eyes, concentrating briefly on the weapon. The man just stared at his eyes, wondering what was happening, not attempting to move. The gun shook and then floated in other air, out of the man's reach. He backed away a few paces as Christian smiled widely, beaming with pride.

"Get out of here," I said as I took the man's gun and slipped it in the waistband of my jeans. "I don't want to kill you if I don't have to. Our fight is not with you."

He shook his head and made the mistake of lunging at me, not noticing the blade I held in my left hand. He gasped and crumpled to the ground like a sack of potatoes.

"Let's go," I said taking Christian's hand again.

"Won't he just get back up?" he asked, looking behind him as the vampire lay still on the ground.

"Probably, but it will be a while. He'll be too weak to fight. He'll need to feed and then find a place to hide until he recovers his strength. I didn't kill him but I did take him out of commission for a while, thanks to you."

"It would be nice if they were all that easy," Christian said.

"Yeah, that *was* way too easy."

"I'm pretty sure that was just a warm up. I don't think the rest will be like this. Wait." He stopped walking. "Can we get the blade back?"

"Oh, I guess I will need that," I laughed. I was feeling a little too self-assured but I knew that couldn't last. Nothing I ever did was easy.

"How did you get your blade out so fast? I didn't even see you do it," Christian said as he pulled my blade out of the man's stomach, wiped the blood off with his shirt, and handed it back to me. The vampire rolled to his side moaning.

"Instinct, I guess. I knew he wouldn't give up that quickly though he had the chance to save himself. He had orders to follow. Thanks for your help, by the way. That was impressive."

"Glad I can finally do something useful," he said as we started walking again. I squeezed his hand and was about to say something when a commotion came to sight and brought us to a halt.

Bodies flew every which way and from where we stood, I couldn't discern who was who. I looked at Christian and leaned in for a kiss, needing to feel his warmth before joining in the melee. *I'm ready when you are…*he thought as we parted. I nodded and grabbed my blade in one hand, the gun in the other. As we stepped closer, I noticed a few bodies already lay lifeless on the ground, their shapes twisted and broken. I stepped over one when something to my right caught my attention.

Kalia grabbed the man she was fighting with and, in one smooth, quick move, snapped his neck and released him. He crumpled to the ground and she wiped her hands on her jeans, heading toward another. I guess I really didn't have to worry about her. Though I saw her as a warm, caring mother, it was just her exterior. She could be a vicious fighter.

Someone grabbed my braid and pulled me to the ground. A woman threw herself on top me and landed a fist to my jaw. I roared from the pain. I heard a loud pop and felt her full weight on me. Shoving her off me, I looked up to see Christian still aiming his gun at her. The blood on the back of her shirt was already showing signs of stopping, making it clear she was not human. I got to my feet and shoved her onto her back with the tip of my boot. "Shoot her in the heart. She's a vampire," I told Christian. With a shaky hand, he aimed at her chest, took a deep breath, and pulled the trigger. Her body jerked as her eyes flew open and never closed again.

"Great shot," I complimented as I looked for either Maia or Jose Luis. I saw neither. "I have to find an opening to talk to Kalia or Aaron."

"Aaron's over there," Christian pointed to a group of four that were fighting each other. Among that group was Riley. She grabbed a woman by the arm and I watched as the woman's eyes bulged and her hair stood on end. She fell to her knees before falling face first to the ground. Riley disposed of her by sending electricity through her body. Turning back to Christian, I saw a man running toward us, sword drawn. "Go! I got this," Christian said and turned to face the man, his own sword drawn.

I hesitated a moment but realized I did trust him to take care of himself. I ran to Aaron's side, kicking away a man aiming a gun at him. "Aaron, Maia is on their side," I yelled through the commotion. "She's not a captive at all."

"That can't be true," he yelled back as he slashed the throat of the man he held by the hair. I gasped at seeing my sweet, gentle Aaron doing something so brutal.

"It is true. I talked to her before coming here," I yelled. Aaron stopped moving but wasn't looking at me. His face was turned to the side and I followed his gaze. Surrounding Kalia and Raul, the sand and soil was starting to lift off the ground, creating swirling tornadoes. The shouting was replaced by what sounded like a freight train as tornadoes picked up dirt, dropped weapons, and a few bodies. "What the hell is this?" I shouted to Aaron.

"I don't know," he shouted back over the rumbling noise. "Look! Up there!"

I followed his pointing finger to where a woman stood on the outskirts of the battle, her arms and face raised to the sky. She chanted in a language

I didn't recognize. "What is she saying?"

"I'm not sure. It's been a long time since I've heard Quechua. It's gotta be a spell of some sort," he said as he watched the woman.

"So what do we do?" I yelled over the roar.

"I'll try to counter her spell," Pierce yelled from behind me. I turned to see his face raised and his arms open to the sky. He began his own chanting.

"Up there!" Christian screamed as he ran to my side, bloody sword in hand.

My eyes scanned where he pointed. It was hard to see with all the debris but, at the top of the cross, a body hung from the rafters. From this distance, I couldn't tell who it was, only that it was male. "Jose Luis!" I screamed as my knees weakened. The condor landed above him, its wings spread to their full width. It was impressive. "Aloysius!"

"Right here," he answered as he ran to my side, his bow already drawn and loaded, aiming at the massive bird. He released the arrow but it missed by inches, hitting a steel beam instead, and bouncing in the opposite direction. He shot another that I hadn't even seen him draw. This one embedded in the condor's left wing and its screams rang over the rumbling of the tornadoes. Pierce seemed to be having no luck stopping the witch creating them. He stood in concentration, looking toward the sky, arms raised, completely vulnerable.

As we watched the condor fold its right wing close to its body, it started changing shape. Its taloned feet changed to human legs, its feathers to skin. Humans and vampires alike gasped in awe as everyone momentarily froze to watch, leaving Pierce to his work. Before our eyes, balanced on a beam in the wind, stood a totally naked Melinda, a vampire with one arm and one wounded wing. Her hair no longer blond but brown, blew in the wind. Her eyes narrowed as she looked down on us. "You cannot kill me!" She screamed. Still, no one moved. All we could hear was the roar of the whirlwinds and the two witches chanting against each other. Untying the boy from his metal prison, she cradled him in her arms before setting him on a crossbeam. She held his shoulders, steadying him. He looked at her face for a moment before looking to the ground. His eyes grew wide before he turned back to face her, shaking his head.

Still no one on the ground moved as everyone concentrated on the odd scene about forty feet in the air. Jose Luis stood with his arms relaxed at his sides, his expression completely blank, and his feet planted dangerously close to the edge. Melinda's lips moved, but because of the tornadoes on the ground, I couldn't hear what she was saying. Christian came to stand at my side since no one was bothering to fight while fixated on the couple above. Finally, Jose Luis made some movement. He shook his head again and turned away from her.

"What are they doing?"

"I don't know but I don't like it one bit," I yelled into Christian's ear. I could barely even hear myself.

Melinda smiled and nodded. He continued to shake his head without looking at her.

"Can't you get up there?"

"I wish I could but I don't know how. I would have to climb," I admitted.

"No!" Jose Luis finally screamed over the deafening wind.

"Oh, God! What is she saying to him?" I stepped closer to the base of the cross, alarming one of the hunters. I knocked him to the ground with my fist.

Jose Luis looked at Melinda one more time before he stepped off the beam, plunging to the ground. Raul ran toward me in a blur of movement, pushing me to the side as he raised his hands. Words in Spanish came so fast from his mouth that I caught none of them. Several gasps surrounded me as Jose Luis lay suspended in the air about twenty feet from the ground.

"Raul, move!" I screamed as a whirlwind came barreling toward him. He dove through the air, landing on his stomach just out of reach. Jose Luis wasn't as lucky; his body was thrown by the wind, disappearing from sight, blocked by the darkened building just behind the cross.

Reacting without thinking, I ran in that direction only to hit the side of the tornado. It threw me away from itself, hurling me onto my back at Christian's feet. He bent down to help me up and then his full weight was on me as he slumped on top of me. In that same instant, I saw Maia's face as she watched Jose Luis's body fly about ten yards away as he was picked up by another funnel. She had no weapon in her hands as she ran to Melinda's side.

Arrows flew from Aloysius's bow as the tornadoes slowed, and finally dissipated. He had hit the witch creating them. Pierce fell to his knees, panting and exhausted. I lifted Christian's weight off me and set him down on the side. A scream tore from my throat as I stared at the stake protruding from his back, blood soaking his shirt and being swallowed by the earth around him.

⤳ THIRTY-FIVE ⤳

The witch casting the storm on the weather lay on the ground, her open eyes staring at the sky. Maia stood next to Melinda. On Melinda's other side, Arturo, who I presumed was the leader of the hunters, held a gun aimed at Kalia. No one else moved or even spoke, except me, of course.

"Maia!" I screamed as I watched for the rise and fall of Christian's chest. My heart leapt as I saw him breathing, but it was labored and shallow. Jose Luis still lay untouched and I couldn't tell if it was his heart I heard or all the other humans. "What did you do?" I screamed as I scrambled to my feet.

Melinda threw her head back and laughed, the arrow still protruding from her injured and bloody wing. My eyes settled on her bare hip, where a tiny condor was tattooed. "Nothing she shouldn't have done. You deserve to lose him. It's only fair, after all. Don't you think so, Lily?"

I looked to the other vampires in my group and they stood with mouths open, eyes wide. Was no one going to do anything?

"Ian did love me!" Maia screamed as she took a step toward me. Kalia took a step toward her and reached for her arm. Maia pushed her away with such force that she landed yards away, a hurt expression on her face. Aaron ran toward her as everyone turned to look. I took that opportunity to advance, my sword held to the side. Ryanne came from behind Melinda, a wooden stake clutched in her hands. I swung the sword and slashed her side. She dropped the stake and clutched her bloody side.

"You killed my Fergus," she muttered weakly. "I loved him." She fell to her knees as a shot rang through the air.

"He was killed in battle while he was trying to kill someone I love," I countered. I turned to check on Christian and saw him drop his gun as he laid his head back on the ground.

"Kill Melinda!" I screamed.

"I don't think so," she said. Her body shifted back into the condor and she took to the air, flapping one wing wildly while the other still had the arrow lodged in it. Shots rang out again as guns trained on her but missed.

"Melinda!" Maia screamed. "What about me? You can't leave me here!" Her arms stretched in the air, waiting for a rescue that didn't come.

The condor squawked but stayed in the air.

"I did everything you said! You can't just leave me, please..." she pleaded, staring above her.

"How long have you been doing everything she said?" I screamed.

Maia lowered her glare to me. "What difference does that make? You deserve everything that happened to you. You deserve to lose and suffer. You deserve to be stuck with a weak man like him." She motioned toward Christian with her head.

"He is not weak!" I screamed. "You're the weak one. You're the one who can't even think for herself. You follow orders, and not very well obviously since we're both still alive."

"Then why is he laying there bleeding to death and I'm not? He's going to die and leave you with nothing! He wasn't even smart enough to hang on to his money!" She laughed but continued to scan the sky, her arms raised, waiting for rescue.

"It was you! You're the one who stole his money!"

"No, dear sister, it was not me. I just helped. Ian and I went to his apartment and took what we needed. It wasn't my fault the idiot kept his checkbook in his night stand drawer. I even got his social security card and his birth certificate from there. Why would someone be so stupid as to keep them all together where anyone could find them?"

"You had no right to steal from him! Just as you had no right to steal from Kalia and Aaron!"

She glanced at Aaron and Kalia but said nothing. She dropped her arms and ran at me, a stake aimed at my heart. Before I could think twice, I instinctively swung my sword. Kalia had risen and pushed me aside but I managed to cut Maia's throat. Her body fell to the ground and she clutched her neck, blood spilling out through her fingers, a gurgling sound escaping her parted lips. Everyone gasped.

"What the hell did you do?" Kalia screamed. Vampires and humans backed away. Kalia's enraged face twisted into something unrecognizable.

She looked nothing like the mother I loved. She tried to run toward me but Aaron held her tightly. She kicked at him trying to break his grasp as he struggled to restrain her. "You tried to kill my daughter!"

"She tried to kill Christian…and me." I dropped the sword from my shaking hand. "She lied to you. She lied to all of us. I tried to tell you that. Aaron, I tried to tell you. You wouldn't listen."

"She is mine! I love her. You have no right to take her away!" she cried. The hearts beating around us grew fewer and fewer as the humans hastily retreated from the scene. The only heartbeat left was a weak one, from Jose Luis. At least I knew he was still alive, though just barely.

"She tried to kill me and my husband!" I screamed, hurt and confusion replaced by anger.

Aaron's eyes softened as he looked at my face with a tenderness I remembered. He would understand. He had to. But his expression slowly became one of stone. "You could have done things differently," he growled through gritted teeth as he clutched a fighting Kalia to his body. "You didn't have to do it this way."

"Please don't do this. Please understand," I said, unable to respond to his comment. What else could I have done? "She was going to kill me next. Is that what you wanted?"

Aaron's mouth opened and then closed again. He looked down at his wife. "You have a week to get your stuff and get out of our house," she screamed at me.

I dropped to my knees, pain in my chest overtaking my body. "Kalia, please…"

"Get out of our lives! I never want to set eyes on you again!" Aaron clutched her tighter as she screamed and he stared me in the eyes, but said nothing. "We did everything we could to help you! We gave you love. We gave you a home. We gave you family. And this is how you repay us?"

"I know you gave a lot. I don't question that, but Maia lied to everyone. She was using you from the beginning," I argued.

"Things were easy before you came into our lives. We were a happy, loving family. We never should've gone looking for you." She wasn't screaming anymore. She sounded mechanical suddenly, unfeeling and cold.

"I never meant for any of this to happen. Maia is the one who brought Ian back into my life. Please don't take my family away from me. I love you both," I cried. "So much."

"It's over, Lily. We never want to see you again," Aaron said without looking at me. My dead heart felt like it was going to break. I couldn't breathe, couldn't force my legs to get me off the ground so I could go to Kalia and plead with her.

"Aaron, let me go to her. To Maia," Kalia pleaded. He slowly released his hold and she ran to drop by Maia. She slumped over her and cried, her body shaking with every sob.

"Lily," Aaron said, his voice soft, bringing me hope again.

"Aaron," I answered, hoping things weren't as bad as they seemed.

"Get your people and get away from here," he ordered.

"Aaron, you can't mean that," I pleaded.

"Now! It's over!" he screamed, his face turning ugly with rage.

I looked at the other vampires who stood surrounding us. Riley looked at the ground when my eyes reached hers. Pierce had no expression on his face, his eyes staring straight ahead. Raul and Beth turned away. Only Fiore met my eyes. She walked over and helped Christian to his feet, draping his arm around her shoulder. I forced myself to my feet and walked to where Jose Luis was laying on the ground. I picked him up and cradled him in my arms. He was still breathing but it was very shallow. As I walked past Aloysius, he whispered, "Go to a hotel. I will be in touch as soon as possible." I nodded.

My eyes drifted again to Aaron as we passed. He turned away from me. A lump rose in my throat and I couldn't swallow, let alone speak. I wanted to plead with him, beg his forgiveness, but I said nothing as I followed Fiore to the path that would lead us off the mountain and away from my family forever.

✐ THIRTY-SIX ✐

The hotel room was as dark as the drapes would allow. I kept them closed all day and all night, not wanting to cheered by the city or the glowing sun that didn't mourn with me. Christian was hanging on, taking blood from both Fiore and me, depending on who was in the room at the time. Jose Luis was in a hospital room in downtown Lima, fighting for his life. Fiore and I took turns with both, never leaving either alone for more than an hour.

It had been days since the horrible events that led my family to cast me out. I was just someone they had felt sorry for and decided to embrace into their family, temporarily, as it had turned out. I wasn't their daughter and never had been. Despite everything she had done, Kalia and Aaron considered Maia their only true daughter.

I tried to focus my thoughts on Christian and Jose Luis's recoveries instead, tried not to think of everything I had lost, but it was useless. The pain and loss was real. It was physical and emotional. I felt it in every fiber of my being.

"Lily, you need to feed," Fiore warned as I swayed when I stood from Christian's side to prepare to take my turn at the hospital.

"There's no time. I'll be fine. I have to get to the hospital," I protested as I leaned against the dresser to steady myself.

"No, you won't be fine. You need to feed. You've been giving Christian blood and haven't taken any for yourself. You'll do neither of them any good if you're too weak to even walk," she said as she stood to steady me. The room was spinning worse than I had anticipated. "It's starting to show on your face and your hair. You're starting to age. Is that what you want?"

I shook my head. "I'll feed when there's time."

"It seems to me you're doing this on purpose. If you don't feed now, today, I will hold you down and force my blood into your mouth. Christian will just have to wait for his."

"No! Please," I argued. "You can't do that. He needs it more than I do."

"Then promise me you'll feed before you go to the hospital. Or are you slowly trying to kill yourself?" She raised a perfectly manicured eyebrow.

"Of course I'm not."

"Good because I would hate to see you do something so rash. You still have a family. Jose Luis, Christian, and I are your family now and we do not want to lose you." She raised her lips to my forehead and held them there. I closed my eyes and swallowed the lump in my throat. She was right. I couldn't do that to Christian, not after how hard we had fought to stay together. I couldn't give up like that. I raised my arms and wrapped them around her waist, squeezing her gently.

"I'm sorry. It just hurts so much, you know? But you're right; I can't give up now, for his sake."

"How about for your own sake?" She backed away to look at my face. "Never mind. I don't care who you live for as long as you live. The Lily I know and love is not weak. She's a fighter. I saw that from the moment I met you. Please don't prove me wrong."

"I will try harder. I promise," I said.

"I believe you." She put her fingers under my chin and raised my face. "I love you. Don't ever forget that."

My stomach did a flip, remembering her argument with Christian. "I won't. I love you too."

SITTING BY JOSE Luis's bedside at the hospital, while his broken bones healed, I couldn't help but think back on all the things I could have done differently. I should have grabbed Maia, restrained her. I didn't have to do what I did; after all, she was just a child. Maybe we could've talked some sense into her. However, again Maia had missed her mark when she plunged the stake into Christian's back. It had taken him a few days, but he was conscious again and slowly regaining his strength. And I had missed my mark; while I had no news, I was sure Maia would recover, just as Christian would.

"Lily, please don't torture yourself over this," Christian said as he heard my thoughts when I sat by his bedside again in the apartment. Fiore had left the room to call Aloysius. The doctors were hopeful that Jose Luis would fully recover from his injuries. He would need a lot of care since he was almost in a full body cast and I was more than willing to do that. "You had no choice."

"I lost the people I love."

His hand wrapped around mine. "You have me. You have Fiore and Jose Luis," he said. "And somehow, you also have Aloysius. He doesn't hold anything against you. Maia survived, remember? It will take some time, but she will heal."

"I know." I blinked over tears. "But I love Kalia and Aaron and they never want to see me again."

"Maybe in time, they'll come around," he whispered. "Let them have some time to clear their heads."

"I guess so. But what do we do in the meantime?" I asked raising my face to his.

"Fiore said that Aloysius will let us stay in his apartment as long as we like. We'll go there when they discharge Jose Luis. We can start our lives over again, together." He kissed my forehead.

"Yeah, you're right. I'm not alone and I hope I never am again," I said and kissed his lips. He sighed and closed his eyes.

"Not a chance. You will never be alone again. That's a promise." He wrapped me up in his strong arms as the door opened. Fiore walked in smiling from ear to ear.

"What is it?" I asked, turning to look at her from Christian's embrace.

"Umm…well…" she started, trying to keep control of her smile.

"Spit it out!" Christian and I said together. She laughed.

"Aloysius is going back to Italy for a couple of months. He wants me to go with him. But I'll stay if you need me to," she said, still not able to wipe the smile off her beautiful face.

Christian and I looked at each other and smiled. "No, of course, go. Just make sure you keep in touch," I said.

She rushed over and wrapped her arms around both of us. "Always," she said and kissed the top of my head. "I need to go pack. We leave tonight."

"I love you," I said. "Never forget that."

"Me too, Fiore," Christian said, surprising both of us. "Take care of Aloysius. He's one of the good ones."

She kissed us both and then kissed Jose Luis' forehead before bouncing out of the room. It was great to see her so happy. Aloysius was a perfect match for her.

"And I'm the perfect match for you," Christian said, looking at Jose

Luis. "And, we have a son now."

Jose Luis stirred in his sleep and we both went to his side. He was our main concern now and he deserved the happiness we planned to give him. I sighed as I looked at Christian who tenderly held Jose Luis' hand in his. One day, we would make Kalia and Aaron understand what Maia had done, but for now, I had my husband, my hero, at my side.

The rest could wait.

END

ABOUT THE AUTHOR

LM DeWalt is a Peruvian American who has been living in the US for 30 years. She works as a teacher of ESL, Spanish, French, and accent reduction and is also an interpreter and translator. She has written for several Spanish language newspapers but her passion was always to write novels. Her love of vampires, and all things paranormal, started when she was seven years old and saw Bela Lugosi's Dracula.

She currently resides in Northeastern Pennsylvania, where it's way too cold, with her husband, three teenage sons and two cats.

ACKNOWLEDGMENTS

I would like to thank my mom, my husband, and my three sons for their patience and encouragement through this process. Thank you also to all my family and friends for their continued support. Thank you so much to Michelle at Central Avenue Publishing, the Greater Lehigh Valley Writer's Group, my critique partner, Bob Janis Dillon, and my wonderful editor, Meghan Tobin-O'Drowsky. A special thanks goes out to Aloysius Dragovits, Daniella Juhasz, Lee and Krista Sandt for their time and inspiration. Last but not least, I would like to thank Oscar Ramirez Barcelli and Carol Rodriguez for their help with the research.

Printed in the United States
by Baker & Taylor Publisher Services